CW01390949

Praise for Jo Piazza

'I was gripped and entertained from start to finish'
Ashley Audrain, *New York Times* **bestselling author of**
The Push and *The Whispers*

'Instantly gripping, gorgeously written, ingeniously plotted,
filled with complicated, fascinating characters, both timely and
timeless . . . Remarkable, astonishing, and just plain wonderful'
Joanna Rakoff, bestselling author of *My Salinger Year*

'A gorgeous, propulsive read that keeps you guessing until the last page'
Janet Skeslien Charles, *New York Times* **and internationally
bestselling author of** *The Paris Library*

'Strong women, rich history and page-turning suspense make for a
rich and satisfying read'
Pam Jenoff, *New York Times* **bestselling author of** *Code Name Sapphire*

'With lush prose and airtight plotting, Piazza's novel made me
laugh, cry – and start planning a trip to Sicily'
Andrea Bartz, *New York Times* **bestselling author of** *We Were Never Here*

'Equal parts riveting mystery and engaging family saga'
Emily Giffin, #1 *New York Times* **bestselling author of** *Meant to Be*

'A gritty and whip-smart read'
Amanda Geard, author of *The Midnight House*

'Captivating'
Woman&Home

'Brilliantly entertaining with a fabulous heroine'
Best magazine

'Jo Piazza's book is a charming page-turner packed with wit and
wicked twists that will keep readers engrossed'
Town & Country

'Masterfully constructed, fast-paced plot . . . A page-turner'
Historical Novel Society

Jo Piazza is the international bestselling author of twelve books, including *The Sicilian Inheritance,* and the *Good Morning America* Book Club pick *We Are Not Like Them* with Christine Pride. Her work has been published in ten languages in twelve countries and four of her books have been optioned for film and television. Jo is also the host of the critically acclaimed *Under the Influence* podcast, and her podcasts have garnered more than twenty-five million downloads and regularly top podcast charts. An editor, columnist, and travel writer, her work has been featured in the *New York Times* and the *Wall Street Journal,* among other publications. She lives in Philadelphia with her husband and three feral children.

ALSO BY JO PIAZZA

FICTION

The Sicilian Inheritance
The Knockoff (with Lucy Sykes)
Fitness Junkie (with Lucy Sykes)
Charlotte Walsh Likes to Win
We Are Not Like Them (with Christine Pride)
You Were Always Mine (with Christine Pride)

NON-FICTION

How to Be Married
If Nuns Ruled the World
Celebrity Inc.

EVERYONE IS LYING TO YOU

JO PIAZZA

HQ

ONE PLACE. MANY STORIES

HQ
An imprint of HarperCollins*Publishers* Ltd
1 London Bridge Street
London SE1 9GF

www.harpercollins.co.uk

HarperCollins*Publishers*
Macken House, 39/40 Mayor Street Upper
Dublin 1, D01 C9W8, Ireland

This edition 2025

1

First published in Great Britain by HQ,
an imprint of HarperCollins*Publishers* Ltd 2025

Copyright © Jo Piazza 2025

Jo Piazza asserts the moral right to be identified as the author of this work.
A catalogue record for this book is available from the British Library.

ISBN: HB: 978-0-00-875664-2
TPB: 978-0-00-875665-9

This novel is entirely a work of fiction. The names, characters and incidents
portrayed in it are the work of the author's imagination. Any resemblance to
actual persons, living or dead, events or localities is entirely coincidental.

All rights reserved. No part of this publication may be reproduced, stored
in a retrieval system, or transmitted, in any form or by any means,
electronic, mechanical, photocopying, recording or otherwise,
without the prior written permission of the publishers.

Without limiting the author's and publisher's exclusive rights, any unauthorised
use of this publication to train generative artificial intelligence (AI) technologies
is expressly prohibited. HarperCollins also exercise their rights under Article
4(3) of the Digital Single Market Directive 2019/790 and expressly reserve this
publication from the text and data mining exception.

Printed and bound in the UK using 100%
Renewable Electricity by CPI Group (UK) Ltd

FSC
www.fsc.org

MIX
Paper
FSC™ C007454

For more information visit: www.harpercollins.co.uk/green

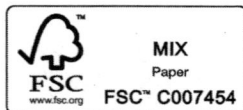

For all the influencers.
May you wield your immense power for good.

A man can work from sun to sun,
but a woman's work is never done.
—PROVERB

I will not give them the kiss of complicity.
I will not give them the responsibility for my life.
—MARY OLIVER, *The Leaf and the Cloud*

TRANSCRIPT OF DETECTIVE JIM WALSH
INTERVIEWING WITNESS ELIZABETH MATTHEWS

E. Matthews: *First off let me tell you that I have no skin in the game here . . . Shit. Sorry. That's probably a bad metaphor given how he was . . . how he was killed, right?*

Det. Walsh: *It is in fairly poor taste.*

E. Matthews: *All I am trying to say to you is that I don't really know them. Together, I mean. I don't know anything about Bex and her husband—what is his name again, Guy?*

Det. Walsh: *Grayson.*

E. Matthews: *Right. Again, no disrespect. I'm nervous. I knew his name was Grayson. I never met him. Until yesterday I hadn't seen her in about fifteen years.*

Det. Walsh: *But you did attend college with the deceased's wife. You used to be friends with Rebecca Sommers.*

E. Matthews: *Yeah, I knew Bex back in the day. That's what we used to call her. Bex. No one ever called her Rebecca. I think she hated being* called Rebecca back then . . . but it seems like something he would have liked.

DET. WALSH: *He? Her husband? The one you don't know?*

E. MATTHEWS: *Yeah. From what I've seen of him on her Instagram account. He just seems like the kind of guy who would be more into a Rebecca than a Bex. Rebecca sounds more proper and sophisticated . . . more wifey.*

DET. WALSH: *Wifey?*

E. MATTHEWS: *Yes. Wifey.*

DET. WALSH: *But you said you didn't know the deceased, you never met him.*

E. MATTHEWS: *Exactly. I've never met him.*

DET. WALSH: *And until recently you hadn't been in contact with Mrs. Sommers.*

E. MATTHEWS: *A couple of weeks ago she reached out asking me if I was still a journalist and if I would be interested in writing a profile about her.*

DET. WALSH: *And that is what you were doing with her on the night he was killed.*

E. MATTHEWS: *Yes. We were hanging out. I had plans to write something for the magazine I work for. We were attending the conference and then I was supposed to go with her to her ranch.*

DET. WALSH: *Were you with her all night?*

E. MATTHEWS: *No.*

DET. WALSH: *When did you last see her?*

E. MATTHEWS: *Around eight-ish.*

DET. WALSH: *Do you have any idea where she is now?*

E. MATTHEWS: *Do you?*

DET. WALSH: *I'm going to be the one asking the questions for now. Grayson Sommers was brutally murdered in his own barn and you are the last person to speak to his wife before she disappeared. Do you think she would be capable of that sort of thing?*

E. MATTHEWS: *No. I mean . . . I don't think so. I don't know what she's like now. She did use to be one of the most capable people I'd ever met. She used to be able to do anything.*

DET. WALSH: *How about you start at the beginning . . .*

CHAPTER ONE

LIZZIE

Two weeks earlier

There are things I know I should be doing before bed in order to get a "good" night's sleep.

I should wash and moisturize my face with at least five different products, turn the temperature in my bedroom down to slightly chilly, put all my screened devices in another room to charge.

I should meditate and then engage my husband in some sweet and meaningful conversation about our days. Or maybe the conversation comes first, then the meditation.

I can't remember.

I should light a candle and write in a journal. I should think about what I'm grateful for.

I should just be.

But I'm not doing any of that. Who actually *does* any of that? I'm scrolling Instagram like any normal thirtysomething woman with a dirty face in a too-warm room while my husband reads the news on his phone next to me, sometimes murmuring in disgust, sometimes chuckling for no discernible reason, since absolutely nothing in the news is funny anymore unless you're a sociopath.

I must have made a noise during my scroll because Peter leans over and places his scruffy chin on my shoulder.

"Are you creeping on that girl you went to college with again?"

"Nope."

"I see her chickens on your screen." I tilt the phone away. "And that three-legged goat. Why doesn't someone shoot that thing?"

"That goat has its very own Instagram account with 1.2 million followers," I reply, even though I've explained this to him before. "Tripod is their own influencer."

"What's her name again? Skanky Betsy?"

Back in college we all used to call her Slutty Bex, not Skanky Betsy. And it was a nickname she fully embraced. She owned it. I realize that it isn't politically correct to call someone Slutty anything anymore, but when that person gets their own T-shirt made with the nickname Slutty Bex on it and they wear it on senior day, then I think it's okay to remember them like that in your own head or, in a moment of weakness when you feel weird about looking at their social media account all the time and even stranger about how your friendship ended terribly, to tell your husband about the nickname Slutty Bex and maybe laugh about it.

I really haven't talked to her in fifteen years, not since Bex ghosted me after college. It's funny how a slight like that can still sting so many years later, but it does.

Back then she wasn't the person she is now, the one I only let myself peek at once or twice a week because her Instagram account infuriates me for no rational reason. Or maybe it *is* rational. The issue is that Rebecca Sommers, or rather @BarefootMamaLove, bears absolutely no resemblance to Bex, the woman who once did a forty-five-second keg stand in the basement of Sigma Chi with her top off. Or the woman who befriended me the first day of college by ordering two pizzas to our shared dorm room and watching *Sliding Doors* with me because I was too nervous to go out to the frat parties. I'd never had a single sip of alcohol before and she didn't make me feel dumb about it. She bought me some fruity wine coolers and taught me how to handle my booze. Rebecca Sommers has absolutely no resemblance to the girl who convinced me to pierce my belly button with her even though I had never even pierced my ears.

In her new life, the one I watch on social media, Rebecca now lives in a renovated farmhouse on a ranch somewhere out West where she raises fluffy heritage chickens, cows, sheep, and goats. No one in her family ever wears shoes but their feet are somehow never dirty. She makes her own cheese, milks her own milk, and bakes enough bread to feed a small army. These days she's very, very blond, not the dishwater-blond variety from college, but like a honeydew-meets-a-gold-doubloon kind of yellow. It's a blond that costs money. Bex didn't have money in college. Like me she worked in the cafeteria as part of her work-study program. We were the only ones in our sorority who had actual on-campus jobs. None of the other girls needed them. Their parents were the type who paid their tuition in full, who bought them off-campus apartments and rented out the rooms to other students because it was a "good investment."

It was Bex who got me to rush for our sorority because she said it would be "a hilarious social experiment," and she was probably the reason they let me in. She charmed all those fancy Tri Delts with her off-color jokes and her ability to score drugs from a townie. We were a package deal, so they accepted me too.

Bex was also an RA in one of the freshman dorms like I was because it gave her free housing. It wasn't cool, but it was cheap. Being lower middle class gave both Bex and me an edge, it made us weirdly chic to the trust fund girls from NYC and LA. We weren't exactly charity cases, but we gave the sorority street cred. We were inseparable back then, and our friend-breakup, if you can even call it that, still has the ability to make me overwhelmingly sad, especially when I'm scrolling social media after one and a half glasses of wine.

I've never met Bex's husband. But it seems like she married up in a big way. I, on the other hand, just got married.

That's unfair. I married well. I married a man who is funny and tender and a good father and who still thinks I'm interesting after a decade of marriage. I married a man who knows how to change a tire, find my G-spot, swaddle a baby, make my mom laugh, and do our taxes. He's a man who can tell when I'm sick of small talk at a school-parents party and always finds a way to extricate me from a conversation with the head of the PTA. These are not trivial things.

But I also married a man who is now unemployed despite being overeducated at one of the top schools in the world. A man who has never worried about saving or investing. A man who might never work again because he's too proud to take a job he considers beneath him.

But he's still a good man. I have to remind myself of that.

And he's still stupidly handsome as he pushes forty. If I weren't so tired from work and raising our two small kids, I would happily have sex with him more often than the once every two weeks we seem to be managing these days.

Bex and her husband apparently do it every single day. I know this because they crafted a reel on Instagram with their pastor (their actual pastor) about how they decided to reignite their sex life for their thirty-fifth birthdays. They encouraged their followers to participate in the #WhoopieWithYourSchmoopie challenge. That video got something like eight million views and the comments were uncomfortably supportive and also slightly sad, filled with women who I assumed were complete strangers to Bex bemoaning their lack of a sex drive or their husbands' affairs or their closeted sexuality. I gobbled them all up like a grocery-store romance novel, all those secrets spilled onto a small screen.

If I called Peter my "schmoopie" he would likely divorce me. And rightly so. I would respect him for that. It would be the correct decision. I made the mistake of showing the whoopie challenge to him, which led to my having to explain how I knew Bex in the first place, which led to his scrolling through her account and then calling me out every time he caught me looking at her or Tripod or her six beautiful kids.

"She seems terrible," he said the first time I showed him her profile.

I loved him even more for hating her as much as I do now. That's one of the best things about Peter. He hates what I hate and that's a real turn-on for me. Some people want to like the same things as another person, but give me a man who also despises work birthday celebrations, loud chewers, and people who talk on wireless headphones in public and I swoon.

Hate is the wrong word when it comes to Bex. I'm wounded in ways I can't properly explain. I miss her and that ache turns into frustration, which turns into disdain. Her feed riles me up with misplaced envy because there is no way in hell I would ever want to live on a farm with six children. I want to say that scrolling her Instagram is not some regular thing for me. But that would be a lie. I swear that I have my own fully functional (mostly) adult life and priorities that do not include her. I just sometimes get sucked down the rabbit hole and then I feel all the feelings.

Both Peter and I hate influencers, but as magazine editors— or in Peter's case, a former magazine editor—we have a reason to. They did sort of help destroy our industry. I don't think any of them meant to. In fact, I know they didn't wake up one morning and get together in one of their beautiful McMansions or rustic off-the-grid cabins or anti-vax communes and say, *Oh, I want to kill print journalism and the careers of thousands of reporters,* but that's what happened over the past five years. I'm still holding on to my managing editor job at the magazine by a wisp. When Peter got laid off we used our savings to move out of New York and over to the Philly burbs, where our kids could go to public school and my mom could help us with childcare. Everyone at the magazine is remote now anyway so I only need to be in the office one day a week, if that. Peter is allegedly working on a novel. I'm trying to keep my job so that we all have health insurance.

I scroll Instagram so often because I'm looking for stories that will keep the magazine relevant, or so I tell myself.

Peter nuzzles my neck in a way that I usually enjoy, but I'm too exhausted to think about what leaning into the nuzzle might lead to. It's not that I don't like the sex. It's wonderful once it gets going, once everything is firing. It's just that getting there can be tedious. Even though I've wasted an hour on social media, the ten minutes it will take to get everything situated for sex with my husband (the stroking, the rearranging of the pillows, more stroking, the lube) doesn't seem like the best use of time when I could be failing at trying to fall asleep.

I lean just slightly away, and he knows I'm not into it tonight. When you've been together as long as we have you only need to make the slightest bodily movements to indicate your mood. It's one of the things I appreciate most about marriage, the shared sign language. He rubs the sore spots in my shoulders and my neck instead and that is almost as good as the bygone orgasm.

"Her farm does look lovely," Peter says. "Is it a vineyard or a farm farm? Do they actually grow things or raise things?" Peter grew up in central London. I don't think he's ever been on a farm except for the scraggly pumpkin patch we take the kids to in October.

"Her profile now reads, 'Building our ranch from the ground up with the help of God's grace.'"

"What does that mean? Growing the ranch from the ground up? Don't most things begin on the ground? You wouldn't construct something from the sky down, would you?" Peter is a stickler for both grammar and proper use of language. I think it's in the genetic code of most British people. They can't help themselves. It's like they all learned to read from the *Oxford English Dictionary* while we Americans got our first sentences from *Hop on Pop*. His dictatorial command of words served him well at the hard news magazine where we met and where we both worked at the start of our careers. I left after I had the kids, when I was politely told that my time constraints as a mother would be incompatible with going out on the campaign trail and doing long-form investigative pieces. Peter left when the time constraints of all our readers precluded them from reading the magazine anymore and it shut down.

"I honestly don't know what building it 'from the ground up' means. It seems like it's been there for quite some time," I say. "No one is building. I think she's just being poetic. There's the high protein grain. Apparently, it's made with pig colostrum. Gross. There are cows. They love raw milk."

"Do they also love salmonella?" Peter scoffs. I ignore him.

"I think they started making soap. Definitely organic eggs. And she seems to breed those chickens. You can actually buy baby chicks. They ship them in the mail. Seems cruel to me. And sheep for wool, which she uses to knit, and they also sell lamb meat. She has a whole online store. You can buy everything in her pictures. Look, I could buy this baby carrier right now!" I click an Instabuy link.

"We have a carrier," Peter points out. "And besides, Ollie is getting too big. He hates it."

We do have one, but it's nothing like this one. We have a secondhand BabyBjörn that's been passed through my mom group and probably seven babies. It's frayed on the top where it's been chewed on and there are stains from various bodily fluids that will never come out.

Rebecca's baby carrier, the one that is almost always strapped to her chest in her photos, looks like it's been spun from the rawest of raw silk. There are no stains, no teeth marks. It fits her like a couture gown as she sweeps the porch, hangs the sheets on a line in the fields, bakes everything from scratch. Her pristine carrier looks blessed by the gods. It costs an otherworldly amount too: $575.

Her audience adores the carrier except when she has one of the babies facing out in it. Then they're enraged. Then they rail on her for being a terrible mother because everyone ought to know that letting a baby face outward is a massive safety concern. Her audience seems very fickle. They love her one day and hate her the next. I think she must just let the baby face out for the camera. It makes better photos. Who wants to stare at the back of a baby's head in a picture?

"Was she always a Jesus freak?" Peter asks. We are not a religious family. Peter's religion is soccer and mine is lapsed Episcopalian. I don't remember Bex being religious at all. In fact the only time we talked about religion was when she told me her mom had been ostracized by her very Catholic parents for having Bex when she was a teenager.

"Her husband must be religious. She wasn't into that at all in college. But she does mention God a lot in her stuff these days."

"You know quite a bit about this woman for not having spoken to her for over a decade," Peter says. He has said this before.

"Probably about as much as you know about your favorite sports dudes," I snap a little. "Stats and whatnot."

"But she isn't a professional athlete. She's just some girl on the Instagram."

A woman, I want to correct him, *a woman with eleven million followers*, but the semantics aren't worth getting into when it comes to social media and influencers. Peter has no patience for any of it. He never even joined Twitter back when it was still called Twitter and almost all of us at the magazine were required to use it. "The people who want to read my writing will find it," he always said. They didn't.

I'm about to drop the phone on the floor and shove it under the bed like I do every night since I don't have the energy to get up and go plug it in in the bathroom as Goop recommends. But then I get a notification.

Shit! Can someone now tell if you've been looking at their profile too long? Did I accidentally like that last picture of Bex and her six kids milking that cow? Six feels like too many children to me. Two children feels like a lot of children to me. I don't even know how your vagina would handle that many kids. But thinking about Bex's vagina feels invasive now that she's sending me a direct message.

> Hey Lizzie, is this you?

> It is, right? I have been totally insta-stalking you for a few months now, so I know it is. Hiiiiiiiiiiii

She has been insta-stalking *me*? Well, that's sort of nice to hear. But what is she even looking at? The sad backyard birthday party I had for Nora with the recycled balloon arch I borrowed from my cousin's baby shower, or did she see my taco Tuesday reel where I very cleverly made a train of taco shells for my twenty-month-old to follow into the kitchen? (In hindsight that was a terrible idea. We'll be finding pieces of those taco shells until the kids go to college, but there were five minutes when it looked pretty damn cute, and it got a ton of likes from my small coterie of followers from the neighborhood, which gave me an endorphin boost that I enjoyed too much.)

What am I supposed to write back? And why does her casually cheery tone piss me off so much? The answer to that is painfully obvious. She was the one who chose to end our friendship. She was the one who didn't show up at the airport to pick me up like she was supposed to or answer my calls or texts afterward. She was the one who outgrew me and tossed me aside. She said the cruelest things to me that anyone has ever said.

Yet, I answer her. And I am cheery as fuck when I do it.

> Oh my gosh! It's me. Oh wow, this is such a blast from the past. :) How are you? What have you been up to?

We live in such a strange time where we have to pretend not to know exactly what a person has been up to even though they post about what they have been up to nearly daily—or in Bex's case, hourly. Am I supposed to pretend I don't know about the ranch, the six children, the three-legged goat, all that whoopie, while we message each other on the very platform where I've seen all these things?

> Oh you know. Just living

> Ha. Me too.

The banality of it is soul crushing.

Peter is staring at me now. I'd be staring at me too if I were him. What expression must be on my face as I furiously type to this random person while lying in our bed in the middle of the night?

Emily, I mouth my sister's name. My younger sibling has been working in Asia for the past six months so it's never inconceivable to get texts from her at all hours. Peter rolls his eyes and then blows an imaginary kiss my way before turning over. I hate lying to him. And he hates it when I keep tapping away at my phone once he goes to sleep. We both do. We have an unspoken rule that once one of us shuts our eyes the other puts down the phone. I type a quick bye.

> It's late here . . . going to bed. Great to reconnect though.

> Sorry. I always forget about time zones. You're in New York. I'm such a turd

I smile at her use of the word *turd* because it doesn't seem at all like the kind of thing she would ever post in one of her captions and I feel like I've gotten a little bit of the real her. I hate the rush that gives me. Also, I don't want to correct her about where I live. Leaving New York feels like a failure. There are a dozen things I want to type, but my fingers are frozen.

She keeps going.

But I really want to talk. It's important. Maybe tomorrow?

Sure.

Great. Life is crazy. CRAZY. And I have been thinking about you a lot. I think you are the one person who can actually help me

CHAPTER TWO

REBECCA

There's a right way to be authentic and a wrong way to be authentic. It's the first thing you learn when you start doing the kind of work I do. But also, the first thing you learn when you marry the kind of man I've married. I'm supposed to appear a certain way to certain people. I'm supposed to speak the right words in the right tones. Sometimes I'm not supposed to speak at all. I'm almost always performing, and I have gotten very good at it.

The right way to be "authentic" online is to give away bits and pieces of yourself that seem real, to gently mock yourself, to reveal tiny imperfections, but never big ones. Talk about your stress as a mom, but never your depression (you'll lose followers real fast). Show a dirty dish, but not an entire messy countertop. Look melancholy at times, but *do not cry*. Never let them see you cry.

Thursday is media day for us. It's the day when we create almost all my content for the next week. Does that shock you? That

I'm not snapping and filming and posting every second of every day in real time? That what you see isn't exactly my real life?

I used to make all the videos and take all the pictures back in the very beginning, when this was more of a hobby, something to do when my first babies were little and I felt lost and lonely. That's how all this started. It feels like a lifetime ago.

We moved out to Grayson's family farm a year after we got married. His dad had just had a stroke and needed someone to take it on. The move seemed like a big, awesome adventure, also a way to make a new start, to begin a new chapter of our lives and leave all the terrible things that had happened with the two of us in San Francisco behind.

So, we moved out here and set up the farm, or rather, what was left of it. Farms aren't cheap to operate and most of the land had been sold to big factory farms owned by Tyson and General Mills by the time we got it. But there was still a chunk remaining, a sizable lot in the middle of nowhere. The farm, or "the ranch," as we now call it, is at least a ninety-minute drive from the nearest city and forty-five minutes away from the next town. When Grayson grew up on his dad's land there was more of a community, even a Main Street of sorts with a hardware store and a doctor's office and a grocery shop, but most of the local farmers sold their land to the big corporate guys, and when they left, the little stores and most of the people did too. By the time I finally got pregnant after more than a year of trying I was all alone with my first baby, Alice. Gray was traveling constantly, trying to get his various start-ups off the ground. He was always at some conference or another.

So I did what was recommended by the pastor of the church

Gray had been going to since he was a kid. I began to journal, and I put my journal up online as a blog.

Then I had another baby. I somehow kept blogging through it all and then switched to Instagram.

That's how it started. It sounds so basic, but early on it was just me and my babies, all of us crying more than I've ever cried in my entire life, me writing and posting pictures to try to feel better because it was nice when strangers told me that I was doing a good job.

So yeah, back then I took my own photos of our life together. I made the videos of how to bake for a bunch of kids. Those got me a lot of attention. Baking bread from scratch! Pain au chocolat and perfect éclairs out of a rustic kitchen with grain I had harvested myself! The Internet ate that up. But it was our kids who always got the most attention. Babies and pregnant bellies are what the algorithm loved and I gave it so much of both those things.

But I can't keep up with it on my own anymore. It's been years since I could. My audience is a hungry beast. It wants more, needs more. We need to produce photos, videos, captions, content, content, content, to keep the views, to keep the sponsors, to keep the money coming in. We aren't just on Instagram. We're on YouTube, TikTok, Discord, Pinterest, Telegram, and a few other places I have never even heard of but my content coordinator says will be the next big thing.

So Thursdays! Media day!

My kids hate Thursdays.

The big kids are so over all of this, except for Bella. My eight-year-old daughter loves performing in a way that is both adorable and slightly creepy. Alice, my oldest, hates it and begs me to keep her out of everything. I do what I can. Despite what many of my haters think, I do have boundaries when it comes to my children.

This is what happens on Thursdays: First we shoot a "get ready with me" reel. This is our most lucrative asset of the week. It includes seven sponsored products that you might not even notice, but which pay upward of $25,000 just to be mentioned in my daily routine. I get the kids up in the morning like I usually do. Kiki helps. She's our nanny. You'll never, ever see her on the socials, and Gray hates her and hates that she is here. He has told me over and over again that his mom raised him and his seven siblings without any help so why can't I do it? He needs me to know that my lack of self-reliance is a moral failing.

Well, his mom wasn't supporting their whole family and keeping a farm solvent while his dad flew all over the place desperately trying to find the next big investment to make him rich. So Kiki is here, and she is my absolute savior and, if I'm being honest, my closest friend. I'm not even sure if she likes me, but I love her.

Kiki and I get the kids up and we get them fed. If Gray's around he avoids this part of the morning. He's usually up with the sun, but not because that's what farmers do. We have a staff for that. He's working out in the gym down by the barn. He's been on an ultramarathon kick that consumes most of his waking hours outside of work. He only joins us at breakfast when I tell him he absolutely has to be in the pictures because at the end of the day he knows where his bread is buttered right now. I would never say it out loud. There would be consequences for saying it out loud, but we both know the truth. On media days we also have Stacy, a professional photographer from the city, come out. She used to be a photojournalist for the newspaper but now she exclusively does influencers. She just bought a Tesla. Stacy is killing it.

I try to shoot all the things involving the littles as soon as I get them up and fed because they have about an hour, maybe an hour and a half, of performing for the cameras before they get pissy and moody and I can no longer get anything good out of them. Stacy is great with camera angles and blending in with the wallpaper, but it's still a lot of work for the kids.

Stacy arrives while we eat, and we take a couple of shots of me preparing breakfast. It's mostly made well before we start shooting, but there is always some dough I can pop in the oven. Yes, I still make my own sourdough. It's easy and pretty and people love it. And yes, I enjoy doing it. I'm a baker. It's all I ever wanted to be, and the moments when I get to create food from simple ingredients, the way I used to when I thought that doing that would be my entire life, are some of the happiest moments of my days.

I guzzle coffee and then promote the non-caffeinated coffee alternative we have a low-six-figure brand deal with. I'll caption it: *I am not a coffee drinker, but I crave my morning pick-me-up ritual. I sip my DiRT/Wooter in the mornings. Don't worry, you fasters. It's totally compatible with intermittent fasting. It gives me the boost I need, and the benefits from superfood mushrooms deliver immune support and focus. I like to dress it up with vanilla Lively Proteins collagen for my skin.*

After all the kids are fed, they crawl back into bed, and we shoot me re-waking them up in their matching pajamas. It's also #sponsored, of course. One of our first big brands to sign on was an organic linen sheet company, and the matching pajamas are my own brand that comes in seven different prints and is sold on my website.

Then we take a video of me getting them out the door and into the cabin that we use as a schoolhouse. We have a teacher who comes in to oversee the homeschooling, even though I genuinely try to be as involved as I can, especially with science and math since they were my favorite subjects when I was in school. You'll never see the teacher though. I let people assume I do it. The audience likes that. They seem to appreciate self-reliance in a mother as much as my husband. Then, with the baby in tow, we shoot some images in the barn with the animals. I strap him to my chest even though he hates it and wants to walk. The carrier is getting tight. For as much as my followers and the brands I work with love babies and big round pregnant bellies, I can't have another one. I just can't do it.

We gather eggs from the chickens, pet the lambs, say hello to Tripod (who is honestly a massive dingus of a goat and I would get rid of him if he wasn't such a fan favorite . . . if he had four legs he would definitely head-butt me in the ass). We pose for cow-milking pictures, but we have people and machinery to do the actual milking. I've attempted to breastfeed six babies (with a 50 percent success rate despite what you may have seen of me feeding the twins, one dangling off each boob) and getting milk out of a nipple is difficult no matter who or what is doing the lactating.

The big kids start school. The baby goes with Kiki. I head back inside and do some reels of me getting my face on for the day with the organic eco-friendly makeup brand that's a new sponsor, and doing my hair with the Dyson Airwrap and raw sugar multi-miracle hair mist. We do some diaper changes with the baby for the new biodegradable diaper brand that is testing us out. We tried something called elimination training with the twins when they were babies and the engagement was incredibly high on it, but to be honest, the house smelled like shit all the time and I just couldn't do it again. Gray was constantly complaining about it. We shoot some stills and videos out in the schoolhouse. I change outfits seven times to make sure I have something different on for every video. The kids wear monochromatic linens every single day. We sell them in our online shop so it's good promo, but also it makes it hard for the audience to tell what they are wearing and whether they have actually changed clothes since it's impossible to get them to change their outfits seven times on Thursdays.

Some commenters have gotten irritated with the "sad beige" way that I dress my kids, but it's really about convenience and other people love it. The clothes sell out every time we have a new drop.

For some reason my audience gets jazzed about watching me make beds and hang laundry, so we always shoot a couple of those videos. In reality we have a heavy-duty industrial-sized washer and dryer and I don't hang the family sheets on a line like Ma Ingalls. They'd get dusty and filthy in five minutes with all the dirt and wind around here, but it works for the socials. We put those videos in slo-mo with a quote over them about loving life and living simply and getting back to our roots. The engagement goes bananas.

We always make sure to shoot Gray off in the fields somewhere, on the tractor, riding his horse. The audience seems to get off on the fact that they don't know that much about Gray, that he's a cipher of a cowboy. I think it makes it easier to imprint their own fantasies on my husband, which is fine with me. They don't need to know the truth about him or about us.

Sometimes, late at night or early in the morning when I can't sleep, I open my own social media accounts and wonder what I would think of myself if I were an outsider looking in. Would I be intrigued? Angry? Calmed? Irritated? Would I be a fan or a hater, because I have both and they're equally ravenous for my content. My account has grown exponentially in just a few years. There's an intense hunger for content like mine, for #Homesteading and #PrairieLife, for #BackToYourRoots and #TraditionalLiving. I've leaned into it and there is no going back.

The audience loves looking through the fun-house mirror I have so meticulously created on my social media.

I wonder what people would think of the hashtag #MyPersonalHell.

Here is what we don't take pictures and videos of:

The kids and I always eating dinner alone because Gray gets triggered by how noisy and chaotic it is at mealtimes.

Me feeding each of the kids a different meal because none of them eat the same thing even though we always photograph one wholesome hearty stew, soup, or hunk of meat.

Our caregivers, house cleaners, or the farm staff. To our audience we do it all ourselves.

We don't show Gray and me sleeping in separate bedrooms or the knock-down-the-walls fights we've been having lately.

You'll never see my bruises.

No one ever sees me cry or hears me scream.

CHAPTER THREE

LIZZIE

Things I Have Seen Bex (um . . . Rebecca) Sommers do on a small screen in my hand:

1. Castrate a three-legged goat.

2. Potty train her twins without diapers.

3. Give birth to her children in a tub on the floor of her restored barn.

4. Extol the virtues of the rhythm method of birth control even as she seems to be pregnant every couple of years.

5. Churn butter.

6. Commit to a thirty-day "intimacy challenge" to have sex with her husband every day for an entire month.

7. Give all of her children haircuts that look amazing.

8. Deliver a baby lamb.

Every picture that Bex posts has the same captions and hashtags. Things like #DreamsDoComeTrue, #RomanticizeYourLife, and #SomeonePinchMe. If you don't think too hard about it, those captions can work for anything.

Did your toddler poop in the pool? #SomeonePinchMe.

Did you not tear your perineum while giving birth in that tub? #DreamsDoComeTrue.

I'm thinking about this before I even pick up my phone while lying in bed in the morning when I feel a sharp pain on my toe like I've been bitten by a rat.

"Jesus Christ," I yelp, waking Peter as I snatch my leg away from the offender's fangs.

My first thought is that our geriatric basset hound, Bethany (don't ask), is curled up at the foot of the bed and got hungry but didn't know where she was. It's happened before. But no. The wound was inflicted by our toddler, who has inexplicably taken to biting people's toes like a rabies-infected raccoon. Ollie laughs in glee as I yank up the blanket and do the only thing I can possibly do as I grit my teeth through the pain and check to see if I'm bleeding. I grab him, tickle him, and cover him in kisses while asking him to "please stop biting people, especially Mommy," and inquire about when exactly he ended up curled at our feet.

"Darktime," he replies simply. "Nora snore."

"Fair," I say. "But wake Mommy up next time and maybe sleep at the top of the bed. And also do not bite toes. It's not polite."

"And terribly unsanitary," Peter says as he grabs Ollie around the waist and hoists him over his head to tromp down the stairs to wake up Nora to start the day. Peter can get away with saying things like "terribly unsanitary" and not sounding like a douche because he is well-accented and everything his people say sounds charming and smart.

With both of the men in my life occupied for a hot second, I lean over and grab my phone from where I shoved it beneath the bed.

I figure I won't hear from Bex again. She was probably tipsy or something when she texted me, even though I don't think she drinks much anymore. They don't exactly seem like party people. Maybe she'd taken an Ambien. I do weird shit when I take them. Peter said I once stood up on the bed in the middle of the night and rapped "Funky Cold Medina" after taking a whole pill during Nora's sleep training.

No messages. I get up and pee, relishing the quiet in the bathroom, and go through the motions of making sure the kids are dressed in clean clothes and presentable for camp. I lose the argument with Nora about whether she can wear the purple princess dress she's worn for the past ten days. It smells like a rest-stop bathroom and the sequins are falling off. I know that the Montessori counselors will silently judge me in their smug Montessori way, but I've learned to pick my battles. I eat half a waffle left on Ollie's plate and get to my desk in the corner of our bedroom just in time to start Slacking with the rest of my team for eight hours. I miss the newsroom. I miss being around actual people and bitching about crazy bosses while getting our coffee in the morning. Talking to someone on Slack feels like talking to a robot that's always a little pissed off at you.

And then to my surprise, Bex messages me bright and early West Coast time, nine A.M. my time.

Hey you

I am now a "you"? And I merit a "hey"?

My fingers hover over the keys of the phone, but I wait to answer and go to the bathroom again and do Wordle before writing back. Why I'm treating Bex like I would a middle school crush, I have no idea.

My New Year's resolution this year was to stop bringing my phone into the bathroom with me because it is both disgusting and contributes to my overabundance of anxiety-inducing screen time. The initial joy of opening the phone typically lasts about three minutes and is quickly replaced with dread. But I've failed miserably at this resolution. It was easier to quit smoking in my twenties than to not stare at my screen while I poop at age thirty-six.

And that's what I'm doing when I reply to Bex.

Oh. Hey you. It's early there.

Two can play at the "hey you" game.

I get up at 5 so I can get grounded and have me time before the kids are awake. Also we get up with the sun. Farm life. Haha

You live on a farm?

I don't even know why I'm pretending that I haven't seen her cows' nipples.

Yeah. Just a small place. 125 acres. It's gorg. You would love it

I never once indicated that a farm is something I would love during our college friendship. Neither did she.

Cool.

So you're an editor at Modern Woman. That's amazing!!!!!!!!!!!!

My inner copy editor tries to ignore the surfeit of exclamation marks.

Still there!

Exactly one exclamation mark.

I do get a little thrill that she knows this about me and I want to make it sound better than it is, better than a whittled-down team of writers, editors, and designers chugging away at a magazine half its previous size, all of us working from our bedrooms, and some from their parents' basements, everyone hoping to get another year or two out of it before the inevitable next round of layoffs.

Just prepping for the big September issue. Always a slog, but #worthit.

Who the fuck am I?

So much cooler than my days. Running after kids CONSTANTLY and baking bread. You have littles too though right????????

I hate the word *littles* the same way I hate the word *hubby*. I don't say that part of me would maybe love to chase them around all day instead of dropping them off at their "camp" or their "preschool," both of which are essentially glorified and over-priced day care that will drain our bank account until the start of public kindergarten. We paid all the deposits for these things a year in advance, back when we thought Peter would have a job by now. And of course they are nonrefundable so we put our children in the daily holding pens and pay through the nose so maybe Peter can eke out enough of a novel that someone might want to buy it.

I don't say that sometimes I long to be with my kids, chasing them through a field, at the same time as I long for intense soli-tude where I can be blessedly alone without anyone touching me or needing me, so that I can work and feel like a productive person in the world. All of these things are all true at the same time.

I've always had this question about her Instagram account. *Does* she run after her kids all day? Six is a fuck ton of children. And I don't know how anyone manages raising any number of kids without help, especially while posting as many pictures and stories and reels as she does on three or four different social media platforms. I noticed the other day that Bex just started a newsletter. I imagine she has the kind of invisible help that celebrities have. I once interviewed the team of nannies who cared for the kids of a world-famous reality television family. Their NDAs had expired and they told me that whenever they spied a paparazzo in the bushes they had explicit instructions to hand the children to the mother and essentially dive out of sight like a CIA agent avoiding a sniper.

I don't respond to Bex for a few minutes while I head back to my desk and try to put out a fire about a cover story that hasn't been turned in on time. When I return to my phone Bex has sent a barrage of what seem like harried messages.

> I don't want to take up too much of your time. I'm sure you are CRAZY busy. But I had this wild idea and well . . . No it's probably stupid

> But I have been working on something out here. Something new and we are trying to get some press for it and I thought about you

> You're like one of the best writers I know and you know me so I think you would get this and get me and be fair about it and everything

And well I'm pretty private about things these days so I don't want to invite just anyone into my home

Is there any chance . . . No probably not . . .

I feel weird for her when I read all this. It's like watching a teenage boy ask someone out on a date over text and failing miserably. I also kind of like it, which makes me a terrible person, but I don't actually care. The thrill outweighs the shame.

What's going on?

I write it in as breezy a tone as possible.

Is there any chance you might come out here and maybe profile me for your magazine? There's a lot happening and I would feel most comfortable with you being the writer. You'll get an exclusive. You can stay in our guesthouse and I promise you it will be BIG news. Please say yes. PLEASSSSSSSSSSSSE

Something isn't right about this request. And even though I'm overjoyed that the ball feels like it's very much in my court,

I'm also pissed that she hasn't even mentioned the reason we haven't spoken in more than a decade. No explanation. Just this? Does she think she's so famous, so important, and so fancy that I don't deserve at least the smallest of apologies?

I stare out my window at our neighbor Marvin's yard and see him outside in his bathrobe for a secret smoke, far away from his wife, Judy. His robe falls open as he sits in a lawn chair, but he doesn't care. He just lets his balls air out in the breeze while he inhales. I see Marvin almost every morning. I see Marvin's testicles almost every morning. I desperately need a change of scenery.

I book my ticket before even asking my boss if I can write the story.

* * *

I adore being on planes without my children. Work travel has never felt so luxurious as right now, even squeezed into an economy seat at the back of the plane, just one row away from the bathrooms.

Absolutely no one needs me. No one is asking me to fix the volume on their screens or get them a snack or scratch their right foot. I'm in heaven. It feels like I have twenty-seven hands and all of them are free to do whatever I want.

There's a mom behind me balancing a baby on her lap while a toddler draws a butt with a bright blue marker on her knee. I'm so happy I'm not her, and yet when I pass her to go to the bathroom, I want to count every single one of her baby's naked chubby toes and maybe put them in my mouth.

Over the past two weeks I've been going back and forth with Bex about the details of this trip. She's been tight-lipped about the announcement she's making, the big exclusive I'm supposed to be writing about. "Can't be too careful, even with you," she messaged me. But she ended up reimbursing me for the plane ticket and then paying for all the other expenses.

Bex asked me to meet her at something called the MomBomb conference at this insane resort out in the desert where rooms start at $2K a night. It's close to her ranch and she's apparently making her big announcement there. She promised we would head to the farm the next day. I'd never heard of MomBomb, but apparently it's the number one conference of female influencers in the world. Bex thought it could be a nice way for me to get the lay of the land.

Why am I so eager? I keep coming up with new ways to explain it to myself. It's a good story for one thing. Anything written about Bex has been going viral for the better part of a year now. She's a lightning rod in the mom socialsphere but has also become something of a piñata in the culture wars. An exclusive interview with her (she never does them) would do great things for our website and maybe I could convince her to do something in print too, even though no one reads us in print and the magazine is leaning toward becoming only digital to save money.

There's also something else newsworthy here, something that's even more interesting to the old hard news reporter in me, the person I was before I had my kids. According to some of the influencer chat boards on Reddit (they're insane and highly detailed and it's no wonder that traditional news is in the shitter when people can just read these conspiracy theories all day), there's local speculation that Bex's husband might be gearing up to run for office, maybe even Congress. That's a real story.

The existing congressman for the district is approximately 107 years old and keeping an iron grip on the seat with every ounce of Viagra coursing through his mottled veins, but the local party is hungry for fresh blood and a reboot of optics (this is according to one intrepid redditor named DesertFoxStormTrooper). Grayson Sommers has everything they want in a candidate. Excellent hair, traditional values, a pretty wife, and a gaggle of children who all live off the land. I wonder if I'll get to meet him, and maybe interview him too. It could be a story for one of our publishing company's other magazines, the newsier ones. It could be a chance to do some real reporting again.

I could really go for a Bloody Mary. I cut down on drinking liquor when I had the kids, because I couldn't hack hangovers while parenting, but being alone on a plane seems like an excellent time to indulge. I order one and ask for it to be extra spicy even though I know an airplane Bloody Mary is just cheap vodka and tomato juice. I say it because I want to feel like I'm in some fancy bar. I pay the thirty dollars for in-flight Wi-Fi so I can research MomBomb as I sip, and to be honest, the conference is way more intense than I expected.

There are more than two hundred panels and breakout sessions on growing your business, courting advertisers, reinvention marketing, and pivoting your personal brand. It's a master class in entrepreneurship and I can't say I'm not intrigued considering my career in magazines is a sinking ship and I have no life preserver.

Could I become an influencer? Is it an alternative to working at Trader Joe's, something I have actually strongly considered since learning about their generous health benefits for families and because I truly enjoy their early 2000s playlists (so much Weezer) and Hawaiian flowered shirts?

There's actually a panel entitled, "Content Creation 101: How to Start Monetizing Tomorrow." I click the sign-up button.

But what the hell would I monetize to my 347 followers on Instagram? Here's a picture of the secondhand water sandals from Target that I snagged from the pool lost-and-found rummage sale the other day. #Blessed. Let me show you my toenail that fell off after the kids gave me hand, foot, and mouth disease twice in two months. #TheJoysOfMotherhood. I'm a person who currently edits spam listicles for a women's magazine about how to perfectly shape your eyebrows to look like Karlie Kloss, so I shouldn't be such a judgmental asshole, but I still can't wrap my head around what it would be like to monetize my actual life.

It's only been two weeks since Bex first messaged me, and we never got on the phone to talk about the plan for the next few days. We organized all the details over DM. It was intensely efficient, which I appreciated, but left me no time to ask her any real questions. I did tell her I wanted to dig into all the online vitriol that gets slung her way in the comments section of her posts and on a variety of different Internet forums (and also my own personal moms text chain, which I left out). She wrote back with a shrug emoji and said that would be fine.

"We're old friends," she wrote. "I'll be an open book."

But will she? Her image is so carefully curated, her accounts so well-orchestrated. Am I going to get Bex or Rebecca? I have no idea what I'm in for.

CHAPTER FOUR

REBECCA

Everyone is lying to you about something.

I look around at all the insanely accomplished women here at the MomBomb conference, all of them posing for photos, schmoozing with brands, closing deals, and streaming every second of it onto their platforms, and I think of all the things I know they're lying about.

The rumor mill is constantly churning in our world, but we also usually keep one another's secrets from the public because we all have something to hide.

I spy Marybeth Kelsey. She's got more than three million followers on her account about finding true love when you least expect it after divorce. Except she's currently separated from her second husband in real life and continuing to post about their happy union because it will destroy their brand if she tells anyone they are splitting before their big five-year vow renewal at Disney in the fall. They've got it all planned for Cinderella's castle and no one ever says no to that sweet, sweet Disney sponsorship money. Once it starts flowing it will keep going for years unless you take a shit on Space Mountain.

Marybeth is chatting with Amanda Meery, who has just under a million followers watching her homesteading in the Alaskan wilderness with her three kids. Except all three of those kids are actually away in boarding school because teenagers have no interest in living without electricity, running water, or Netflix, and she shoots all their content in a single week when they return in the summer. The rest of the time she boats around the Aleutian Islands with her girlfriend, Carol.

Dixie Simmons got famous for making breast-milk ice cream and yogurt on her channels and she rails on about how preservatives and additives in grocery store foods cause cancer and ADHD in kids, but I've seen her crush the processed food aisles of Costco while sucking down a full-sugar bottle of Coke.

During Hurricane Eliza last year, Jenn Thayer became Internet-famous for sticking out the storm with her three kids and geriatric dachshund in Florida, but I know for a fact she was streaming from in front of a green screen in the Chicago suburbs.

Erin Sayers claims she lost a hundred and thirty pounds by eating nothing but meat for a year and doing a hardcore weights routine, but we all know she's on Ozempic.

Veronica Smith sells training courses for how to optimize your life as a stay-at-home mom of four boys using vaguely militant tactics and self-improvement tips from Tony Robbins and Dale Carnegie. Her husband is a professional baseball player, a massive douchebag, and my husband's best friend. Veronica loves waxing poetic about raising "masculine men" who aren't "snowflakes," as she details her morning routine of ice bathing and weight training to be a #MentallyStrongMama.

I could write a book about everything Veronica is lying about. And I'm pretty sure she slept with my husband.

But who am I to throw stones? I'm lying about practically everything.

The MomBomb conference is sorority rush on steroids meets Harvard Business School. You have never met a more ambitious crowd of women who are so meticulous about their beachy waves and personal branding. It feels like you're being judged and scrutinized every single moment. Mostly because you are.

I've been coming to MomBomb for ten years, since before it was such a massive thing, since way before the big sponsors signed on, back when it was held at a Marriott in Orlando and we all paid for our own rooms because we were hungry for community, friendship, and swag. Back in those days we were still paid in free products so we were drowning in BPA-free Tupperware, linen swaddles, and vitamin D supplements. That was before we knew what we were worth. Before we all started to fight for it. These days MomBomb is at an insane resort right in the middle of the desert with a view of the mountains. Each suite has its own infinity pool and there's a meditation labyrinth designed by James Turrell and constructed out of oyster shells. The architecture is sleek and modern, using stone and wood that seem to whisper, *Nature, but make it fancy.*

It's like your Instagram feed came to life—if your feed was filled with million-dollar views and impeccable design, which many of ours are at this point.

I don't take too many pictures or videos when I attend things like this, which could be a missed opportunity for content, but it's really about self-preservation. Anything I do on my own without the children always leads to the inevitable comments about "who is watching your kids?," which is difficult to answer honestly most of the time. It's inevitable that someone will post and tag me while I'm here, but I try to avoid it by saying no to selfies.

When people ask me that question about who is taking care of my kids on a daily basis, any time I do anything without a child strapped to me, I would love to say, *They are with their other parent.* But that's also not the truth. Even when Gray is home he isn't doing much parenting, especially lately. He wanted these kids, so many of them. He wanted even more. He loves the idea of many, many children in the house, but the reality of them always seems unpleasant to him. Besides, now that I know the truth about what he's done, having more children will be impossible.

Plus, I could never pin childcare on Gray, even if he were up for it. In our world the husband doesn't do domestic labor.

The fact that I can never reveal that I have any sort of help at the ranch is insane but necessary. Parenting this many kids with a full-time job is no joke. I think parenting two kids would be no joke. It *is* work, but no one wants to hear that. They see me as a "good" mother because they see me "do it on my own."

So my kids are happily with one of their caregivers right now and they will be for a few days while I handle Gray.

MomBomb kicks off in earnest tomorrow, but everyone arrived yesterday to "pre-conference" and there's a little bit of a moms-gone-wild vibe since the event is strictly no kids allowed (unless you're breastfeeding). When I arrive it's already cocktail time even though it's barely past noon. This year's conference has a tequila sponsor, several wine sponsors, and a hard seltzer sponsor. Also plenty of gummies, CBD, THC—you name it, you can ingest it.

When I look at the bar menu I notice there is also a collagen creamer sponsor. This means that many of the cocktails are an eggy white. Anything to keep it tight.

But there's also a variety of nonalcoholic beverage sponsors for the more traditional and conservative crowd. I would be considered one of them. But that's not why I don't drink much anymore. Gray and his family abstain for religious reasons (and to save face in the community). Gray also can't handle his liquor. I learned that lesson the hard way.

I stopped drinking because I hate feeling out of control. If there was one reason I married Gray in the first place it was because he gave me a sense of safety and stability that had been lacking in every other part of my life. It's the best thing about him and most of it had to do with his money. Money can equal stability, and it definitely gives you power. I know that now and I will never forget it.

The theme of this year's conference is *Motherhood, Enhanced*. There are coasters and T-shirts and stickers with the tagline on every available surface. I'm not totally sure what it means. What exactly enhances motherhood? Are the products made by the sponsors enhancing motherhood? Are we enhancing motherhood? The single biggest complaint from my followers is that I make motherhood look too simple and easy and frictionless. But they don't want friction. They don't follow me for stress or for the lows of parenting and wifedom, or womanhood. They want the pretty shit and it's why they keep coming back. I am, in many ways, *Motherhood, Enhanced*.

I cut through the crowd and say hello to the familiar faces. I can feel eyes on me from all around the pool. It might be what celebrities feel like when they mistakenly decide to go to a Starbucks or the farmers market like a normal person. I have no idea. But I know these eyes are watching me and judging me. All of this is a performance.

I look around for her, for Lizzie, but I don't see anyone who looks like her. It's embarrassing to admit that I've been following her life and career as closely as I have. I know she follows me too. It says it right beneath her profile . . . LIZZIE MATTHEWS FOLLOWS YOU. So her pretending not to know anything about me when I messaged her was funny and it also bummed me out. But I get it. I'm the reason our friendship, the closest one I've ever had, is over. I'm the one who disappeared, who just left Lizzie hanging with no explanation. But I could never tell her why. I was so embarrassed and ashamed when it happened, and then the longer I waited the more impossible it seemed to reconnect. I'll tell her now. If not tonight then tomorrow. She deserves an answer and she deserves one in person.

Maybe I'm being too self-absorbed when it comes to Lizzie. Maybe she really doesn't know anything about my life or follow my actual feed. That would be strangely refreshing. Maybe she just followed me as a courtesy when I followed her and she never looks at Instagram anyway. She probably has other stuff going on that's more important with the magazine job and the handsome husband who is from London or Wales and looks a little like nineties Hugh Grant with his charming but slightly pervy smiles. She's also got two little ones, which is so much work. For me, the first two were the hardest. Going from one to two nearly broke me, both physically and mentally. I want to ask Lizzie about it, about how she's doing, about how she managed the transition from not being a mom to being a mom. I want to grab her and hug her so hard. But I won't. I tell myself to be cool. Stay cool. I need her on board for everything if I am going to pull this off.

I keep scanning the crowd for her wild brown curls, which in her online pictures seem just as unruly today as they were fifteen years ago, but there's nothing but honey highlights in every direction I look.

I spy @SingleDadDan by the tiki bar surrounded by a scrum of women three deep. He's doing a card trick, an actual card trick, and the ladies are loving it.

A few years back one of the MomBomb founders thought she was being inclusive by inviting @SingleDadDan to the conference even though it literally says *Mom* in the title. I think she regretted it after that first year, when the rumor mill started that he slept with at least three of the #FitnessMoms. Apparently, the next year he moved on to the #OrganizationMoms and then the #WineMoms. There was also talk of an orgy.

The women here are divided into their cliques, or rather their categories—fitness, luxury fashion, vintage fashion, renovation, DIY, Jesus, wine moms, and newly sober moms, who are having a big brand moment right now.

I overhear an overserved #AnxietyMom complaining to an #ADHDMom about how she never knows who her real friends are anymore since she hit a million followers. "Do they love me or do they love my following?" If you have to ask, you know the answer.

I honestly can't wait to get out of here. If I don't see Lizzie soon, I'll just hang out on my own. It's what I've been desperate for. Time alone to regroup. To plan. To go over everything I have to do in the next forty-eight hours. I want to get to the gym, sit in the sauna, and then go to my room and order room service. I need to get my nerves settled. I know that after tomorrow everything will change.

Everything will be better. I know it. It has to be.

It can't get much worse.

Out of necessity I keep my sunglasses on as I circle the pool. The bruise around my left eye has mostly faded but I'm not taking any chances. That's not the story I want to tell. My phone beeps in my bag and I pull it out hoping it's Lizzie telling me where I can meet her, preferably a quiet corner away from the crowds. But it's not her.

It's him and he's not happy.

CHAPTER FIVE

LIZZIE

Blippi is the last person you want to see in the midst of a day-drunk hangover. I curse myself for having two Bloody Marys on the plane as I cross through the immaculate lobby of the Sensoria Hotel only to be greeted by every parent's least favorite YouTube star.

It takes me a beat to realize that Blippi is a sponsor of this shindig and he, or someone who bears an intense likeness to him, is here for the content exposure offered by a thousand influencer mothers. As I rummage through my bag looking for a stray Advil, he's miming throwing a rope in the air and lassoing me around the waist. I've never wanted to punch a human being in the face more. I sidestep him to get to the check-in desk, passing through a massive arch that spells MOMBOMB in hundreds of balloons arranged in a rainbow pattern. Both Blippi and the blatant branding are a direct contrast to the minimalist design of the lobby with its natural stone and wood and the massive windows offering views of the surrounding canyons.

Blippi persists. He mimes taking out my phone and getting a selfie together. I shake my head no as I try to hand my driver's license to the woman behind the check-in counter, who looks at Blippi with similar ire.

"Go away. Scram," she hisses so quietly no one but the three of us can hear. I love her.

Check-in is swift. Bex has taken care of everything, which I'm grateful for. The magazine's meager budget could possibly have swung an economy flight, but not these insanely expensive hotel rooms. All I want to do is get upstairs and take a hot shower, maybe a bath. I'm not scheduled to meet Bex, who I should practice calling Rebecca, until the morning and my interest in attending tonight's "get to know you" welcome circle is fairly low. I should be more into all this, given that influencing is the next frontier of journalism and all that, but despite the allure of the money, the very thought of turning myself into a personal brand continues to make me want to swallow glass. I tried to pinpoint it while sipping my second Bloody Mary on the plane. Why not join in? Make that money? Get it, girl? I think it's because I don't want my career to be all about me. Most days I'm bored of myself. Why would anyone else find me even remotely entertaining? What would I say or do to perform for an audience?

The young woman behind the counter clears her throat and I look up, assuming she's warning me about another Blippi encounter. I brace myself.

"Before you go to your room you'll need to check in for the

conference. Everyone needs a wristband to be on the property this week." She holds up her own wrist to show a pink rubber bracelet that clearly reads STAFF. "The conference rented the whole space and they're big on security so if you could check in with them that would be great. Straight down the hallway and in front of the grand ballroom. You can just leave your bag with me."

The energy in the hotel is electric. The space is entirely filled with women, not a man in sight. I stroll down the short hallway to the check-in desk, where I'm greeted by the same black-clad, clipboard-carrying assistants I've seen thousands of times at thousands of event check-ins.

"You're Lizzie Matthews," one of them announces to me as I approach.

"I am," I agree, startled until I look down and see that her clipboard has pictures of attendees and their estimated check-in times on it. Whoever runs this thing has the efficiency of the Swiss guard.

"Okay, so you're press, which means you get an orange band and that will let you into the greenroom for interviews before all of the panels. There are a few sessions that are creator only so that everyone has a safe space, but the orange band will get you into most everything. I also have a badge for you."

She hands me a standard conference badge on a lanyard, also with my picture on it, and my Instagram handle. Thank god it doesn't have my follower count. I wonder if in addition to the color-coded bracelets tied to job functions there are also tiers of follower count in different shades. Turquoise for ten thousand, magenta for fifty thousand, all the colors of the rainbow for a million plus. You are a queen.

"And your welcome bag." She hands me a reusable canvas tote with MOMBOMB embroidered on the side along with my initials. Classy. I don't dig through it, but I can see it's packed with stuff. T-shirts, vitamins, skincare samples, period panties, which I am vaguely excited about.

A line is forming behind me so I start to hustle away, but one of the check-in ladies stands.

"Let me give you a quick tour," she says cheerfully, and links her arm through mine. I change my mind. These young women are the opposite of the clipboard girls who police Fashion Week check-in, the ones who usually sneer and evade eye contact unless you're Zendaya or RuPaul.

She takes me toward what looks like a wall of glass but is actually a door that slowly swings open as we approach.

There's a bar with white stone firepits and lounge chairs draped in gauzy blankets in an abundance of muted tones. Exotic plants mix with sago palms and robust lavender bushes.

"Notice the feminine lightness of the details."

I try hard to notice. I pet a blanket.

"It's baby alpaca," she whispers. "This way."

I'm beckoned toward what appears to be a modern version of a swinging rope bridge. I gasp in terror as I glance down at the chasm below, my heart hammering, toes curling over the tops of my flip-flops. I can't take a full breath. We appear to be on top of a gorge with at least a thirty-foot drop or maybe more. Beneath my quivering legs is a canyon of jagged rocks so sharp they could pierce right through the unlucky soul who slips from these wooden planks.

"The property embraces every bit of the natural landscape

here, offering a modern twist on old-school glamour and adventure," my guide informs me. "This bridge was first constructed by the original owner, a Spanish countess at the turn of the century. Of course since then it's been modified and updated with the latest in safety protocols and materials. This way to the pool," she beckons.

Heights terrify me. I gasp and stutter, grasping the thick rope railings with my fingers tensed into tiny lobster claws, but somehow I manage to cross the ten yards of swinging bridge without having to resort to crawling on my hands and knees. I'm woozy and trembling by the time I'm back on solid ground.

"The pool here is built directly into the mesa," I am told as we approach the next patio. "If you take any photos or videos out here we ask that you tag the Sensoria and also hashtag #MesaPool. They've been very generous with us and we want to give back."

She says this in the same tone Sally Struthers once used to encourage everyone to send money for starving children. What she refers to as the mesa is a startling rock formation jutting out of the navy-blue water that stretches to the edge of a concrete expanse and then seems to fall off directly into the desert. The pool is crowded with well-appointed ladies, many of them in oversized straw hats. I see faces I recognize, way more than I expected, and it's almost jarring to see them in person. There's my favorite bento box lunch influencer. *Five things in five minutes* is her mantra. If you are making lunch for six minutes, it is absolutely taking too long, she insists. She somehow manages to make gorgeous lunches using only leftovers. And the smoothie lady. I have to restrain myself from asking how exactly she gets the rainbow layers of the banana-berry smoothie so perfect when mine looks like brown sludge. She's talking to this one pelvic-floor trainer who I've been following since Ollie was born. I can't look her in the eye. Not after what we've been through virtually together.

Over there is the woman who meticulously organizes closets and pantries. I honestly can't get enough of her. I watch her videos, rapt with envy, and every time I'm done, I swear I will organize just one junk drawer, just one. Her obliteration of clutter is so strangely soothing that I feel like I know her intimately, like she's a friend I can just walk up to and say, "Do you really think I could do a capsule wardrobe?" It sort of reminds me of the time that I covered the Golden Globes for the magazine and I found myself in a room filled with celebrities all talking to other celebrities like they'd been best friends since high school. Taylor Swift was sharing a piece of chocolate cake with Naomi Watts. Ryan Gosling handed Ryan Reynolds some ChapStick. None of it felt real. I had awkwardly tried to fist-bump Meryl Streep before I interviewed her as she munched a chicken satay skewer. She only nodded at me in return, my fist hanging in the air like a lost balloon at a birthday party. I will not fist-bump anyone at this pool.

When my phone buzzes my heart flutters with anticipation. Bex?

But no. My sister Emily's face fills the screen. In her photo she's sticking out her tongue and making jazz hands on a beach somewhere in Bali. I think that's where she is now, but I'm never sure. This brilliant woman is five years younger than me and constantly on the go. Her interest in having a husband or children is less than zero. All she wants is to be a top anthropologist in the field of matriarchal studies now that she's finally finished her dissertation. I had no idea matriarchal studies was something you could focus on or make a career out of. But Emily seems to have always known.

"I have to take this," I say to my handler. She makes prayer hands and bows slightly in goodbye as she returns to check-in and sets me free on the pool mesa.

As I turn around, I run directly into a statuesque woman staring at her phone.

"I'm so s-sorry," I stutter to the smoldering brunette, who barely glances up at me. She's wearing a red gingham dress that looks like a picnic blanket. It's got a sweetheart collar and is cinched at the waist with a massive matching ribbon and bow. Her hair is pulled into an exquisite French twist. Her makeup is flawless, bronzer accentuating her sharp cheekbones. She's June Cleaver meets a Kardashian.

"You should watch where you're going." Her eyes catch on my orange wristband, which announces PRESS in bold black letters, and then she softens her tone and reaches out a hand to shake mine.

"I'm Veronica Smith. Who do you write for?"

Modern Woman," I say, craning my neck to look at her since she's also wearing four-inch black heels.

"Interesting. I always see that magazine on the newsstand and think, 'What the heck is a modern woman?'" When she laughs, I laugh because it feels like the polite thing to do. I've also wondered the same thing. "Maybe we should talk later. I have lots of answers to that question." She sashays away before I can say a word.

"Right," I murmur to her back as I walk to the edge of the deck to return the call.

"Hey, Emmy."

"Could you put my godchild on the phone? I had a dream about Nora where she turned into a purple dragon and I need to tell her about it." Emily doesn't even say hello to me.

"I'm not home. I'm on assignment."

"Where? I thought the magazine didn't send people on assignments anymore."

"It's . . . I guess it's a special case."

I explain MomBomb as best I can. Talking through it sort of feels like explaining the *Jurassic Park* franchise to an alien, but Emily gets it right away. She has a fascination with Internet culture, but she claims it's only from a sociological point of view and she doesn't keep any of the apps on her phone.

"Will you send me lots of pictures of women taking pictures of themselves?" she asks.

"Absolutely."

"You're a really good sister."

"I know."

I mention Bex. "Do you remember her?"

"Yeah. When I visited you in college she gave me her Wonderbra and my first joint." Of course she did. It amazes me that there is so little information out there about Bex from college given the public's current intense fascination with her, but she's managed to bury her wild-child past quite well. All that money must help.

"You were fifteen when you visited me at school!"

"I was mature for my age. I think I still have that bra."

"I miss you," I say with a sigh.

"I miss you too. I wish I was with you," Emily says.

"Me too. The spa here looks incredible. You'd love it. I think they make you eat crystals or something to fix your karma."

"That sounds right. I've gotta run but will you tell Nora about the purple dragon or should I call Peter?"

"You should definitely call Peter," I tell her, because I love it when my sister annoys my husband.

"Okay. Love you so much."

"Love you so much too."

I'd never explained what happened between Bex and me to my family. It didn't make sense to me so how could it make sense to them? She was a fleeting memory to Emily, just a college girl who gave her a padded bra and some dank weed when she was fifteen.

There's a crew of ladies waiting by the elevator, four of them in the same flower print beach cover-ups, each holding a Stanley Cup the size of a newborn baby. Peter has a theory that everyone these days is overhydrated and it's leading to their brains drowning in idiocy. "I drank nothing but beer and weak tea for three years in university and I passed all my exams with flying colors," he says every time a teacher chastises us for forgetting the two water bottles required for each child for day care.

These women clutching their half-gallons of water have clearly been indulging in something else at the pool bar and have lost their ability to use their indoor voices.

"She's so smug."

"She thinks she's better than all of us."

"I heard she got a boob job and a tummy tuck after that last baby."

"She's wearing those sunglasses to hide her eye job. They've been looking a little bit droopy lately."

"So were her boobs."

The women cackle like crows. One of my favorite facts that Nora tells me on repeat from her animal encyclopedia that she can't quite read yet is that a group of crows is called a murder. A group of ravens is called an unkindness. Both are fitting here.

Still, I lean in a little closer. I love gossip and shit talk about strangers.

"I've heard her marriage is on the rocks."

"Can you blame that poor husband of hers? She seems like such an ice queen. I don't understand how she has such a huge audience. She hardly speaks."

"You heard about him and Veronica . . ."

"For a while I thought BarefootMamaLove was created by AI."

As a shadow approaches behind us the murder of cackling crows grows strangely quiet.

When I turn, I realize exactly who they're shit talking about.

I didn't think I would feel strangely protective of Bex after all this time. My mom friends and I have talked enough crap about her Instagram account over the past couple of years even though they don't know about my direct connection to her. It's just one of those cultural things that moms talk about, like whether or not Brad and Angelina really hooked up before he was separated from Jennifer Aniston or whether Ronan Farrow is Frank Sinatra's kid.

The most recent texts from them had a list of questions they wanted answered and conspiracy theories they wanted laid to rest.

Does she have a nanny?

Does she have an army of nannies?

Will she tell you what that fancy oven in her kitchen cost? If not, get a good picture of it. I'll figure it out. I have sources.

Has she gotten fillers?

Is she taller than Gray? Does he stand on things in family photos?

And then from Kelly, who is a staunch @BarefootMamaLove defender, the one person on our group text who tells us she falls asleep watching Bex's videos because they are peaceful and she wishes her life were that simple and easy. Kelly has three questions and a request for me.

What does she smell like, what mascara does she use, what's her secret meatloaf ball recipe, and can you get me a set of her matching mommy and me gardening aprons that sold out last month. Please and thank you.

When we were in college Bex smelled like Clinique Happy perfume and Parliament Lights. Now I sniff the air for the familiar scent, but only get a nostril of cedar and tangerines from the essential oils being pumped into the lobby.

Seeing her in the flesh and knowing she heard what these crows just said about her, I want to rush over and give her a massive hug and then tell these ladies to fuck off.

My old friend is wearing sunglasses indoors, which *is* pretty affected, but whatever. She probably just got back from the pool and it sort of gives off some sexy and mysterious Jack Nicholson vibes.

"Hey, Cricket, it's good to see you," she says politely to one of the women.

"Hey, Rebecca," Cricket says too enthusiastically. Despite her nastiness, it's clear she wants Bex to like her. "You look great. How are things? Is everything great? I'm so happy to be here. Are you? Everything is just so transformative and invigorating and great."

It's a lot of great. I would almost feel bad for Cricket if I hadn't already decided she was a massive bitch.

"So great . . . Lizzie." Bex turns to me and she smiles, what looks like a real smile, not the forced one she was giving these women just seconds earlier.

Something swells inside me. It's not dissimilar to the feeling I get when I'm at the playground with my children and I see any other kid start to cry or get hurt. My mom instinct creeps in and I want to run to comfort the strange child, even the worst of them, even the ones who are otherwise total little bastards who throw sand in your face and spit in the sandbox. If one of them is in pain I'm compelled to do my best to help.

57

That's what I do now. I wrap Bex in a massive hug and look pointedly at the other women so that they know I know exactly who they were talking about.

"It's *so* good to see you," I say. Even with her sunglasses on she looks grateful and melts into my body with such need that I feel embarrassed for her.

Once we're alone in the elevator, Bex slumps against the back mirror and takes off her sunglasses to rub her eyes. I notice a light purple bruise under her left eye, the kind that's impossible to perfectly hide with makeup. I know this because my mom tried for years before my dad passed away.

"There should be a German word for sneaking up on someone just as they're saying the worst things about you," she murmurs, instantly flooring me.

In college we learned from an Austrian hallmate that there was a German word for someone you immediately want to slap when you start talking to them—*Backpfeifengesicht*. This immediately became our favorite inside joke. We were endlessly searching for German words for strange things, and if one didn't exist, we would invent our own. There should be a German word for a guy who gets much cuter after three vodka sodas, for the freedom and giddiness you feel when someone cancels plans at the last second and you have a free afternoon to yourself, a German word for the grossness of discovering you put a new tampon in but haven't taken the old one out.

"Or a German word for how two shots of tequila and a THC gummy make you believe you're whispering shit talk to your friends instead of broadcasting it to the whole room," I say in the elevator. If this is where she wants us to start, right back in our shared intimacies, I can match her.

She giggles.

"Or for women who think massive water bottles are a fashion accessory. Did you just get here?" she asks, making direct eye contact with me so that I can't look away from her bruise.

"Yeah. About half an hour ago. My plane was delayed."

"Do you have plans for tonight?"

"There's a welcome circle, right?"

"Did you want to go to that?"

"Not at all." I don't feel like lying to her.

"Me neither," she says. "It's a lot of self-congratulatory selfie-taking and a circle jerk of brand placement."

Her tone and crass words catch me off guard. Much like the women talking about her outside the elevator I realize that I haven't heard Bex's real voice in years. Her videos have captions. She hardly speaks. But it's all done in a way that I hadn't noticed. I'd felt like she was speaking directly to the camera for the years I have peered at her on the phone, but now I realize it was all a sleight of hand. I heard the words in my head and not out loud. Her real voice is as low and gravelly as it ever was. Her tone is perfectly tinged with sarcasm and skepticism. She is the same girl I fell in love with during that first week of college. She's still in there.

We arrive at my room before I even realize she was walking me here all along.

"Can I come in and sit down? Maybe we could order a drink?" she asks almost shyly.

The familiarity continues to be jarring. *Why did you ditch me?*

I scream in my head, despite how ridiculous it sounds to my adult brain. *Why haven't I seen you in nearly fifteen years?*

"Sure," I say, remembering she's the one who paid for the room, and that has to give her some privileges. Once we walk in, I realize I will be sleeping in a mountain-view suite with a massive king bedroom, a sitting area, and a balcony the size of my nursery that leads out to a private infinity plunge pool.

"Wow, Bex. Thanks for booking this."

She waves her hand in the air like it's nothing, which I guess it is for her, and a twinge of jealousy tightens my throat.

"I didn't book it. The conference offered as many rooms as I wanted if I would do the keynote talk tomorrow."

"Yeah, about that. Why are you doing it?" I sling my suitcase onto the bed, but don't unzip it. I'm embarrassed at the early-morning packing job I did in the dark so I wouldn't wake Peter. My clothes are balled up in little bundles. I have no idea if the underwear I threw in is clean or dirty.

"The conference? Or the keynote?"

"Both, I guess. You don't do that many of these, right?"

She sinks onto what looks like the most comfortable sofa I've ever seen.

"I always come to the conference. It's a good way to get in front of sponsors. But no, I don't ever do any of the big speeches. I always figured no one wanted to hear what I had to say. Could we order a drink and some food before we start talking? I'm dying for french fries and a burger and a martini."

"I thought you didn't drink," I say.

"A lot of people think a lot of things about me." She raises a perfectly groomed eyebrow at me. "You heard those women at the elevator. They all have their opinions and none of them are nice. What do you think about me, Lizzie?"

It doesn't feel accusatory. In fact, she seems to genuinely want to know. Still, I stutter a little. No one has ever asked me so directly what I think of them except for Peter once during an argument right after he lost his job. "Do you think I'm a failure?" he had asked. *Only a little,* I didn't say. I avoided telling him I thought he could have hustled a little harder, that he was too set in his ways, that he could have found a way to save himself if he had tried just a tad more. I hate being asked what I really think of people.

"I think you seem lonely." I don't know where it came from. The words just vomited out of my mouth before I could process them.

Even though she's drowning in lovely-looking children and money and land and has that stone fox of a husband, something about her perfectly curated life seems sad.

"Yeah. I am," she says simply, and heads for the door. Now I've gone and insulted her with my big fucking mouth.

"Hey, Bex, I'm sorry."

"I'm not offended. And it's nice to be called Bex. Gray prefers Rebecca so that's what everyone has called me forever now. I was just going to head to my room to change. I hate this bathing suit. It's riding up my ass. I'll put in a drinks and food order while you unpack and freshen up. What do you want?"

"Whatever. Same as you."

"Easy. It's nice to be with someone who feels so easy."

It does feel easy. It's not at all what I expected. I certainly didn't expect to fall back into the comforting rhythms of the friendship we established as roommates at age eighteen. Not after the things she said to me in that last email. The reason I never reached out wasn't just that she ghosted me, but that she humiliated me and abandoned me. Maybe that's dramatic, but it was how I felt at the time and how I still feel when I conjure the memories.

"Be back in twenty," she says, and swoops out the door.

I barely have time to move my scrunched-up clothes from the suitcase to the dresser, swipe a washcloth under my arms, and take a pee before Bex returns in a T-shirt and sweatpants, her hair on top of her head in a messy bun. She's still got on plenty of makeup and these fake eyelashes so long they seem like they could reach out and tickle you. But she looks less photo-ready and more, I don't know, more normal.

"Snacks will be here in a few." And with that, a bellhop is knocking on the door. He brings in a cart with more food than I would order for my family of four.

"I'm starving," she says.

There are two burgers and fries and onion rings. A platter of nachos and a brownie sundae—the exact opposite of the home-grown and nutritious snacks on Bex's Instagram.

"Are we expecting anyone else?" I had wondered on the way out here if she would have a publicist with her all the time or an assistant, perhaps a mini me who looked exactly like her in the same prairie dresses and golden curls. Bex, but slightly smaller. The next size down of a Russian nesting doll. I've never seen any of these people on her account, but they must exist.

She shrugs. "Nope. Just us. I wasn't thinking straight when I ordered the ice cream. It's gonna melt. I guess we have no choice but to eat that first."

There's also a massive shaker on the cart, out of which the server pours two martinis the size of small fishbowls.

Bex grabs a glass and begins digging into the brownie sundae. I don't admit that I've been attempting a carb-and-sugar-free diet that is foiled every day by the scraps of chicken nuggets and cookies on my children's dinner plates and I grab a spoon and drip hot fudge onto my tongue.

"Remember when we always had dessert in the dining hall before we ate an actual meal?" Bex says.

"Or Froot Loops. Because we could. Because there was a never-ending supply of Froot Loops in the dining hall and when there's so many of them you have to eat them."

"Exactly," she says. "I think about those days a lot."

I don't want to tell her I do too. Instead, I scoop the last of the brownie from the bottom of the sundae into my mouth and pretend to focus intently on chewing.

"Let's sit out on the balcony," Bex suggests. "We can watch the sunset."

I hadn't even noticed that the sky had turned a cotton-candy pink and orange behind the craggy peaks.

"It's beautiful out here," I say. "You live close, right?"

"Not far. It's flatter where I am. More desert prairie vibes, but we have these massive weird rock formations that just appear as if from nowhere. It's a little like Mars. But these mountains are so dramatic. I love them. We did our honeymoon at a little place over there. We hiked to that peak."

"Do the two of you still hike together?"

"No," she says flatly, and heads outside while balancing two plates like a waitress.

Once we're out on the balcony she shovels fries into her mouth and then polishes off the burger in about three minutes before turning back to the martini and starting to pick at the nachos. I don't match her speed, but I'm pretty hungry myself and dive in with relish.

"It's nice to be away from my kids," she finally says.

"Do you miss them?" I ask.

"Every other second, but it's still nice. There should be a German word for the phantom cries you hear when you aren't with your kids."

"Or the relief you feel when a kid cries and you realize it isn't yours . . . something like *Nichtmeinkinder*." I don't realize I've been storing up these quips for years, just waiting to tell her. Maybe she's been doing the same.

"Oh my gosh, I love that one! *Nichtmeinkinder!*"

I love that she loves it. "It's so crazy. I can't wait to get away from my kids and then the second I'm on the airplane I'm scrolling my phone looking at pictures of them," I say.

"Same," she laughs.

"And you have twice as many as I do. More, actually."

"Gray always wanted a big family."

It's the second time she's mentioned her husband with a grimace.

"What about you? Is that what you wanted?"

"For a long time, I wanted what Gray wanted." She takes a sip of the martini and stares at the sun as it kisses the horizon. "But not so much anymore."

"No?"

"No," she replies, and says nothing else.

"Tell me about your kids," I finally say.

The joy returns to her face. "I'm surprised at how beautiful and messy motherhood has been and how much it has reshaped my identity," she says.

"That sounds like one of your captions."

She cringes. "You're right. It's hard to turn it off sometimes."

"Do you write them? The captions?"

"Some of them. A lot of them are scheduled way in advance but I look over everything. I'm hands on. Always checking that we're on brand."

It's a reminder that she isn't just the housewife frolicking in the field with the barefoot children or the mother baking bread in the kitchen and then drying the linens on the line. She studied finance and management in college. She's a brand.

"Okay, how about this," Bex starts over. "You know that scene in the Harry Potter books where Ron is reading Harry his tea leaves to tell him his future?"

I nod. I'd grown up obsessed with the Harry Potter books but Bex had never read them. I'd brought a couple to college as comfort reads and she devoured them.

She keeps going. "Okay, so Ron is predicting the future to Harry and he says, 'You're going to suffer . . . but be very happy.' That's how I feel about having kids sometimes."

It's so perfect that I want to cry.

"So tell me about your kids. Really," I press her.

"They're wonderful. I mean also hard and a lot, but mostly wonderful. They're all so different. I guess I kind of thought they would all be more or less the same. But they are all exactly who they were when they came out of my body."

I can't help but look at her body when she says it. Because it's perfect. She doesn't look like she had one baby, let alone six. I've only had two and nothing is in the same place where it started.

"You were right earlier when you said I was lonely. I love being with my kids more than anything in the world, and it's also the loneliest thing I've ever done, raising them the way that I have."

"How do you manage with so many?"

She chews on her thumbnail for a second as if she's deciding how to answer.

"Once you get past three, it gets easier. They're like a tribe. They take care of one another. It's beautiful to watch." Again, this does not feel like the truth.

"Really?"

"Oh, I got you with that one. That really was a caption at one point. God no. It's bananas. And we have help. There are babysitters and a nanny."

I don't mention that I never see those people on her social media as I mentally check off one of the questions from my moms text group.

"In some ways it does get easier when they're older. You're in the thick of it with two under five. Alice, my oldest, is twelve and she's brilliant. She can play the piano like no one else you've ever heard and she composes her own music. Entire sonatas and also pop songs. I wanted to send her away to a special school where she could focus on it, but . . . Gray wouldn't . . ."

She clams up again at the mention of her husband and I don't press it. Instead, I ask if I can see a picture of Alice and she shows me two dozen of them, including a video of this little angelic redhead singing along as she plays on a baby grand.

When my phone rings I grab it, excuse myself, and do a quick check-in with Peter. He sounds tired but happy, relieved that both kids are finally in bed. I chatter a little tipsily about how insanely gorgeous the hotel is and my ridiculous encounter with Blippi. He tells me that Nora built a boat out of marshmallows and toothpicks and floated it in the bath and then ate it and we chuckle about the strange genius of our daughter. It's so nice to talk to him without the constant tit and tat of who is doing what for the children, without the can *you* just get up to check on that cry to make sure they didn't choke in their sleep, did *you* pack the lunches and the water bottles and the snacks, are the bathing suits still wet, where are the socks, why are there no socks, why are there never any fucking socks for the love of god!

It's always the negotiation of it all that's the worst. Should you? Should I? Can you? We live with the unspoken dictum, *We both do it all.* But in reality, there's no job description in so-called egalitarian marriages: It's the Wild West when everyone's supposed to be doing all the things. The division of labor is simple right now. He's doing all of it because I'm not there, so we can't bicker and I like him more for it.

I mention this to Bex when I get off the phone and she snorts. Actually, snuffles like a pig, but in a weirdly cute way.

"I think that has always made it easier with Gray and me. There was never any expectation that he would ever do anything for the kids or in the house. He made that very clear from the beginning. It was my job—my 'duty,' as he called it. So it's hard to resent him for not doing it. Our roles were always very clear once the kids came."

The two of us are quiet as the sky gets dark and the first stars start to peek out of the twilight haze. We dip our toes into the infinity pool.

"Remember that time we took the train into New York but had no idea how much a hotel room would cost so we had to sleep in Central Park?" she asks.

"Yeah," I say. "And that guy who worked at the zoo found us sleeping on the bench and thought you were hot so he let us in to see the sea lions." Bex had loved those sea lions. She was enamored with them. The dude, who was probably a janitor, was enamored with Bex and kept sputtering off facts like how sea lions can dive seventy feet below the surface of the water.

"Of the ocean?" Bex had said in amazement. "You know, I've never seen the ocean," she added, mostly to me.

I took her to Coney Island later that day. We rode the subway and got sunburnt and drank margaritas out of plastic yard glasses before getting the last train back to Philadelphia. I ask her if she remembers riding the Cyclone.

"Of course." She places a hand on my knee. "It was one of the best days of my life." We both take a moment then, but she keeps the memories coming.

"What about the time we entered that hot-wing-eating contest at the stadium and you came in third?"

"Ewwww. Or remember the pasta 'sauce' we made out of parmesan cheese and Tabasco?"

"How about the time we dressed up like slutty Wayne and Garth for Halloween?"

We go back and forth like that until the first martinis are done and she pours us two more, which I know I'm drinking as quickly as I downed the Bloody Marys on the plane because I'm so unpracticed at this. Thankfully, it seems like she is too, and I can see her getting as squiffy as I am.

Halfway through my second, I blurt out, "What's it like to be so rich?"

She laughs. A real big, huge laugh and I'm reminded again how much I used to love it when I made her laugh like that.

"It's not my money. Or at least it wasn't for a long time. It was all Gray's family money. They made it a hundred years ago from mining and oil wells and it kept trickling down like water from a river that is being tapped dry from overuse. And they did eventually tap it out. Or most of it anyway. The new money's mine. Now I'm making real money."

"How much?" This question is insanely bold, but if I don't ask these things I'll start to ask her the other things that I might not want the answers to. *Why did you abandon me? When did you start to hate me?*

"A lot. It'll be more soon. That's what I wanted to talk to you about, or part of what I wanted to talk to you about. I got a deal, a big one, and I'm gonna announce it tomorrow."

"So will you be Rodrigo Aguilar rich?" Rodrigo Aguilar was the richest kid in our class at school. He showed up with a new Bentley every semester and had his own personal assistant who actually sat in class and took notes for him.

"Did you hear his dad went to prison? Pyramid scheme!" Bex says.

"I saw that. But what's he doing? Rodrigo?"

69

"Running a hedge fund."

That makes sense. Money makes money, even if your dad is a felon. "So this deal of yours . . . how does your husband feel about it all?"

"That's the problem." She pauses again and massages her temples. It's dark on the balcony now and her face is only illuminated by the light inside the room. I can still see the dusky outline of the bruise.

"He doesn't know about it," she finishes. "And he isn't going to like it. He's . . . he's traditional about a lot of things."

"Obviously," I snort. It's the closest I've come to expressing any kind of judgment about the life she's chosen.

"Yeah. I know."

"And he doesn't want you to do what? To work? You're already working, aren't you?"

"But no one knows that. Or if they do they don't believe it. People are happy to think I just take pictures and videos of my life as a homemaker, right? They don't think it's real work and Gray kind of takes that attitude too. But this, this would be a job, a big job, and I know he won't like it."

"So what are you going to do?"

"I'm still figuring that out. I would love for you to write about it as it happens, when I announce the deal, I mean, get it up as soon as possible. And then we can do the whole profile, but I want to make it so that this is something he can't take away from me. I want it out there in the light and I want everyone to know." The words catch in her throat. She chokes on them. "Too many things are hidden and secret in our lives. I want to change that. I want something better for my kids, especially the girls."

I reach over to place my hand on top of hers. I get it. I want opportunities for my daughter that I never had. I want her to have all the things, even if I don't know exactly what that means.

"You're brave," I say.

"I've never been more scared in my life. But I have some leverage. There's some things Gray would rather I not know. Rather no one knows. I don't want this to get nasty. But I have ammunition."

She shivers and it isn't because of the cool breeze coming in from the desert.

"Want to go inside and watch a movie? Finish off a bottle of wine?" she says, deliberately changing the subject.

"Yes please," I say, and mean it. I want nothing more than to grab the insanely fuzzy blanket from the foot of the bed and pop open the expensive wine that welcomed me on the counter and check if *How to Lose a Guy in 10 Days* is on the hotel TV. It seems like the kind of movie that's always on a hotel TV. I want to snuggle with my old friend the way we did in college. When was the last time I just sat on a couch and watched a movie with a girlfriend? It's been years. I don't think I've done it since I went away with my sister right before Nora was born for what we called our sistermoon. And that's my sister, not even a friend. I talk to my mom friends mostly on text because even though we all started out having our babies in the city, now we've scattered to various suburbs and even new states. I've made some new friends since our move, but it feels like we're still auditioning each other. Plus, it takes dozens of texts to get a single mom date on the calendar and even then childcare falls through for half of them.

But I yawn. I'm exhausted and drunk and also hungover at

the same time and I'm already yearning for my first cup of coffee in the morning as I dread the headache that awaits me.

Bex sees it in my face. She's always been able to read me. I miss that.

"I forgot about the time difference again," she says quietly. "You must be exhausted."

"Yeah. But maybe I could rally."

"No. No. There's time for us to catch up. You're here for the week. So much time. Get some sleep and let's meet up in the morning before the main event. I'll order breakfast to my room. I'm just down the hall."

"You're sure?"

"Of course. I need a good night's sleep too." She stands. "Ohhhhhhh, but I do need to use your bathroom before I head out. I've got insane mom bladder, especially after those martinis."

"Trust me. I know. I leak when I laugh too hard, and I have to cross my legs when I sneeze. It must be worse after six."

"You have no idea. My vagina is the size of the Grand Canyon."

It's such a Bex thing to say. Something that I would never imagine coming out of Rebecca's mouth or being in one of her captions. I wonder how long I'll get to have this version of her . . . if it's only for tonight.

"I'll wait to stand up until you get out of the bathroom 'cause I'm gonna have to go real quick too," I say.

I lean back on the rocking chair as she opens the sliding door and steps inside. The haze has cleared and the stars are something else out here. I think I see Orion and maybe Lupus, the wolf. Peter is very into astronomy. It's one of his many hobbies.

I don't have hobbies anymore and I don't even know what they would be if I had the time. But Peter loves mastering a subject just enough to sound smarter than most people in the room. He put one of those constellation finder apps on my phone. I reach for it so I can tell him what I've seen when we talk in the morning.

It's not until I pick up the phone and put it in front of my face to unlock the screen that I realize I have the wrong device, that I'm staring at a message that definitely is not meant for me.

Even without fully unlocking the phone I can see the start of it.

> You won't get away with this
> you fucking bitch

It's from someone saved in the phone as G.

Gray?

It buzzes again. The device practically leaps out of my hands and clatters onto the concrete floor of the balcony. I look behind me before getting down on my hands and knees to pick it up. I gather both phones, mine and Bex's, and walk into the living room, hoping her device goes back to sleep before she comes out of the bathroom.

I place it on the coffee table face down anyway, to make it seem like I just tossed it there casually when I brought it in. I pour a glass of wine for her, hoping to stall her from picking it up so that the screen will definitely go dark.

"Hey." I hand her the wine when she walks out. "I had a change of heart. One more nightcap." Her eyes are slightly glassy from booze and probably exhaustion. She takes it from me politely, but I know she's not gonna sit down. Suddenly I pull her into one more fierce hug, and it isn't just to stall. I want to hug her, to remember what it felt like to touch her. She hugs me back just as hard.

"Let's get wild tomorrow night," she says, laughing as she pulls away and walks over to the coffee table. "Let's have three drinks instead of two and maybe smoke a cigarette." She slides her phone into the pocket of her sweats without glancing at it.

"Bex . . ." I start, wanting a few more minutes. "Why . . ."

Her shiny expression crumbles. Our eyes lock. *We're going to do this.* Then she holds up a hand the way I do to shush my children, but it doesn't feel condescending. "I know what you want to ask and I owe you so much. So many explanations. So many apologies and I want to tell you everything. Tomorrow. I promise. Tomorrow night. We'll really talk. But I need you to know that I am sorry. I'm sorry for all of it. What happened . . . You didn't deserve it."

As she opens the door she turns around and shoots me the Crest Whitestrip smile I now know so well from her Instagram. It's so different from her cautious smile in college, the one where she kept her lips closed most of the time to hide her bad teeth.

"We have all the time in the world."

But we don't. We don't have any time at all.

CHAPTER SIX

REBECCA

I want to tell you about the beginning of my marriage. It began as a love story. I need you to know that.

You probably won't believe me when I say that. I barely believe me.

Especially since I left Lizzie's hotel room and texted Dan (@SingleDadDan) and asked if I could come over. I needed to blow off some steam and Dan is always game for blowing anything. There are lots of rumors in the influencer world about Dan, but I started most of them so that no one would know I was the one he was spending after-hours time with at these conferences. The #FitnessMom orgy rumor I made up would have been a bit much if there hadn't been a scandal a couple of years ago where a group of the conservative influencers were all swapping spouses at house parties and dry-humping like high school kids. When they got caught, they made it clear that what they were doing was "soft swinging," or everything but penetration. It was very confusing.

So because of the rumors I started everyone believes Dan is a cad and something of a nonstop sex machine, and I don't think he minds at all.

Our thing has been pretty transactional since the beginning. The one time a year I get away from my children at this conference, all I want is to feel like a woman with a body that is all my own again.

He *is* sweet and funny though. I have to give him that. The first time we met at MomBomb San Diego years ago I had asked him to grab me a drink at the bar because I thought he was a waiter.

"I can try. I'm trying to get a drink too," he'd said.

"Sorry I thought you were a server," I replied.

"Because I'm handsome enough to also be an extra in the next *Mission: Impossible* movie?" He delivered a thousand-megawatt smile and raised his eyebrows. He had dark tousled hair and baby-blue eyes that had already looked me up and down. I could tell he liked what he saw.

"No. Because the only other men at this mom conference are the ones serving drinks."

He was sheepish and explained why the conference organizers had invited him, how he was weirdly enjoying himself in San Diego for the first time since his wife passed away three years earlier.

"I guess I feel less alone here," he'd admitted once we had gotten a couple of beers.

"That makes sense," I'd said. "Me too."

"I'm so sorry." He looked genuinely chagrined. "Are you a widow too?"

"No. I just don't have any actual friends."

We laughed even though it was my truth. Talking to him was

always easy and we had a good time joking about how weird the entire world of social media was, how it was so strange that this was an actual job.

"My mom always wanted me to be a doctor," he said.

"What does she think about you doing this?"

"Oh, she has no idea. She isn't on Instagram. In real life I'm still a podiatrist."

He wasn't joking. That's part of what was so charming about him. On Instagram Dan did funny dances with his daughters and joked about not knowing how to braid their hair. In everyday life he scraped bunions.

* * *

But he was clingier than usual when I went to his room after Lizzie's. Also drunker than usual, which was irritating to me because it made him sloppy in bed.

"We should get married and become a modern-day Brady Bunch," he joked. I gave him a polite laugh and handed him a Red Bull from the minibar to try to perk all of him up.

"I'm serious. Imagine the engagement we'd get off an engagement." He giggled at the homonym. "And a wedding. We'd make so much money off of a wedding."

I usually love talking about money, but not with Dan, not then. I would have preferred that he didn't talk at all, and I pushed him down on the bed, pleased to see that the Red Bull had given him wings. Dan usually let me be in charge, and I enjoyed it immensely. He rested his hands gently on my hips and lowered me slowly on top of him, reaching up to run his hands over my breasts, pinching my nipples the way he knew made me crazy, and I clenched around him and lost myself in the pleasure.

I peeled myself out of his sweaty sheets right afterward to leave and do what needed to be done, to put everything into action.

"Hey, B," he murmured. He had called me B since I revealed I actually hated being called Rebecca.

"Yeah?"

"I meant it. We could do it. Be together. It would be nice." His voice was slurry and dreamy.

"I'm married."

"Divorce him."

I almost told Dan my plan then, almost spilled the whole thing because it was already bursting inside me and I wanted someone else to tell me it was going to work out.

"It's not that easy. You know that."

Dan gripped me around the waist and pulled me back to the bed, kissing my hip, my back.

"I'll do whatever you need me to do to make it easier. We could always kill him," he said with such innocent humor that I flinched.

"I gotta go."

My future wasn't going to be easy or pretty, at least not for a while, but there was no turning back. I had a plan.

But before I tell you about that, I need to tell you about Gray. We were in love once. Painfully and crazily in love.

When I graduated college I had these big plans to move fast and break things, to lean in and be a girlboss. I had gone to the best un-dergraduate business school in the country and that's what the girls in my class there were told to do. Never mind that a lot of the women I was friends with at that school had moms who hadn't set foot in an office since before their maternity leaves, after which they promptly quit. Those mothers were on boards and ran charities. That wasn't leaning out, not really. Not working becomes more respectable based on the number of zeros in your bank account.

My bank account was at zero, actually less than zero, when I moved out to San Francisco after graduation. I owed more than a hundred grand in student loan debt even after working my butt off to pay for school as I went along. I tried not to worry about it, but debt is like a paper cut that never goes away. It stings when you least expect it.

But I had a plan. I was going to work for a tech start-up and save all my money in order to do what I really loved. I wanted nothing more than to open my own pastry shop and bakery and then a chain of bakeries and finally a mail-order delivery service for artisanal baked goods, a monthly box delivered right to your door. I would be the CEO and the master baker. I was good in the kitchen. So fucking good. My mom had passed that down to me. When she wasn't working two jobs to support the two of us on her own, she lived in the kitchen, lived for baking. Making bread cut down on grocery costs, but she also adored it. Sometimes it seemed like the only thing that brought her any joy.

Joy was in short supply during my childhood, but we nearly had it together during those moments in the kitchen. Mom was strict because she didn't want me to end up like her, pregnant and alone at sixteen without an education or a penny to her name. She worked insane hours cleaning houses and stocking shelves at big-box stores, but it still felt like we never had enough cash to pay for new clothes or all the doctors' bills when her diabetes got bad.

And then she was gone. Dropped dead right at work and I was left to pay for life on my own starting at age sixteen. I quietly moved out of our apartment before the landlord evicted me for not paying rent and slept in the backseat of our old Mazda to avoid getting put in the system. My grades were good. I was varsity in track and on the debate team. I'd always kept to myself because Mom had instilled in me an intrinsic fear of everyone and everything, but it became a necessity senior year so I could fly under the radar. On paper I was an ideal candidate for a good school, and I didn't hold back in my personal statements to college. The unstable mother, her untimely death, living alone in the car. You might even say it was practice for my future in confessional blogging.

Getting to college after having such a difficult and joyless upbringing was like walking onto a movie set, like opening up one of those cakes that someone jumps out of and screams *surprise*. I liken it to what the Amish kids must feel when they go on their rumspringa, their year of self-discovery.

From the moment I got to campus I loved being in love. I was desperate for it. It was all I wanted and maybe sometimes I went about it the wrong way. Maybe sometimes I said yes to things I shouldn't have in the hopes that doing so would lead to a real date and not just a night in the frat house. Did I deserve the names they called me? Maybe. Did I own them? Absolutely. Because what the hell else was I going to do? And besides it felt like a massive *screw you* to the world to wear a T-shirt emblazoned with the words SLUTTY BEX that I ordered for myself on the Internet.

I made my bed, and I lay in it. And plenty of others. I make terrible jokes when I'm nervous.

Other girls mocked me, some of them feared me. Some were

jealous. But never Lizzie. She loved me straightaway despite all my flaws and all the various costumes I tried on over the four years of college. I thought being in a sorority would bring me a gaggle of giggling girlfriends like I saw in the movies, but our connections were pretty sterile. Not with Lizzie. She was the first person who made me feel completely comfortable just being me. Lizzie believed in me when no one else did. We could sit comfortably in silence or snort-laugh for hours.

Grayson was different from other people too. He treated me like a lady, which sounds old-fashioned and ridiculous but it's true. He had these manners out of another century. I was only at my job at BlueNet for a year when we met, and I was already burnt out on the tech world.

I was working more than eighty hours a week. Fifty of them in an open-plan office filled with the same rich kid douchebags I'd gone to college with. Then I did another thirty hours as an assistant pastry chef at an up-and-coming spot in Hayes Valley, making no money and getting no respect and not giving a damn because it was the only thing that made me feel whole.

When my friend Jamie invited me up to Sonoma to a wine-tasting event at some fancy vineyard on the one Saturday I had off in months I jumped at the chance. Getting dolled up in San Francisco meant putting on my sleek black hiking pants and fancy fleece vest instead of the nubby one I usually wore on Saturdays. I paired it with some nice wedge heels and blew out my hair. You could never look like you were trying too hard in that city. It was the opposite of going to college on the East Coast, where you were supposed to major in trying too hard just to go out to get a bagel in the morning.

Jamie was a friend from the tech job. She worked in marketing for BlueNet and said it was a little bit better over there since her department was about 80 percent female as opposed to the 5 percent (me) in finance. But the hours still sucked, and she was just hanging on to the job until the company went public and she'd get paid out for her stock options.

I smelled Grayson before I saw him. Is that gross? It's a little gross. But it's true. He smelled better than anyone I'd ever met. We were standing thigh to thigh at the bar trying to get a drink and suddenly I was overcome by the scent of pine needles and leaves burning and salty sweat after a long day's work.

Maybe I describe it like that now because I know it so well. I don't know what I thought at the time except that it smelled delicious and I wanted to swallow it.

"Oh excuse me," he said as we knocked gently into each other. His bright green eyes met mine and I was a goner. "Can I get you something? I think I have this young lady's attention." Of course he had the bartender's attention. He had the attention of every woman in the room. I could feel everyone watching him and, by extension, watching me.

"I'll take a tasting flight," I said, thrusting my shoulders back and my boobs out. "The red. What are you having?"

"Diet Coke for now. My drug of choice." He said it so sheepishly that it was cutely weird. I assumed he must have been driving. The bartender had been listening to us and my wine flight was ready in less than a minute.

"Do you want me to explain the wines to you?" she asked. I didn't. I wanted to stare at this gorgeous man a little longer and think of something brilliant to say to make him fall in love with me. I also wanted to down that first glass to get my hands to stop shaking.

"You can explain them to me. I'll take a red too." Jamie slid in next to me.

"There are a couple of seats open by the firepit if you want to take them, babe," she said to me. Jamie was a truly excellent wing woman. I wish I'd stayed in touch with her when I left the Bay Area, but I didn't stay in touch with any of those women. I regret it now. Not as much as I regret what happened with Lizzie, but I do regret it.

Gray eventually ended up hating Jamie and all the girls like her from the office. He hated any woman I got close to. Now I know that he wanted to keep me all to himself, or at least keep me away from anyone I might confide in. But at the time he told me those girls were all trashy and ridiculous, that I was so much better than them and hanging out with them would only bring me down. He told me I had so much potential. Why would I waste any energy on people like that? "I just want the best for you, and I think you deserve the world," he'd said over and over through the years. Pathetically enough I believed him.

I barely remember what Gray and I talked about for the next two hours at that winery, but it *was* two hours. All around us everyone was drinking and dancing to the bluegrass band that had been flown in from Austin. Jamie brought me another wine when the flight was finished, and I didn't even clock that Grayson only drank water and soda. What I *did* notice was how he kept bringing me water and how he stood when I stood to go pee and remained standing with his hands behind his back until I returned. He asked me questions about myself, and he seemed truly interested in the answers. There was lively conversation and giddy laughs at dumb jokes, shared interests in mountain biking and musicals. A strange but earnest detour into our favorite childhood Disney movies.

And then Jamie stumbled over singing "Sweet Caroline." Before I knew what was happening she spilled a goblet of red wine down the crisp white front of Grayson's shirt.

"Oh my god. I'm so sorry," I mumbled, holding on to Jamie with one arm and trying to mop up Grayson's chest with a Kleenex I found in my pocket with the other.

"Good time never seemed so good, so good, so good." Jamie belched in Grayson's face.

"Nothing a proper soak won't get out," he said with an honest smile.

A proper soak? Who the hell was this guy and why did it turn me on so much to think about him taking off that shirt and soaking it in some big old farmhouse sink somewhere? Maybe it was because the wine was making the fabric cling to his fantastically cut stomach in a way that would have been obscene if not for his goofy grin and the blond curls flopping into his face.

"I'm fine. You should take care of your friend," he whispered to me.

And because he told me to, I ushered Jamie into one of the taxis waiting in the circular drive and directed it to the motel room we had rented for the night on the banks of the Russian River.

A staff member chased after the cab, tossing two gift bags into the backseat, because he would be damned if we didn't depart with our complimentary bottles of their brand-new rosé.

I expected Jamie to crash once we got to our room, but she was fired up with a second wind and pouring us glasses of wine by the time I got out of the shower.

"Your phone is buzzing," she said, dangling the device between two of her fingers.

"Probably work," I said.

"Or a handsome man in need of a new shirt."

"I can't believe you spilled wine all over him, Jamie. I'm mortified. And it isn't him. I didn't give him my number."

"I did. As you were dragging me away, I passed him your business card. Because. I'm. A. Good. Friend."

I tried to snatch the phone away from her, but she was shockingly fast for a person with the blood alcohol level of a rodeo clown. Before I knew it, she'd dashed out the screen door in the back of the motel room. I followed her in just a towel.

"You can't write back yet. You've got to play hard to get, Bex. Trust me on this one."

Everything in my body burned to get to that phone, to see what he wrote, to call him back and beg him to meet me at my motel that very minute.

"Time to cool off. Come on." Jamie placed my phone on a rock on the riverbank and wiggled out of her jeans. Before I knew it I'd dropped my towel and dove in after her. She was right. It was the only way I could play it cool.

And now all I can wonder is how that man went from someone I had to jump into an icy cold river to get out of my mind to someone I would do anything to escape from.

CHAPTER SEVEN

LIZZIE

I should be hungover but I'm not. Probably because I went to bed at nine P.M. and got to sleep until the decadent hour of seven forty-five. And when I woke up, I merely opened my eyes, looked around at the beautiful room, saw that no one needed me, and closed them again.

There is no child at the foot of the bed gnawing on my toe and no husband to give thirteen directions to in order to get the day on track.

It's pure fucking heaven. I consider room service, but remember I told Bex we could have breakfast in her room. I text before I get in the shower, but there's no answer. After three unanswered texts the glow of our reunion from last night wears off and I remember that this is a woman who once begged me to fly to California to visit her and meet her new boyfriend and then disappeared. The same woman who abruptly ended our friendship in a six-line email that was so cruel I can still quote from it today.

The memory stings more than I want it to. Yes, back then I'd paid for the plane ticket to California with my own money and it wasn't cheap. Yes, I'd planned on staying with Bex and instead had to book a ridiculously expensive room at a grungy hotel by the airport for three days because everything in the city limits cost more than my monthly rent, and yes, I had been insanely excited to see my friend, to hug her and, if I am being totally honest, to make sure she was okay, because she had been fading from my life for a year and I wanted to know why. But when I arrived . . . nothing. She didn't answer my calls or texts. I took the train and then a bus to the address I had for her and her boyfriend and banged on the door. No answer even though I could hear that someone was in there.

I went to her work. They gave me some lame excuse about why she wasn't there. And then, right before I was ready to do something like call the police (not that I actually thought they would do anything), I got that email from her.

Last night I'd been too giddy at our pleasant reunion to push her for an explanation, and she probably wants to kick the can of our backstory down the road until I write a glowing profile of her for the magazine so she can make even more money.

I keep thinking about that one line from Bex's email all those years ago, the one that haunts me the most.

You're obsessed with me and it has to stop.

That single line was the reason I never reached out after that.

I'm pissed off all over again before I've even had a proper cup of coffee.

Avoiding the big conversation, I decide, is classic Bex. Nothing has changed despite the fact that she made me belly laugh like a toddler last night. Despite the fact that being with her made me feel like me again in a way I didn't even know I was hungry for. I'm annoyed, but also somehow vindicated at the fact that nothing about her has really changed.

I dress in the most Instagrammable thing I packed, a maxi dress from a Dôen photoshoot that I brought home on a whim even though nothing about it was practical or felt like me. The material was slightly too sheer, the ruffly lace on the ends of the cap sleeves and neckline screamed Disney princess, and the calico print made me look like a sexy Mennonite. That's how Peter described it the one time I tried it on in our bedroom. But when in Rome you do as the Romans do. This dress will absolutely help me fit in here, and for some reason, I want to.

In the elevator I overhear one woman say, "I feel so great. This place is totally mom spring break. We know how to party and network and celebrate and be in bed by nine-thirty!"

"I got four new sponsors last night and I did the vodka ice luge."

"It's because that vodka is organic."

I stifle a laugh. Both women turn and assess me. They take in my orange press bracelet and my badge and decide not to over-engage.

"Nice dress," Ice Luger says, and resumes her own conversation.

I wind through the exhibit tables set up en route to the ballroom, stopping every so often to hear a spiel and get a free thing.

The hotel's main ballroom is packed and the first morning session is in full force. Servers roam the room bearing sponsored snacks on silver platters. They're all the kinds of foods that moms would buy in the supermarket and serve to their kids for break-fast. Eggo is apparently a major sponsor of this event, at least as far as I can tell from their signage all over the place. But the child food is dressed up fancy for the adults. Eggo mini-waffles are topped with artisanal local goat cheese and heirloom mini toma-toes. Individual egg bites, the kind you pop in the microwave for a minute, have dollops of caviar on top. Caviar! The level of ex-travagance, the money spent at this event, I haven't seen any-thing like it in years, not since magazines actually shelled out for Fashion Week parties and book launches. Those days are long gone, or at least I thought they were, but now the money is here and it's flowing.

Four women are on the stage beneath an archway of fake greenery and a neon sign that screams I AM WOMAN.

Roar, I think as I snag a mini muffin from the buffet and sit at a table in the back of the room. There are notepads at every seat with MOTHERHOOD, ENHANCED on the top. Enhance me, I think. Happy to let you do your best.

The moderator of this particular talk, an excessively tall woman in a pastel yellow sundress and blond extensions that nearly reach her butt, smiles wide as she addresses her panel. "In-troduce yourself, ladies, and tell me about your zone of genius."

A brunette with a massive pregnant belly and a calico dress quite similar to my own begins. "I am a multi-hyphenate human who goes with the flows of the moon to show up authentically for myself and my community. I love speaking from the heart and showing up for my authentic self because that is the way to honor the purpose of my life."

I have no idea what any of it means. It's a word salad of self-help speak. But I swipe through my phone to her Instagram account, @B0ssBabe$$$, and see that she has more than three million followers and is the CEO of a "digital brand agency" that was recently named one of *Forbes'* fastest-growing companies in the United States.

"I am here to nerd out with each and every single one of you about what you are creating and how you can scale it," she continues. "Just remember, as entrepreneurs—and all of you are entrepreneurs—*you* get to choose who you show up as every day!" The crowd screams in unison: *"BOSS BABE."*

It's slightly culty, but I find myself clapping along, because who doesn't want to show up as what you choose every day? When was the last time I did?

The panel continues in rapid-fire chatter about growth strategies and optimization, about leveraging artificial intelligence for balance and success, about utilizing a variety of platforms to engage your following. Everyone around me is taking notes, and maybe I should be too. There hasn't been this much energy in magazines for a decade. Part of me, a larger part than I would care to admit, envies all of them, these women who seem to be on the cutting edge of media while I'm riding a dinosaur into the asteroid.

When the panel ends, I head to the bathroom to text my family and apply more mascara. This is a very lash-forward crowd. I attempt to reach Bex again and the radio silence is too eerily familiar.

My prairie-chic dress, with its many tiers of fabric, is impossible to pee in. I scrunch it up around my waist as I do a quad-burning squat, careful not to let the back of the gown fall into the toilet. I haven't used this particular maneuver with a garment since my wedding day.

When I return the stage is set for a single speaker. At first I worry that maybe I've gotten everything wrong . . . maybe Bex has her big talk now and not at noon. Maybe she wasn't blowing me off at all but preparing for her keynote.

I find a table with a couple of empty chairs.

"Hi," says a woman about my age wearing bright green overalls. "I'm Haisley."

"Lizzie," I say.

"You're with the press?"

"I write for *Modern Woman*."

"Are you interested in chickens?"

"Excuse me?"

"Do you ever cover the chicken vertical?"

"*Modern Woman*," I say again. "Not *Modern Farmer*."

"Right. But, chickens?"

"I'm sorry. I have no idea what you're talking about." I glance down at her badge and see that her Instagram handle is @HenfluenceGirl.

Is there truly an influencer for everything?

"I don't cover chickens." Words I never thought would come out of my mouth.

"Well, if you ever change your mind, I have stories."

"I bet." I turn and look the other way. "Who's talking now?" I ask the petite brunette next to me. She's furiously pecking away at her laptop with one hand while hoovering down a chocolate croissant with the other.

"Ughhhhh," she groans. "Marsden Greer."

"Who is that?"

"Right? Who even is he?" Sarcasm drips from her tone. "Of course they would give a prime speaking spot to a guy like him and not a woman . . . even at a conference like this because they just want attention from a celebrity . . . Maybe they could give it to a woman who has been sweating away on a platform that truly improves the lives of working women, working moms. Nope. They're going to give it to some dude who plays for a professional baseball team and just, like, announced that he created an app and wanted to talk to some moms about it."

"I'm Lizzie." I introduce myself in response to her tirade.

"Katie."

Her hair is pulled up into a sloppy ponytail and she's wearing simple jeans and a black tank top. I glance down at her feet in dusty Converse sneakers and suddenly feel incredibly overdressed even though she's the one who is out of place in this room. "I assume you have a platform that improves the lives of working moms?" I say, gulping down the coffee that is set in front of me by a harried server.

"I do." Her serious expression lights up. "It's like Airtable and Slack combined, but for the family business unit. It's a way to make sure dads are involved in the project management of the family. I was inspired to do it because I see so many women, my sisters included, losing their minds over constantly giving their husbands the same simple instructions for the most basic things, like how to log into the pediatrician platform or what kind of Popsicles their kid likes."

"How many kids do you have?"

"None! I'm more of a childless cat lady." She laughs. "I saw a hole in the market. I'm here for the networking, but keep that on the down-low. If they find out I don't have kids, they might run me out with torches."

"Your secret's safe with me. I often prefer childless cat ladies. The app sounds great," I say, meaning it, although the last thing I want is another reason to be on my computer or my phone when I don't have to be. I don't think I can stomach another "productivity platform" even if it's life changing.

A woman sitting on my other side chimes in. "It *is* great. And she deserves all the funding." I turn to look at her. She's older than most of this crowd and stands out because she's foregone the muted pastel dresses and onesies for a bright purple pantsuit. Her salt-and-pepper curls have a single purple streak running down the middle. I love her a little bit at first sight.

She conspicuously looks at my name tag. I wonder how far we are from a future where no one needs to clock name badges anymore, but when AI will alert us through a little chip in our brains who we are about to talk to and whether they are worthy of our attention.

Ding, ding, this person is useless for both your social and business climbing. Move along.

Ding dong. This woman is an HR executive at a big firm looking to hire a content director. Turn on that charm. Talk about your personal development journey.

"You're Rebecca Sommers's friend," the purple-suited woman says. Our friendship, if you can still call it that, isn't indicated anywhere on my badge and her shit-eating grin lets me know she likes catching people off guard with an excessive amount of information. Maybe she already has the AI chip in her brain.

"I'm Lizzie," I say instead of validating her claim.

"I know. I work with Rebecca. I'm Olivia Jackson." A look passes between her and Katie, but I can't tell what it means.

"What do you do with Rebecca?" I ask Olivia.

"A little of this. A little of that. I'm an advisor. Accountant. Friend."

Is "friend" a job now? I don't say it out loud.

"Olivia is everyone's accountant," Katie says. "And manager."

"Not yours," Olivia fires back jovially.

"Only because I can't afford you yet, but you will be." Katie rolls her eyes and explains more to me. "About a decade ago Olivia realized that influencers were going to be the future of both media and commerce. None of her old colleagues in LA believed her. So she quit and started her own thing. Now she specializes in accounting, management, and financial planning for influencers who are worth more than . . . What now, Olivia? What's the total amount of money you manage?"

"I don't kiss and tell." Olivia delivers that devious grin again.

Katie waves her hand in the air. "More than, like, a billion dollars. Anyway, she's a baller."

"How is an influencer accountant different than a regular accountant?" I ask, genuinely curious.

"Oh, it isn't really. I just understand how the creator income streams work better than the average Joe Schmo who doesn't get that when you're a creator your entire life is your business." Olivia leans in to explain to me.

"So they can write off everything?"

"Not everything, but a lot. They're always creating content and always marketing."

"And you work with Bex—I mean Rebecca." I stammer to get the name right.

"I do. Have for years."

"The Sommerses must have a complicated tax situation. They have so much going on."

"Oh, I don't work with Grayson Sommers," Olivia says pointedly. "Just Rebecca."

I think about my own relationship with our accountant, Joel Wasserstein, who has a small office in Alphabet City in Manhattan. We only talk in February when it's time to start getting all our expenses and forms in order and we've never actually communicated with Joel except by email. He definitely wouldn't know I was bringing a friend to a work conference.

I decide not to play it cool. "How do you know who I am?" But Olivia is not frazzled by the question.

"Rebecca's one of my top clients. We talked about you coming." She stops and it's clear that's all she wants to say about that.

Before I can follow up, a hidden stereo starts pumping out the eighties yacht-rock anthem "The Final Countdown" and the room goes entirely dark.

"What the hell is happening?" I blurt out. No one else is fazed.

"Good meeting you, Lizzie." Olivia clasps a strong hand on my shoulder. "I'm sure we'll be talking much more soon. Looking forward to it." She turns to the stage with a laser focus.

A slim but well-muscled man with immovable hair fist pumps his way from the back doors of the ballroom. He's the first dude I've seen who isn't working here, and the vibe in the space immediately shifts. The man takes his time getting to the stage. He's got a square jaw and the bushy beard of someone who has watched too much *Outlander* with their wife.

"HEYA, MAMASSSSSSSS!" he shouts into the microphone.

"Is that Marsden?" I ask.

Katie rolls her eyes. "Doesn't he look like a Marsden? When did people start naming their children the things you would normally call beagles anyway?"

"By the way," I whisper to her before Marsden can start speaking, "do you know Rebecca Sommers? I've been looking for her. Have you seen her around this morning?"

Katie taps away at the computer for a second before answering. "Everyone knows her," she says. "I haven't seen her this morning. She's probably getting ready for her big talk."

Another woman, the henfluencer, chimes in. "I assumed she would be here since this Marsden guy is like her husband's BFF since they were kids. Super tight."

"Oh. Yeah. That makes sense," I say because I can totally see Marsden hanging out with Grayson. Their names alone demand it. This dude taking the stage with his perfectly coiffed Ken doll hair and his deep V-neck T-shirt revealing intensely trimmed chest hair and a well-oiled physique has the vibrating energy of a kitten. It's like he can't decide whether to step up closer to the microphone or hurl his body onto the stage and do burpees. He chooses the mic and chants again.

"MOMS ARE THE BOMB!"

He seems to expect a call-and-response.

"MOMS ARE THE BOMB!!!!?"

A few women offer weak claps and half-hearted repetition.

"What does his app do again?" I ask Katie.

"Who knows. People love giving funding to white dudes who are on TV. I bet he doesn't even know."

The music finally fades, and Marsden has to say words that are not a cheer of some sort.

"So happy to be here with you lovely ladies today. I love women. I love my wife."

"His wife is such an asshole," Katie whispers.

"You ladies have been busy little bees. I've been told by my team that you all, that you mothers, control eighty-five percent of household purchases in the United States, that y'all got a spending power of something like $2.4 trillion. I know a little something about that spending. My wife is always racking up the charges on the credit card. But you know what they say, happy wife, happy life."

The room stays mostly silent except for one table in the front that erupts in giggles and hoots. Many of them stand to cheer on Marsden. There are at least fifteen women squeezed around a table that should only seat eight. When they sit back down, I notice a couple are perched on the others' laps. They're slightly different from many of the women here. While everyone I've seen so far has looked like they're ready to appear on high-definition television at a moment's notice in a wardrobe that might cost half my monthly paycheck, these women have gone above and beyond the call of aesthetic duty.

This crew appears airlifted out of a 1950s sitcom, the kind I used to watch on Nick at Nite with my grandma when I slept over at her apartment as a kid. Margaret Anderson, Donna Stone, Harriet Nelson, June Cleaver. These women are all in dresses with fitted bodices that accentuate impossibly tiny waists. Instead of the Pre-Raphaelite waves of many of the other conference attendees their hair is pulled up into intricate French twists or pinned into scarves that match the patterns of their dresses.

I've never seen any of them in person of course, but I recognize a few from my scrolls. The so-called tradwives, the most controversial of the influencers. The worst thing to happen on the Internet since planking. I don't really give a damn if someone wants to play dress-up and service their husband. I do care when they start spouting off about how this choice is a new offshoot of feminism. They cook and they clean and they talk about how a woman's place is in the home and how she must submit to her husband. They homeschool their kids. They claim that women who work in the corporate world have been sold a lie, that it's toxic for women to focus on anything but motherhood. I pray they'll descend into the graveyard of Internet trends past, like the Mannequin Challenge and dabbing, before my daughter gets a phone.

@BarefootMamaLove gets lumped in with the trad influencers a lot online. I think about Bex's captions that claim motherhood is her own highest purpose. Just make it *Little House on the Prairie* instead of Betty Draper. A false nostalgia for a different century.

Marsden is still going on and on. His acolytes are rapt. But most of the crowd is doing what we're doing, whispering in side conversations and tapping away on laptops.

But then, as if Marsden has intuited that the majority of the room has checked out, he decides to go all in.

"Do you want to know why I'm really here today?" No answer.

"I am here for you! All of you are doing God's work. Motherhood is the highest vocation for a woman to aspire to."

I see Katie look up from her laptop for the first time and fix a steely gaze on the stage.

"I know that a lot of you were raised in a world that told you to lean in and climb the corporate ladder and grab that brass ring. But y'all know that just made women miserable. You all want to have your babies and live the good life while your husbands take care of you. Am I right?"

Silence.

Dead silence, even from his biggest fans. They must know this is the wrong crowd for him to preach this kind of gospel to.

"I don't think he knows what this conference is about," Katie says, not even in a whisper.

"To be fair . . . it is called MomBomb," I mutter. "It's fairly innocuous. It could be about any number of things. It could be about your pelvic floor or promoting nuclear energy."

"The women in this room command billions in advertising," she shoots back. "It's a business conference."

"Still sort of a dumb name. Like Marsden," I say, mostly to myself, before turning my attention back to him.

"You all chose to quit your jobs and focus on the most important thing in the world. Being a wife and mother."

"No, we didn't," someone yells.

"We are running companies here," another chimes in.

Marsden is slightly shaken but undeterred, like a robot vacuum programmed to continue moving forward despite running into a brick wall.

"Sure you may be doing your little side hustles and posting your cute pictures and videos. But your true dedication is to your husbands and those little angels. And that's where my new innovative app that you can find on the phones comes in. It's called Stay. Yes, Stay. For all you *stay-at-home moms*. This app will have everything you need to keep staying and momming and loving those little ones."

"I know words are coming out of his mouth, but they don't seem to be doing what words usually do," Katie says. "None of it makes sense."

Before he can explain what exactly Stay does, something whizzes by the side of Marsden's head.

"Was that a waffle?" I ask.

"I think a petite pancake," Katie says. "The Dutch kind."

Marsden is a professional baseball player. He has excellent reflexes. But even he can't dodge the deluge of pastries that are suddenly being slung his way.

"I think some of these women played softball in college," Katie says admiringly, as she picks up a croissant from her own plate and underhands it toward the podium.

Marsden stands there in disbelief. *Why are these women, these moms, so angry? What could possibly enrage these tender creatures in such a profound way?* his confused expression begs. And then he says out loud what's in his brain.

"I am honoring you. I am venerating you."

"You are a condescending prick," one of the moms I recognize from outside the elevator yesterday wails. "I made three times my husband's salary last year and now he works for me. Who do you think you're talking to?"

A splash of vanilla custard drips down Marsden's cheek, forming an obscene trickle. You can feel the energy pulsating through the entire space. It's contagious, to be honest . . . and electric. I want to throw a croissant too but my plate is empty. Even while pastries sail through the air Marsden still has an idiotic smile plastered on his face and his shoulders thrown back with the true confidence of a decently attractive white man who has never been told no.

Suddenly there's a loud thud. We all turn to see men in uniforms streaming through the now open doors.

The police have arrived.

CHAPTER EIGHT

LIZZIE

The cops bumble their way into the ballroom. By the looks on their faces they're bewildered by the room of well-coiffed women chucking pastries.

As one of the officers approaches the stage they step on a freshly thrown jelly donut. Its electric red insides squirt out like a spray of blood across the ballroom's tasteful beige carpet. Soon the whispers all blend together to form a buzz of locusts. More than a few women hold their phones aloft, no doubt live streaming it all to their audiences of millions.

Everything is content.

Finally, the cop makes it to the microphone. His ruby-red-jelly-donut footprints trail him the entire way. He has to bump Marsden away from the mic.

"Is Rebecca Sommers here? Mrs. Sommers." There's a pointed emphasis on the *Mrs.*, or maybe I imagine it. Everyone cranes their necks to look for Bex, but I know for sure she's not here. I've been searching for her the whole morning. And after a beat or two of silence the officer knows it too.

"Has anyone seen Rebecca Sommers this morning?" Disdain drips from his tone as he says her name. I looked around as eagerly as everyone else. A sense of dread flushes through me when the cop repeats his question. What do they want with Bex?

If the cops were smart, or if they had any handle on what kind of room they were walking into, maybe they would have told the hotel to shut down the Wi-Fi before busting through those doors, but they hadn't had that foresight, and within thirty seconds, texts and emails and DMs are shooting around the country, maybe the world, searching for Rebecca Sommers. Everyone is greedy for information and for eyeballs.

"I'd like you little ladies to sit tight," the officer on the stage drawls as the moderator from earlier, the one in the flouncy buttery dress, swishes back onto the stage to regain a modicum of control over a situation that has gone entirely sideways.

"It won't be that much longer," she promises in a carefully controlled tone. "And I'm so sorry for this interruption. The MomBomb staff is diligently working with these gentlemen and we will all be able to adjourn to this morning's breakout sessions shortly."

I look down at my own phone, hoping for a dozen missed calls from Bex, or at the very least a text from her. Nothing. When I glance back up a cop is behind me. Had he been reading my screen?

"Miss Jackson," he says to Olivia. "We need you to come down to the station."

"Why?"

"We need to ask you some questions."

"I can meet you there in an hour," Olivia says in a smooth and practiced tone.

"We would prefer you come with us."

"I don't think so." She stands and makes her way out of the ballroom, the officer trailing behind her like a puppy.

"No one leaves," another cop says into the microphone from the stage.

I comb through Bex's social media accounts, but she hasn't posted since last night, when she'd made a reel of her beautifully manicured toes dangling in the infinity pool in my room, the purple mountains and orange sunset glowing in the distance. Cursive words were sprinkled over her milky white calves: LIVING THE GOOD LIFE AND CATCHING UP WITH AN OLD BESTIE. OUR FRIENDS ARE OUR EVERYTHING. There were already thousands of comments.

Preach sister

Friends, God, children, and chocolate . . . also our husbands . . . lol

I aspire to be as calm and present as you

Thank you for your inspiration

Sexy toes!

Funny how everyone believes everything they see on social media

Where are your kids?

When can I hang out with you?

I want to be your bestie

What is your toenail color?

My dream life

The way I would love to live

The naked longing for a fantasy in most of the comments makes me intensely sad.

Because she tagged me in the reel, I've amassed thousands of new followers in the past twenty-four hours and the numbers keep climbing.

Much to the chagrin of the conference's organizers, Mom-Bomb does not continue as planned. The breakout sessions don't happen, and more police officers show up to keep us all penned in the ballroom even though they probably don't have the authority to do it. Lunch is eventually served. Waiters traipse from table to table with blue cheese iceberg salads and lukewarm salmon as if nothing were amiss.

"Holy shit," the henfluencer finally clucks about an hour into our captivity.

We'd hardly spoken since the disruptions. No one was talking much, but I figured all the influencers were communicating on their phones. I saw nothing but bowed heads and fingers flying furiously over screens. No one touched their salmon.

"Grayson Sommers is fucking dead," she announces. "Holy shit. Someone killed him."

DET. WALSH: *You haven't seen Mrs. Sommers at all today?*

E. MATTHEWS: *No. We were supposed to have breakfast this morning, but she never called or texted. So I went to her room and knocked and she wasn't there. I got worried that she overslept.*

DET. WALSH: *Did you have a lot to drink last night?*

E. MATTHEWS: *Define "a lot."*

DET. WALSH: *I don't like sass.*

E. MATTHEWS: *It was a lot for me. I don't normally drink more than a glass or two of wine.*

DET. WALSH: *Was it a lot for her? Do you think she could have driven a car after what she had to drink?*

E. MATTHEWS: *I honestly don't know. Maybe. But probably not. Like I said, I was worried that she overslept so I banged on the door and I called but there was no answer.*

DET. WALSH: *Did you think that was strange?*

E. MATTHEWS: *I thought she had already gone downstairs, and I went down to find her.*

DET. WALSH: *But she wasn't there?*

E. MATTHEWS: *She wasn't there.*

DET. WALSH: *When did you learn about what happened to Grayson Sommers?*

E. MATTHEWS: *After the police arrived at the conference. It didn't take long for people to start talking and chattering, even as the room got locked down. Eventually someone got ahold of the pictures . . .*

DET. WALSH: *What did you think when you saw the pictures?*

E. MATTHEWS: *That whoever did that to him must have really fucking hated Gray Sommers.*

CHAPTER NINE

LIZZIE

Every time I try to talk to one of the officers passing me in the hall of the police station my throat tightens. It feels as though someone is choking me. The words won't come. I just want to ask when they think I can leave. My phone has no service and I've been here for hours. There are no windows in the station, which feels like such a cliché, but it's true. I have no idea if Grayson Sommers's death has made national news. Not that he's famous per se, but Bex is well-known enough, and more important, she's a beautiful white woman who may have murdered her husband, which will be catnip to every attention-starved news network on the planet.

I've never been interrogated before. It lacked all of the hokey charm of the gazillion seasons of *Law & Order* I've watched since college. Detective Jim Walsh had none of Stabler's charisma or his sexy eyebrows. Walsh was a short, round man with a round head that had hair only around the periphery and none on the top. He didn't wear a uniform, just dirty blue jeans and a denim button-down shirt, more reminiscent of a ranch hand than a detective.

I'm still in shock about everything—the fact that I'm in a police station at all; the fact that Bex's husband is dead, possibly brutally murdered; the fact that she is likely the prime suspect.

I think back to the moment the henfluencer told me that Grayson Sommers was dead.

"How do you know?" I'd asked.

"Eliza Jane, over there." She had nodded in the direction of another table. "She's got a cousin who's a cop out by the Sommers place and he just tipped her off."

The woman continued to stare down at her phone. "This is insane."

"What? What else?"

She tilted her screen toward me and that's when I saw Grayson. Or rather, what was left of him.

"Isn't it illegal for a cop to text photos of a crime scene?"

She shrugged but didn't take her eyes off the small screen.

The photo must have been taken quickly and secretly with a phone. Only the torso was visible and it was slightly blurry. In it, Grayson's plaid shirt was ripped in two. His bare chest was splayed out over the sharp blades of some kind of farm equipment. They had ripped through his entire abdomen, flaying the skin open. The floor of what I assumed was the Sommerses' barn was coated in dark blood, so dark it almost looked black.

I choked back a gag.

"Ohmygod . . . ewwwwwww," the henfluencer squealed.

"What?" everyone around her demanded in unison.

"Someone apparently sliced off one of Grayson's body parts and put it in the kitchen freezer."

"Which one?" I asked.

"Not sure yet. But I bet he got the Lorena Bobbitt treatment."

"Do you think Rebecca did this?" another tablemate had asked me hungrily. "You're friends with her. Weren't you with her last night? It looked like you were with her last night in her photos." This last line came out like an accusation. She moved her chair slightly away from me.

"No. Absolutely not. She didn't do this. And I don't know anything." I stood up, desperate for air. Desperate to leave. I wanted nothing to do with any of it. I wanted to erase those terrible images from my mind. *It isn't real,* I told myself.

"I was with her l-last night," I stuttered when someone else repeated her question.

"Why didn't y'all come to the welcome circle?" another voice asked accusingly.

"I was tired."

"Were you with her all night?"

"Well, right until bedtime."

"So she could have done it."

Everyone close to us was listening. I dropped my voice to a whisper. "But she didn't. She wouldn't."

"How well do you know her?"

I didn't know how to answer that question. Because at one point I would have said I knew Bex better than anyone. But that was too long ago. Suddenly my phone rang with a number I didn't recognize.

I sent it to voicemail and seconds later it rang again. I didn't want to answer it. I wanted to call my husband. I wanted to call Bex. I wanted to get the hell out of there.

But when it rang a third time I walked to the back of the room and answered.

Sure enough, it was the police. They knew I'd been with Bex the night before. "How?" I'd asked dumbly.

"She tagged you on Instagram."

Ace detective work. They asked if I wanted someone in the ballroom to come find me and get me to the police station. I managed a quiet *no*. "I can drive."

The officer on the line gave me the address of the station and I silently thanked God that they hadn't tried to march me out the way they did Olivia Jackson.

That's how I ended up here, being questioned for more than an hour. Now I just wait. When the detective was questioning me, he told me I shouldn't leave just yet and I didn't know if he meant the police station or the state.

I'm greedy for information as I sit beneath these fluorescent lights, constantly checking my impotent phone to see if service has somehow miraculously returned.

"Elizabeth Matthews."

I jump at the sound of my own name. It's Detective Walsh again. "We have a few more questions."

"Have you ever met Rebecca Sommers's children?" he asks when I sit back down in the little room. I shake my head. Though I can name them in age order, and I've seen two of them born on the floor of Rebecca's house on her Instagram reels. Though I feel like I know each and every one of them intimately, which I am only just starting to realize is slightly gross and unsettling,

I don't actually know them. I've never met a single one of them in real life, never touched their bouncy cheeks or smelled their downy heads. I don't know those children at all.

"I don't. Where are her kids now?"

He pauses, as if debating whether to tell me.

"We don't know," he finally admits. "They're gone too." This sharing of information feels strategic. He will give me something and I'm expected to give him something in return. It's a classic strategy, one I've used as a reporter. "We're worried about them."

I am too. The worry scratches at my brain and I can't stop thinking about Bex's face as she told me about Alice and how talented she was at the piano. I'd never seen her so flush with pride. Then I remember what she said next, that it was Gray who wouldn't allow Alice to go away to a special music school.

There's something else about Bex's face in the memory that snags in my mind. The heavy makeup under the eye, the bruise she was trying to hide. She had flat out admitted that Gray was controlling, and I know what I saw. I should mention this to the police. Both of those things could be a motive.

For the first time since seeing those pictures of Grayson Sommers after he bled out in his barn, I can imagine my old friend possibly doing it, but maybe she didn't have a choice.

Jim Walsh watches me intently as I shudder. He knows I have something to tell him and he's going to wait me out with stony silence. I stare at my hands. *Tell him*, I think. *Give him anything at all that might lead them to those children.*

"There is one more thing I should tell you," I say to the detective.

※ ※ ※

I'm intensely unhinged the entire drive back to the hotel. My heart batters against my ribs like a moth trying to escape through a window. I told the police the truth. I did the right thing. I didn't flat out say I thought Bex killed her husband. I don't know if she did.

I know nothing.

All I admitted was that I knew there was tension in their marriage, that maybe he had hurt her because of that tension. Jim Walsh gobbled these details down like a hungry puppy, didn't even hide his excitement at my admission. He let me go after that and when service returned to my phone in the parking lot it flooded with notifications.

I have thousands more Instagram followers. Every person who followed me before last night was someone I had interacted with in real life. But these new people are all strangers. They don't know me, only my connection to Bex, and they want that connection by proxy. They are desperate for it.

The comments on my latest post of the nachos from last night are intense.

Where is Rebecca?

Have you seen her?

Who are you?

Peter has left three voicemails and sent a half dozen texts. There's no way he could know what happened out here yet. But when I listen to them, I learn that Grayson's murder has somehow made the national news already. I do a quick Google search. It even made *The Washington Post,* which described Grayson as a congressional hopeful about to launch an exploratory committee here. In the same article Bex is described as a stay-at-home mom and lifestyle influencer. No mention of her as the breadwinner of that family, the CEO of a company. The headline in *People* magazine reads, "Congressional Hopeful Brutally Murdered, Influencer Wife on the Lam." The news cycle works fast, and it hates women.

I shouldn't read the comments on this story. You never read the comments. No one is meaner or more viscerally cutting than an anonymous troll on the Internet, but I do it anyway.

I'm not surprised at all. She seemed like a crazy bitch ready to crack.

Where are you BAREFOOTMAMA????

We all have your back

Girl, Jesus is the only man you can truly trust!

If you need a place to hide out you can stay with me

Rebecca Sommers is a liar and a fraud and a whore. Now everyone will know the truth.

Her husband seemed so wonderful. I am horrified. He was exactly what I wanted in my future man. RIP GRAYSON

I didn't think someone with that much air between her ears would be capable of pulling something like this off. I almost respect her more.

So much talk of her being crazy and unhinged, a psycho, a whore. All from people who likely followed her every move and post with bated breath until about eight hours ago. All from women who probably bought her expensive baby carrier and matching apron sets. Maybe the same people who posted all of the sycophantic comments on her last reel saying how much they loved her life and wanted to know her toenail color.

It all makes me hate humanity.

It's twilight and the sky is that pretty swirl of colors I saw last night from my balcony while I was sitting with Bex. My insides are as mixed up as the painting in the sky. I'm ashamed for telling the police such personal things about Bex and confused about my strange role in all this. If she did do it, if she murdered her husband, then was I brought out here as an alibi?

I pull over and answer the phone when Peter calls again.

"What the hell, Lizzie? Where have you been? What's going on? Why didn't you call me back? I've been worried sick." My husband's voice, even erratic like this, calms me slightly, and some of the tension melts out of my shoulders. He is real.

"The police station," I say, like he should have known.

"Oh, honey. What happened? What do you need? How can I help?" I only just realize that I hadn't texted him. I'd completely forgotten, or rather I had the thought to text him and then just didn't do it, a thing that happens almost every day. I am constantly texting him only in my mind.

"Where should I start?" The tears come, fat and salty. I miss Peter. I miss life the way it was twenty-four hours ago. I want him here now to hold me and then drive back to the hotel and get me safely into bed. Nothing here feels safe. I spent last night with a potential murderer and I had no idea. I shouldn't be so surprised by this sudden wave of emotions. I'm gutted. I was used as a pawn by someone I didn't think had the ability to hurt me anymore.

I fill Peter in as best I can through my sobs.

"Do you think she did it?" My rational and highly analytical reporter husband will always get straight to the point. No bullshit.

"Yes." I choke back another cry. "No. I have no idea. She was unhappy. I can tell you that. Deeply, deeply unhappy despite what she's posted on social media all these years. It sounds like Grayson was awful to her. It was all a lie."

"You need to come home."

"The officers asked me to stay in case they had more questions."

"I don't think they can make you do that. Do you need a lawyer?"

"No. Why would I?"

"I actually have no idea. I've never gone through something like this."

"Me neither. But no. I don't think I do. I told the police the truth. This isn't about me. I barely knew her." That is the truth. I knew Bex. I barely knew Rebecca Sommers. In fact, I didn't know her at all.

"I know. I know. Okay. Do you want me to fly out there?"

Yes. I want that desperately, but I'm also a grown woman who can take care of herself, and right now our kids need him more than I do.

"No. I can do this on my own. I'll talk to them again tomorrow if I have to and then rest up and come back."

"Do you think Alana will be okay with that?"

Alana is my boss, my editor. Ten years my junior and a rising star in tech, she took over *Modern Woman* when the venture money poured in to save it.

"Alana? Why would she care if I stay here or not?"

"Shit, Liz. *Modern Woman* is all over this story. Have you not talked to Alana yet?"

"No, I called you first. What do you mean?"

"When I read about what happened and I couldn't get in touch with you I went to the *Modern Woman* website, and they have a picture from Rebecca's Instagram on their homepage. It's of her feet. So strange. But the caption announces their editor is on the ground and covering this breaking story."

"No. No." I shake my head. And then I look at my stream of text messages from Alana and from David, our photo editor, sent hours ago. They're desperate for information.

"I can't."

"Tell them that."

"I don't think I can do that either. My job is hanging on by a thread." I haven't said this out loud before. "All of our jobs are. The magazine is."

"It's late here. You don't need to call her back right away." But I know I do. Alana doesn't sleep. She's a machine and she's singularly focused on the traffic we so desperately need to stay afloat. "Fuck," I whisper.

"Don't call her. Get some sleep."

"Okay," I say, though I know I'll call. I'm a good soldier. But not until I get back to my room, not until I take a shower and scrub my body raw with the fancy hotel soap to get rid of the smell of police station—a mix of stale coffee, cigarette smoke, and recycled air.

"I love you, darling. And I'll get on a flight within the hour if you need me."

We can't afford that, but I like that he pretends we can. "I know you will. And I love you too," I say, grateful for this man who has never once told me I couldn't do something or pressured me to be anything other than myself. I'm lucky. I know that.

There are several shiny black town cars in front of the hotel with black-clad security guards at the ready waiting outside them, as well as a number of television news vans with satellites on the tops of them. A scrum of reporters is roped off about twenty feet from the main entrance, a pen of wolves. I know those pens well. I've spent days inside of them. I have to hand it to this hotel and probably the conference. They've mobilized quickly to lock this place down and keep the reporters on the outside. Which means I might be the only press on the inside. I try to ignore that familiar tingle of excitement at being the first to crack a story because this time I'm part of the story. It's a feeling that I've missed desperately without even knowing it.

I can't put on my sunglasses as a disguise since it's so dark, but I've got the tattered Phillies hat I wore on the plane ride out here to cover my greasy head and I can pull the brim low over my face. I'm still wearing the ridiculous dress I put on this morning, and the lace has given me a rash on my neck and wrists.

The journalists bombard me with questions as I approach the property. "Were you at MomBomb? Do you know Rebecca Sommers?" I am certain that all these people know Lizzie Matthews was with Rebecca last night since Bex tagged me in that last

Instagram post, but I don't think they know it's me right now. I'm mostly a ghost online. I don't have a bunch of pictures of myself on Instagram. My headshot on the magazine's website is probably five years old. I keep moving as quickly as I can. The lobby is more of a safe space, at least from the press. But plenty of women from the conference are still here. They probably flew in from all over the country and aren't scheduled to fly home for days. Perhaps, like me, they long to be safe from the questions of the outside world, or more likely, they're seduced by the proximity to drama.

"It's her," I hear one of them whisper loudly, but I don't break my stride as I shuffle toward the elevators.

Once inside I realize I need the room key to get up to my floor. I rustle around in my purse, but it's not in there. Shit. It must have fallen out in the car when I grabbed my phone. I'll have to go back out and get one from the front desk. My hunched shoulders and quick shuffle clearly convey I don't want to talk to anyone and thankfully everyone keeps their distance. When I get to the front desk, I request a new key and the clerk behind the counter types something into the computer and then takes a beat to read whatever is written there. Maybe they want me out of here. Maybe they don't want such a close witness in this case in their hotel.

Or who knows, maybe they want the attention. All press can be good press.

I look up and the expression on the woman's face is nothing but kind and accommodating and I hate that I now suspect everyone of something nefarious.

"Here's your key, Ms. Matthews." She slides the glossy black card my way. "And according to our system it looks like we have a message for you."

"Oh?" I'm genuinely surprised.

"Hold on one second. I'll run into the office and grab it."

My breath hitches with anticipation, though I know it's probably from Alana. When I didn't respond to emails, calls, or texts, she got old-fashioned and likely faxed over a list of questions she wants me to answer ASAP. If I don't call soon, she'll be on the next plane here and then I'll really be in a dumpster fire.

The clerk returns with a small envelope, the paper the palest shade of pink possible. The stationery is expensive and heavy in my hands. "Thank you," I say, knowing I'm being watched by everyone in the room.

I make it to the elevator and use my new card to get to my floor. I somehow manage to make it all the way into my suite before I rip open the envelope and yank out the note card inside.

The paper is the same color and weight as the envelope. It smells vaguely of lemons and basil. There are only two lines written on it, but I read them over and over again until the words blur.

I didn't do it. You have to believe me.

CHAPTER TEN

LIZZIE

Alana wants everything. She wants photos and first-person interviews with MomBomb attendees. She wants all the details about the last night I spent with Bex. She wants to know our entire history together. She wants me to live stream everything from the *Modern Woman* accounts if possible. I tried to tell her that I'm a witness, or something. That I'm whatever you call it when the police bring you in for questioning, that I don't know if I can share anything.

Alana was undeterred. She got on the phone to the magazine's general counsel, who confirmed that if I haven't signed anything, I can share whatever I want with whomever I want whenever I want.

Legal advice aside, it feels wrong.

Alana is a lot of things, but she didn't get to be as successful as she is today by not knowing how to read people. She turned on the empathy when we spoke, said she couldn't imagine what

I was going through, asked what I needed, how she could support me. And only then did she ask for all the reporting.

The most successful hunters are always the ones who make sure their prey are comfortable and unaware before going in for the kill. Alana and Bex might have that in common. I promised my boss two stories. The first is due in an hour.

I sit down at the computer as the sun comes up and decide I have to lie in this piece, or at the very least bend the truth. I will do most of what Alana asks because we need my salary and my generous benefits. But this is different than being a fly on the wall at the Golden Globes or sitting in the audience during a murder trial. This is my life and our shared history. Only yesterday I was bemoaning how I could possibly create content out of my own life. And now someone is begging me to.

The note that Bex left me is on my bedside table and it was the first thing I saw when I opened my eyes after a fitful couple of hours of sleep. I've brewed myself a cup of coffee from the very complicated Nespresso machine. There should be a German word for the intense confusion one feels in the face of new hotel appliances and lighting options.

Despite what the note says, I don't believe Bex. I don't know who or what to believe. I don't know when she'll be in touch again, but I think I have a plan to *make* her get in touch with me faster and it involves writing this article and getting it up on *Modern Woman* as quickly as possible.

Adrenaline has kicked in. I'll write just enough about reuniting with Bex to make Alana happy. I'll write the things that will hopefully make Bex reach out.

Her note feels like a desperate plea, but she's also more calculated than I ever took her for. And let's not forget she may also be a murderer. I can't stop thinking about her kids. Where are they? Grayson's parents have finally talked to the press. They're pleading for information about their grandchildren. How do six kids disappear without a trace? One of them is a toddler who is still breastfeeding. It seems impossible in this day and age that anyone could disappear. And more important, are the children safe if Bex is with them and she's unhinged and dangerous?

I keep thinking of this terrible story we reported at the magazine about two years ago that was so popular it was also turned into a podcast. A Hollywood producer bought the television rights too. I think Emma Stone is slated to star in it next year. At first I was excited to be assigned as the lead editor on such a big project, but it quickly overwhelmed me and put me into a dark place.

The story was about a mom who killed her seven children by driving them all off a hundred-foot cliff into the Pacific Ocean. All of the kids had been given near fatal doses of Valium and Benadryl and were most likely sound asleep at the time of the crash, which was the smallest of consolations.

I was in the thick of postpartum with Ollie. I'd only just started back at work a few weeks earlier and I remember the intensity of my milk coming in as I edited the story. My shirt was soaked before I could get to the bathroom with a useless hand pump. I hadn't slept in weeks. The baby had colic; the toddler had strep. Someone needed me during every minute of every hour of every day. I sat on the toilet then and bawled, and for the briefest of seconds I completely understood why that woman had driven off a cliff. I immediately pinched myself hard enough to make a mark and took it back because what kind of woman tempts fate like that?

One of the things we discovered in our reporting is that prior to the incident the mom confided in a co-worker that she wished she hadn't had such a big family, that she wished someone had given her permission to just stop. It seemed so strange to me at the time, the use of that word—*permission*.

But in hindsight it's clear that mother felt trapped. I know in my bones that no matter what she did or didn't do Bex feels trapped too. It may be one of the only things that I know for sure. But she couldn't do what that woman did. There's no way. Even if she's the one who murdered Grayson in that barn, I don't actually believe she could hurt her kids. And I have to keep telling myself that as I write this story, because I'm putting myself on the line here in the hopes that I'm right.

I bang away at my keyboard, the words flowing easily. I'm in a groove in a way I haven't been in a long time, and despite the subject matter, it feels damn good. I love writing, always have.

I take a break when I need a real coffee and not the weak Nespresso crap in the room. I think it's close to lunchtime and the hotel will probably be packed and Alana wants interviews. I read on the MomBomb Instagram page that the rest of the conference has been canceled as the organizers have been working with the authorities, but people are welcome to stay as long as they need to.

You deserve the space to absorb, reflect, and heal, the organizers wrote.

While writing I've been trying to avoid reading what's already out there, though I know there are a lot of column inches. There are the traditional news stories, but also entire Reddit threads now dedicated to searching for Bex and positing theories about what she's done. They are cruel and often unhinged. The grammar is appalling. The hatred is real. I remember all of the vitriol and outrage in the comments section of the stories about the mother who killed her children by driving the van off a cliff.

I wonder what happened to this woman to make her so sick and sadistic

She deserves to burn in hell

It was warranted. What she did was horrible. It was also like rubbernecking a car crash because you're titillated by something appalling. The commenters were desperate and maybe delighted to be so horrified.

For the current Bex story, which someone has dubbed #BloodyFootMama, there's also a whole tribe of TikTokers who refer to themselves as "citizen journalists," both men and women who claim they will get to the bottom of this case before the police. Who are these people and how do they get their information? Do they have real jobs? Or is this a real job now?

A news alert comes across my computer screen that Marsden Greer, that stupid ballplayer from yesterday, has made a statement about Grayson Sommers's murder. But I need coffee before I can watch it.

There's a knock at the door. Part of me thinks it's Bex, but I'm only slightly disappointed when I throw it open and see Olivia standing there. She looks no worse for wear than she did yesterday, despite the fact that I know she must have spent much more time than I did in the police station. Her purple suit has been replaced with an electric-blue version in the exact same style and cut. A blue streak is now in her hair. She's holding out a cup of coffee.

"It's black, but I brought creamer and sugar. I don't know how you take it."

"It's like you read my mind," I say. "I was about to head down to get some coffee."

"Oh, you don't want to go down there. At least not yet. I think we should talk first."

I'm slightly hesitant.

"Ten minutes." She cocks her head and I realize she isn't asking if she can come in. I step aside and she brushes past me.

"Are we allowed to be talking to one another?" I ask.

"We can do whatever we want."

"I'm just . . . I'm sorry. I don't know the rules here."

Her voice softens. "I get it. A lot of this is new for me as well. But yes, we can talk safely and legally too. And if you want to get your own lawyer you are more than welcome to."

"Do you have a lawyer?"

"I am a lawyer."

"I thought you were an accountant."

"I'm both. And I happen to be Rebecca's attorney so there are things I know due to attorney-client privilege that I do not have to share with the police."

"But you'll share them with me?"

"Not all of it, no. But some."

"Did she do it?" I blurt out.

"By 'it,' I assume you mean did she murder Grayson Sommers in cold blood in their barn?"

126

"No, I meant did she sleep with Bradley Cooper?"

"You're funny. Rebecca said you were funny."

"What else did she say about me?"

"I don't think we're here to talk about you. But we can if you want." Olivia settles onto the couch.

"I would like to know how much she told you about me." That seems only fair here, if maybe self-serving.

"Okay. So let's talk about you first. She said you were old friends. She said you were a great writer and a great reporter, that you might be desperate for a good story."

She pauses here to gauge my reaction and I flinch slightly because it's embarrassing that Bex would know that about me, but anyone who has followed what's been happening in media in the past decade could easily smell that desperation.

I thrust my shoulders back slightly. "I'm always looking for a good story."

"As you should be. And Rebecca was going to deliver one to you. She had big plans. But they didn't turn out the way she expected."

"That's an understatement."

"Circumstances changed. They usually do. I read the coverage so far on *Modern Woman* magazine. I saw them claim you're their boots on the ground here. You'll still be working on this?"

I shake my head. "I'm going home as soon as I can."

"How can you do that if you're on assignment on what looks like it will be one of the biggest news stories this month?"

The truth is that I don't have an answer to that.

Alana wants me here for the week, maybe longer if need be, and if I say no, she can very easily cancel my tenuous two-year contract. That was something she made abundantly clear before we ended our call. She was sweet and understanding until she wasn't. But Olivia doesn't need to know any of that, no one does. Not even Peter for the time being.

"I think you should stay," Olivia says without breaking eye contact with me. "Have you heard from Bex?"

Her use of the nickname is intentional. She knows it's what I call her. She clearly knows lots of things.

"You and I are going to have to trust one another. You don't have to start right now, but soon. And if it makes you feel better, I can sign on as your attorney as well, which means our relationship is also covered by attorney-client privilege." She holds up a hand. "Like I just said, you don't need to decide anything right now. But it's an option, and it's a good one. First let me tell you what I came here to tell you. Rebecca, Bex, was going to give you a massive story."

"I know that."

"But you don't know exactly what it was?"

"No."

"She recently signed several licensing agreements with huge multinational brands. The deals are worth a couple hundred million in total. She would be leveraging her entire platform for a magazine, a television show, multiple lines of home goods. She's poised to be the next Pioneer Woman, or actually even bigger than that. She's poised to be the next Martha Stewart."

I don't mention that not everything has always turned out rosy for Martha.

"She was poised to be," I say instead. "Now she's wanted for murder."

"There's no warrant out for her arrest yet," Olivia says diplomatically. "And I won't let her be tried in the court of public opinion."

"Her husband is dead."

"No one cares about her husband. Do you know anything about Martha Stewart's husband? They've been divorced since the nineties. No one cares. No one will remember Grayson Sommers in a few years."

"He's fucking dead," I shout.

"It's terrible. I know. But she didn't do it."

"Did Grayson know about this? All of these big deals?" I already know the answer, or at least part of it. Bex told me the other night, but I want to know what Olivia knows.

"No."

"How is that possible?"

Olivia sighs. "A lot of reasons. She had tried to make deals like this in the past. Not as big of course. But there have been offers and he forbade her from pursuing them over and over again."

"Why?"

"He claimed it was because they didn't need the money, even though they did. But I know it was because he couldn't handle her getting more and more famous, more and more powerful."

"So she didn't tell him about this one."

"No."

"And she was planning on letting him find out how? Through my story? Through her big keynote speech here?"

"I believe that was her plan."

"And then what?"

"She didn't think he could stop her if she made it so public."

Once again, I feel like a pawn in some game I didn't agree to play.

"He also can't stop her now. Because he's fucking dead. That's convenient for her."

Olivia watches me process all of this and chooses her next words carefully. "I agree that it seems convenient. Of course she also can't pursue any of this if she's in prison so it makes no sense for her to have done what she did when so much is at stake. Have you thought about the fact that Rebecca could be in danger herself? That whoever killed her husband might want her dead too? Everyone has been so quick to demonize her. No one seems at all concerned about her safety."

I have to honestly admit that I hadn't thought about that. I too had been quick to jump to conclusions about who was the perpetrator and who was the victim here.

Dread lurches through my stomach. Bex is missing and of course she could be in danger.

"Can I write about anything you just told me?" I ask.

Olivia shrugs. "I knew I was talking to a reporter when I said it."

"Are we on the record?"

"Sure. I can email you some of the specifics about this deal. We should get that information out there. It drives me crazy that every story written about her so far calls her a housewife instead of mentioning that she's the CEO of a multimedia, multinational brand."

"That's what she's been selling to everyone," I blurt out. She may be an entrepreneur, but she's been selling a traditional life-style, same as all those June Cleaver clones cheering on Marsden

Greer. She's been selling herself as a homemaker and housewife in order to make massive amounts of money. It's fairly genius.

I'm well aware that I am being played again, but the scoop is good, so I'll take it. And it will get Alana off my back. "Anything else you want to tell me?"

"There are a lot of people who hate Rebecca. There's a lot of jealousy in the world, and when you combine jealousy with as much money as she has at stake, it's always dangerous. If I were you, I would talk to the women who are still here. Some of the women from around where she lives."

"Now you're just telling me how to do my job."

I should dislike this bossy woman, but I don't. I respect her confidence and it feels like she has Bex's best interests at heart. She also plans to make a good deal of money off Bex if things work out, so she has a stake in all this.

"All suggestions. We want the same things."

"I need to finish my story. Thanks for the coffee."

"I'm always good for coffee. Text or call me anytime." Olivia heads to the door to let herself out, but she turns slightly before exiting the room.

"Hey, Lizzie. One last thing."

"What's that?"

"Be careful."

* * *

I can feel everyone watching me in the hotel's restaurant. I carry my laptop under my arm and set it up at a table in the corner to work. As promised, Olivia sent over information about the deal that Bex was about to close with a very famous media company. There would be a TV show and a magazine. She would oversee a whole bunch of other shows on the network. The number of zeroes in the contract made me slightly ill, slightly jealous, and slightly resentful. I can't imagine how Grayson would have felt finding out about all that money she was poised to make in an article written by me instead of finding out about it from his wife.

The piece I write is glowing and kind and not altogether true, but it's what feels right for the moment and Alana texted me about nineteen thumbs-up emojis when she got it. I mostly talked about how Bex, who I called Rebecca, and I reconnected online after growing apart when we moved to different parts of the country. I wrote that we bonded over our children. The lie about the reconnection is intentional. I want Bex to read it. I want her to know that, for right now at least, I am on her side. I want her to reach out to me again and I'm hoping my lie signals that I am here to protect her secrets. I'm still not sure if that's true.

I write about the deal and about how awed I have been by her success. I throw in a cryptic line about how she was worried Grayson wouldn't let her take on such a big new job. But I don't mention her bruises.

Alana is satiated for the moment, but it won't last.

I go back to my room, slide into the plunge pool, and try to forget everything for a couple of hours. I call my babies. It's irrational but I still worry they'll forget me every time I go away. Ollie screams when I try to get off the phone and my heart cracks in two. I can't stay here. I'm a terrible mother. The shame is a rock lodged in my stomach that remains until Peter texts me minutes later with a picture of Ollie happily gnawing on the corner of the couch. He writes:

> Never forget that small children have less of a short-term memory than a hamster. We're fine.

I keep digging and reporting. I go downstairs for dinner.

A shadow of the conference is continuing without the formalities. Many of these women probably couldn't, or didn't feel like, changing their flights. Plus, the hotel rooms were insanely expensive. Most of them remain, huddled in groups all around the dining room, still lounging at the pool, still walking the James Turrell–created meditation labyrinth.

From my online reading, I gather that Grayson's political campaign was further along than I thought. He had an office in the city even though he hadn't yet officially announced he was running. A snappy young man who referred to himself as a campaign manager for "Gray for America" released a statement about his intense sorrow, his thoughts, and his prayers and a call for justice. "We will do everything we can to catch this brutal killer and lock them up for the rest of their life."

"Hey." I look up to see one of the women who was talking shit about Bex in front of the elevator two days ago hovering above me. How was that only two days ago? She has a blond braid hanging over her shoulder and a white eyelet blouse with a high neck that looks expensive. She's paired it with a long denim skirt and the vibe could either be the pastor's wife from

Footloose or the founder of a natural wine company. Fashion has gotten so confusing.

"Hi," I say.

"Can I sit with you for a second?"

"Sure."

"I'm Cricket." She reaches out a hand to me. "Crazy name, right?

"So you were Rebecca's friend from back in school?" she says. As she settles into her chair, I see a table of her friends watching us. I wonder if she lost a bet and they made her be the one to come over here to talk to me.

I nod.

"I saw that in *People* magazine." All I can think is what a strange way for me to end up in *People* magazine.

"And you're also a creator?" I ask.

"Oh yes. An OG. Since the early days."

"What's your specialty?"

"I'm a whimsical playroom mom."

"Oh. That's highly specific."

"You have to be these days. People love my whimsical playroom. I built it from scratch. But I also have a lot of homesteading, homeschooling, natural crafting, but I try to make it funny. I'm also getting into chickens. I'd love to be a henfluencer one of these days."

"I didn't even know that was a thing until yesterday," I admit. Now I know there is an influencer for everything. Much like porn, if you can name a kink there's an influencer for it.

"It's huge. Chickens are big for engagement. Audiences love them. Rebecca started a lot of that. She's had them forever. I think I can even name all of them." She starts ticking names off on her fingers—Mary Lou, Brynnsleigh, Coley, Aimee, and Hennifer Aniston.

"How well did you know Rebecca?" I ask, and then correct myself. I have chills that I used the past tense about Bex. "Do you know her? Are you friends?" I ask even though I know the answer is no.

"Such good friends." She taps her perfectly manicured fingernails on the table and seems to forget that I overheard all the nasty things she was saying about her good friend Rebecca less than forty-eight hours ago. I've noticed that there are two camps of these influencers right now. The ones who are amplifying whatever modicum of friendship they had with Bex and the ones who are pushing forward all their conspiracy theories about her being a killer. Both camps are getting a lot of attention. Like me they're all surely seeing their follower count and engagement on social media increase.

But I play along.

"How long have you known each other?"

"So long. We both had our first babies around the same time. Of course, she went on to have more than me. I only have four."

Only.

"We've been trying for a boy, but we haven't been blessed yet."

I finally recognize her from her social media. She does these videos where she wears matching outfits with all of her daughters and then raps about being a #GirlMom. If I'm remembering correctly she also promotes a lot of supplements. Her whimsical playroom does indeed look delightful.

"How many kids do you have?" she asks.

"Two." Which to me still seems like an awful lot.

"And you're a reporter. Are you writing a story about this? About Rebecca?"

"I am. Something went live hours ago, but I'm working on another one. Can I ask you some questions for it?"

"Oh, I don't know if I should." She definitely wants to. "I should probably check in with my hubs to see how he feels about it."

This is something I haven't heard before. Permission from a husband to speak to me.

"Sure. Ask your hubs."

I pretend to go back to work while she sends a text.

"Ooooo, Chad—my hubby bubby—says I can talk to you," the woman blurts out after her phone chimes seconds later. "But make sure to get my handle in there. Always be marketing, right?"

"Always," I parrot.

"So I should tell you that not everyone is going to be as nice about Rebecca as I am. I mean I really respect her and everything she's done, but there are some women who are real jealous or who think that Rebecca is always on her high horse, you know."

"Right. But not you."

"Definitely not me. She truly is an inspiration to me—you can use that quote if you want. She's a pioneer in motherhood content. She gave so many of us permission to create," she spews from her gratitude lexicon. "And my thoughts and prayers are with her and her children right now. And speaking of children. Have you heard anything about them?" Cricket is also clearly here to get information from me. I shake my head.

"I hope they're safe. Whatever monster did that to Grayson . . . can you imagine if they get close to the children?"

It's something I've been trying my best not to imagine, but of course I have been.

"Who knows what the police are actually doing—I don't think they're the most competent. But you know that Grayson has some powerful men behind him, behind his entire family."

"Powerful men?"

"Church leaders, politicians, all of the rich guys who support the church and the politicians. We don't live here anymore. Chad got transferred out of state years ago. But I still hear all the tea. A couple of years ago—and you can look this up, it isn't just gossip—the wife of one of Grayson's cousins—I think her name was Amelia—wanted to leave her husband and get a divorce. She was in love with someone else." She lowers her voice for the next part. "With a man that she met online playing one of those virtual farming games."

I express the appropriate amount of shock and surprise.

"Anyway . . . she kept the secret really well, but she confessed it to her doctor, her ob-gyn, Dr. Carmichael. He's everyone's doctor. He delivered all my kids. Loved him. She did it when she went in for a postpartum checkup. Thought it would be safe. But someone in his office must have overheard and called her husband right up and the whole town knew."

"Do you think it was Dr. Carmichael? Who called her husband?"

Cricket flinches. "He would never. The man is a saint. Was probably his secretary, Rita. She loved being up in other people's business. Anyway, the wife apologized and repented, and they went to couples counseling with the church. But a year later she was in a car accident, drove straight off the road into the old oak tree on Route Twenty-Seven, dead on impact."

"Did she do it on purpose?" I think of that mother driving off the cliff.

"What do I know? But . . . I think someone ran her off the road. They wanted her out of the way. Her husband is remarried now, a recent college graduate. She's pregnant already and he was just promoted in the church council. But you didn't hear that from me."

I should be surprised that she is telling me all of this insider information, but I'm not. People love spilling other people's secrets and most of all they love feeling included and important.

"So the police will be useless, but if anyone can get to the bottom of this, it's the women here. They know things. They hear things. But also . . ." She hesitates and then watches me in a way that makes it clear she wants me to prod her, so I do.

"What?" I lean in.

"If Rebecca didn't do it—which I don't think she did—I wouldn't be surprised if someone very close to them had something to do with it."

I must look genuinely shocked at her theory because she seems pleased when she clocks my reaction.

"Grayson Sommers made a lot of enemies in our community."

"Tell me more," I prod again. "We can be off the record. Who hated Grayson Sommers?"

"Some people loooooooooved him." She glances over her shoulder at the group of women huddled in the opposite corner, clearly watching us. "You know how Grayson and Rebecca had that big thing on their Instagram about a year ago. The one where they, you know . . . every day. The Whoopie with Your Schmoopie." I have to give her extra credit for being able to say both of those words out loud with a straight face. I can hardly hear them without snorting so I simply nod.

"Well, I heard they did that because everyone was talking about Grayson maybe stepping out on Rebecca with one of the Smith triplets."

The casual way she mentions it makes it seem like I should absolutely know who they are, that they are a household name. Smith triplets? I try to remember. The name Smith is as ubiquitous as air, especially out here. I've been here long enough to realize that. I glance around the room, as if the answer will appear in front of me if I squint hard enough.

"Look them up." She nods to my computer.

I tap in the name. Millions of hits. Oh right. I've seen them before. One sister is a blonde, another a redhead, and the third a brunette, which doesn't seem like it can possibly be natural, but it makes for an excellent aesthetic.

It's the third one who stops me in my search. She's the statuesque woman from the day I checked in. The one who said we should talk at some point, the fifties housewife clone with impeccable makeup and buttery voice who ran into me as I was checking in. Veronica.

"Did the Smith triplets all come to the conference?" I ask.

"They're here somewhere. They were supposed to do a panel."

"All three of them?"

"Yeah. It was how to use AI to increase output and engagement.

They're masters of it. They produce more content than everyone here combined and apparently they just have a bunch of robots doing it. Artificial intelligence is soooo confusing, but I was excited about going to the panel to learn about it."

"Which triplet might have been with Gray Sommers?" I ask breezily.

"Veronica." Bingo. Was that why she wanted to talk to me? Did she know I'm friends with Rebecca? Did she want to spill about the affair or maybe dig for her own dirt?

I glance at my computer, where I've pulled up one of the many Smith sister YouTube channels. They all have millions of followers and their videos are viewed hundreds of millions of times. More people watch them than the NFL. The blonde is named Betty. Who would have thought a family of missionaries would have a hard-on for *Archie* comics? The redhead is Skipper. Yes, Skipper. It's nearly as ridiculous as Cricket.

I toggle over to Veronica's account now. "Wait a second," I stammer in surprise. "Veronica is married to Marsden Greer?"

"Duh," Cricket says.

The men in these accounts are all interchangeable Ken doll types. I'm not surprised I didn't recognize him earlier. I don't watch baseball and neither does Peter because he insists that soccer is the superior sport of all athletic pursuits and he won't let our children be indoctrinated into the American cult of toxic sports masculinity.

I try to draw the spiderweb of connections in my brain. It's a lattice of familial and carnal interdependence.

"Grayson and Marsden are best friends," Cricket says. "They grew up together and then went to college together. They were both Phi Delts, I think, which makes it even crazier if it's true that Grayson was being intimate with Marsden's wife. But who knows. People like to talk." *And so do you, thank god.*

I keep peeping on the triplets' accounts with one eye. From what I can glean, Christ is king, birth control is the devil, and submission to your husband is paramount. No wonder Marsden felt so comfortable standing up in front of a room filled with women, women who apparently are making a shit ton of money, and telling them their highest calling is to serve their husbands.

How much of what the triplets say and do is real and how much is performance? How much do any of them believe about what they're preaching to their millions of followers and how much of it is derived from what is trending and what an algorithm wants? Or, if what Cricket says is true and the triplets are such masters of artificial intelligence, how much of it is dictated by a robot?

I already know that Rebecca's account is mostly smoke and mirrors, but are all of the accounts on social media?

And if Grayson, clean-cut, god-fearing Grayson, was sleeping with the modern-day Phyllis Schlafly, who, according to her Instagram profile, is married to both his best friend *and* Jesus? Oh the scandal.

I can't write about a rumor for the magazine, not without something else to back it up. *Modern Woman* is still hanging on to that shred of journalistic integrity, though probably not for long if Alana has her way. She recently tried to buy out an anonymous Instagram account that publishes nothing but salacious blind items about celebrities. Our lawyers stopped her, and our accountant assured her they couldn't figure out a way to monetize it, but I think they were wrong. Alana could monetize a funeral if she put her mind to it. In fact, she may monetize Grayson's.

I need more proof. "Who else knows about it?"

Cricket waves her hand in the air as if to say this information just exists in the atmosphere, and maybe it does. "Everyone's been talking about it for a year. It's also all over the snark sites."

The snark sites have become a media ecosystem all to themselves. I only recently found them when I began researching Bex for a potential story. They're simple threads, usually on Reddit, and they're essentially burn books of nastiness and unsubstantiated rumors.

"Search 'Veronica Smith and Grayson Sommers' and stuff will come up."

That's helpful. While I can't write about a rumor, I *can* write about someone else writing about rumors with a link to the sites. A dodgy loophole for sure.

"Wait . . . the Smith triplets? If they're called the Smith triplets that means none of them changed their names when they all got married? That seems completely against everything they talk about online about how their husbands rule their households," I say to the woman who just asked her husband for permission to speak to me.

"Oh, they changed them. Their names are definitely legally changed. The Smith triplets are just like their stage names or whatever you want to call them. Probably their manager's idea."

"Interesting." I'm already clicking over to the snark sites, though I want Cricket to keep talking as long as possible. She seems more than happy to, but she also seems to have run out of information, because she starts fiddling with her napkin.

"The last part of all that was off the record, you said. Right?"

"For sure."

"But you can include the part where I said I idolize Rebecca. I truly do. I respect her so much."

She doesn't. But she wants her name in my article.

"Of course," I lie to her. She won't be in the story unless she answers my next question.

I've made a command decision in the past ten minutes to level with every woman I speak to here and ask them exactly what I want to know. What do I have to lose?

"Do you really think Rebecca didn't do it?"

Cricket bites her lip and looks behind her again. "I don't."

"Do you think Rebecca is in danger?" I ask.

She doesn't hesitate. "If she's alive. Then yes."

We both sit there and let that sink in for a moment.

"Have you been to her ranch?" I ask. Even though I know the two aren't close, I assume the answer is yes since Rebecca and Cricket seem to have run in the same circles in the same tight-knit community. But she shakes her head.

"Rebecca is super-duper protective of the ranch. Or at least she was. I heard she was planning some event there for next month. She's been reaching out to florists and caterers and a big tent rental company. That's what some of the girls told me."

That lines up with what Olivia said about Bex wanting to take her brand more public.

"It looks beautiful on her account though, doesn't it?" Cricket says. "It's always been my dream. That much acreage, all those animals, living off the land. It's perfect. She's truly influenced all of my influencer aspirations."

Nothing in Rebecca's life was perfect. Cricket knows that and I know that, and yet the gauzy fever dream persists.

"I should head out," she finally says. "I've been trying to find a way to get home, but my flight isn't for a couple of days and the airlines are such a pain. We won't get reimbursed for the room either. Chad is so mad. My mother-in-law was watching the kids for me and it's a disaster back there. My husband is a terrible babysitter. But DM me anytime and don't forget to tag me in your story." She stands and then turns to offer her hand for me to shake, like we are making some kind of deal. Her handshake is firm and decisive, yet another surprising thing about her.

"Have you heard anything about, you know, what she cut off?" Cricket whispers while our hands are still clasped. I've been trying my best not to think about the severed body part rumors. And yet I also can't shake the memory of an old video on Rebecca's Instagram from a few years back where she very cleanly and easily castrated a young male bull.

"I haven't heard anything," I say.

When she's gone, I step outside. I want to call Peter again.

I'm on the edge of the patio, creeping my way to that terrifying bridge and the inky blackness below. I don't have the courage to step onto it, so I waver on the edges. Peter answers on the first ring with a jolly "Good evening, my love." I can hear our children screaming in the background and I picture them naked, finding ways to annoy each other while Peter calmly sips his beer. He would never call what he does babysitting. Maybe in the beginning of having kids, but not anymore.

"You want to stay, don't you? You want to report this out," he presumes before I can say anything. Some days it feels like my sweet, handsome husband doesn't know me at all and then he lobs a surprise insight my way and I realize that no one will ever know me better.

"I want to find out what happened to Bex," I say. And I do. I want that, but I'm also now completely activated by the thrill of reporting this out. It's what I've always loved the most, chasing down a story, discovering something before anyone else.

"Of course you do. I just finished reading your piece. You have an agenda there, but I see what you're doing, Drew." It's his old nickname for me. As in Nancy Drew. He first encountered the series of books on a hiking trip we took in Scotland of all places. We made our way up and down the hills of the Highlands all day and then settled in for the night in a small stone cottage called a bothy that was outfitted with two sleeping platforms, a human-sized fireplace, and three yellow hardcover Nancy Drews that some other American tourist had left, probably one with a teenage daughter. Peter was so spooked about sleeping in the bothy, which he insisted was haunted with the ghost of a dead prince, that he made his way through all three young adult novels. Ever since then he's called me Drew when he sees me get deep into a story. It's been years since he called me that. It's been years since I did actual reporting.

When I switched over to the mommy track at *Modern Woman* from the news magazine, I went from political hush-money stories to listicles about "Skin-Softening Shower Lotions That Will Change Your Life!"

I miss the chase. I want more of it.

"Yeah, I want to, but what about the kids?"

"What about them? I'm unemployed. Let's not forget it. Put me to work. And besides. We're supposed to head to the Outer Banks to meet your mom and Robbie on Saturday. I can go early with them. They can help with the kids. I know you didn't want to go anyway."

"She is *my* mother."

"She does like me better."

Score another one for Peter. Mom and her girlfriend have a beach house in North Carolina and always invite all of us to come for a couple of weeks. I am not a beach person. I much prefer mountains or lakes that won't leave sand in all my cracks and crevices, which are only getting deeper and deeper every year. I like vacationing at the ocean for the first twenty-four to forty-eight hours. By then I'm sunburnt and itchy and completely over trying to save a child from drowning themselves in the ocean or swallowing all of the sand.

"Really?"

"Yes. Take your time. The Sandy Bottoms will miss you."

Everyone in North Carolina has chosen the most inappropriate names for their second homes, my mother included. My own backside itches every time I arrive.

"Can I talk to the kids?"

"Nora is very busy covering the baby in Nutella. I don't want to disrupt their bonhomie. I know it's past their bedtime but I'm hoping they'll sleep in tomorrow."

"Fair. But they won't. I love you."

"I love you, Drew. Go do your thing."

Marriage can be a wonderful thing and also a terrible thing. Much like parenting small children. Terrible and great. Terrible and great. You have no idea which it will be on any given day.

Except when you do, I suppose. Except when a marriage is toxic, and you feel trapped. My mind returns to Bex. As much as I can't stand my own spouse sometimes, I have never once feared him, and even though I shouldn't have to count myself lucky, I do. Plenty of women live in terror of the man who sleeps in their bed.

That reminds me . . . Marsden's statement? I pop in my earbuds again.

It's a video taken in his home. He's sitting next to Veronica, his large pitching hand enveloping the top of her thigh over yet another retro dress, this one covered in fat ripe lemons. Her expression doesn't change. Her eyes stare vacantly into the camera as he speaks. She's like a robot that has been powered down.

"I'm devastated," Marsden begins. "I loved Grayson Sommers like a brother. We met on the ball field in Little League and we've been inseparable ever since. My entire family has been deep in prayer since yesterday and we will continue to beg the Lord Almighty for justice to be served. May we all remember Grayson as a man of noble character, honor, and bravery."

That was laying it on a bit thick. The man had run a hobby ranch, not led an army into battle.

"He was my friend, and he will be sorely missed. For now, we will do everything in our power to find his killer, to bring them to justice. We will not let this stand." He bows his head in prayer. Veronica misses a beat, but then she does the same. My eyes move to his hand on her thigh. No one would notice unless they were looking for it, but his knuckles are white. They're squeezing. Hard.

I go back inside, sit down, order a drink and an appetizer. I'm not paying attention when the waiter refills my glass of wine. I'm too engrossed in the screen, but when I finally turn my attention to the beverage, I see it. A pink sachet, the same pale pink as the envelope that was given to me at the front desk. My skin prickles with cold sweat as I glance around, vision blurring slightly at the edges. Which waiter brought the wine? Did they drop off the little pouch or was it one of the women shuffling in and out of the room, their eyes locked on the screens of their phones? I can't tell. My eyes scan the crowd for her, for Bex. The thought of her being so near fills me with both alarm and hope.

I slip the pouch in my pocket and walk back outside. I want to be alone when I see what has been left for me.

When I open it, a folded slip of paper falls into my hand along with two keys. On the paper is an address, a gate code, and the hastily scrawled words *next to the bed*. I know without any more explanation that someone is helping me get into the Sommers ranch.

CHAPTER ELEVEN

REBECCA

When Gray and I first got together we'd play a game before we went to bed. We'd lay there in a tangle of limbs, giddy with the newness of being with each other, and ask questions until we fell asleep. Big and small. What's your favorite color? Do you like mushrooms? What sport are you best at? What does forgiveness mean to you? Do you believe in God? Do you think God believes in you?

Grayson was a true believer in God. That was clear from the very beginning. His relationship with Jesus and the church was intense, but for some reason it didn't freak me out. He was introspective when it came to religion and spirituality. He questioned things and was genuinely curious. He talked about Jesus as a friend, a confidant. It felt so intimate and loving. I wanted some of what he had—the conviction, a place to turn when I needed hope—and wanted it to be contagious.

His childhood running around the ranch with his seven siblings sounded so idyllic and he positively worshipped his mother. When we talked about my childhood, I inevitably clammed up. Our lives were hard, but Mom and I tried to make the best of it. I didn't want to just come out and tell him that she worked until she died, literally dropped dead of a heart attack right in the feminine products section of Walmart.

For my entire life we shared a variety of one-bedroom apartments, always with twin beds in the bedroom. I barely saw her except for the one day she had off a week. You'd think I would have had a lot of freedom with that kind of upbringing, but my mom kept me in line with terrible stories about how I'd go to hell if I ever smoked or drank or, god forbid, let a boy kiss me. It was the Catholic guilt in her. Even though we never attended church she still had the fire and brimstone in her blood from her own strict upbringing, where she was told in no uncertain terms that she would absolutely burn in hell after she got pregnant with me. She was never sweet or affectionate, never praised me when I did well in school. I was always the thing that held her back, the thing that ruined her life, and she usually just looked at me with disdain.

Grayson once asked me what I thought happened when we died. I wanted to give him the kind of answer he needed. Angels and wings and limitless love from Jesus Christ, but it was the anniversary of my mother's death, and I just couldn't do it.

"Nothing," I'd said.

His body stiffened and he stopped tracing small circles on my back. "Nothing?" I'd alarmed him.

"Nothing." I held my ground. "I just think the lights go out and we die. So we need to enjoy the time we have here while we have it."

"You don't really believe that."

My answer pained him so much that I laid my head down on his strong bare chest and sighed. "No. I don't. I'm feeling off today."

But I did believe it and I still do now. When you're dead you're dead. It's over. I would take pleasure from Grayson Sommers burning in hell right now, but I just don't think any of it is true. Because if you believe in hell you have to believe in heaven and that is simply too good to be true.

Gray had been with other women before me, but he told me he'd never been in a serious relationship. I was different. I was special. He wanted to be with me all the time. Spent nearly every night in my tiny apartment because he thought it was cozier than his spacious place that overlooked the Bay. Or at least he did until the night someone broke into my place on a rare evening I was there alone. I never even woke up and they didn't come into my bedroom, but they took everything that wasn't nailed to the walls. I was shaken, but Grayson was enraged and never let me sleep there again. I'd move in with him. There was no question about it. His control of the situation, the way he organized the movers and demanded the landlord break my lease, because why didn't they have bars on the first-floor windows to begin with, all of it made me feel safe, protected, and loved.

Gray was the one who eventually encouraged me to quit my job at BlueNet so he could help me get my bakery business off the ground. He was so supportive of my business aspirations. I rented a little storefront on Divisadero, just down the street from Alamo Square Park, where we would spend Sundays picnicking on a blanket beneath the eucalyptus trees and talking about all the places we wanted to travel together. I tested all of my recipes on him, and he told me I was going to ruin his girlish figure. That was impossible. No one was stricter about their fitness regimen than Grayson. He ran fifty miles a week. On the other days he would bike and swim.

I couldn't wait for Lizzie to meet him. While I was tight-lipped about my own family, I raved about her to him. She felt closer to me then than any of my blood relatives. Grayson said over and over again that he was excited to meet her, even said he would pay for her plane ticket out, but I knew Lizzie would never accept it. She was much too proud to take anything from anyone. I certainly wasn't proud. Less than a year into our relationship Gray was paying for everything in my life. He bought all the fancy commercial restaurant equipment and the adorable shabby chic furniture for the bakery. He even came up with the name I adored, "Whisked Away."

"I'm gonna whisk you away," he whispered in my ear the night before I opened the shop, running his hands up the backs of my legs, pushing my skirt up over my waist as he lifted me onto the marble countertop next to the cash register and slid my underwear down over my ankles.

I leaned my head back and spread my legs wide, letting him flick his tongue along my inner thighs until I was burning to have him inside me. He knew what I wanted and made me wait, made me beg for it. I loved this about him. I loved the anticipation almost as much as the climax.

There was a line out the front door when we opened. The neighborhood was hungry, literally hungry, for sixteen-dollar toast and incredibly Instagrammable almond croissants and cinnamon rolls. I had a local artist paint massive pastries on the blank brick wall outside and it became a destination for anyone planning to picnic in the park. The mural did all my marketing for me. I had to hire two more employees and I was often at the shop baking well into the night.

Grayson didn't like that I was so busy. He didn't like it at all.

That's when Lizzie told me she had gotten her first promotion to staff reporter and with it a modest raise that would just cover a plane ticket out to the West Coast. Could she plan a trip to see me?

"Of course," I texted, stupid with excitement. "You'll stay with me. I can even take off for a day and we can head up to wine country and get squishy."

I mostly quit drinking when Grayson and I got together. Since he didn't indulge, I didn't want him to think less of me when I did. Sometimes I had a couple of glasses of wine when I went out with the shop employees, and we had all toasted with some champagne the morning we opened, but that was it. I was excited for a little one-on-one time with Lizzie, when I could get silly with only her.

A couple of days before she was set to arrive, I got my first real press in the *San Francisco Chronicle*. Their food reviewer had been by, and I'd answered a few questions about what inspired me and my business plan. They were curious if I had plans to expand. "I've only been open a month," I'd said with a laugh. But then my ego got the best of me, and before I knew it I was saying on the record, "We'll end up being the most successful bakery franchise in the Bay Area." The night the article came out I stayed late at the store and celebrated with another bottle of champagne.

I only had a couple of glasses, but I didn't make it to our place until well after midnight. Gray was still awake when I got back.

"Where were you?" he demanded when I used my key to let myself in.

"The bakery," I said, balancing on one foot to unlatch my sandal. It was hard to do in the dark and when I reached for the light switch at the same time I stumbled against the wall.

"Are you drunk?" he asked.

"No." I giggled because I was nervous at the gruff tone of his voice.

"Are you laughing at me?"

"Of course not. Gray, what's wrong?"

"My girlfriend, the biggest baker in the whollllle Bay Area, ditched me tonight and then comes stumbling home drunk like a little whore and laughs in my face."

His words were a sucker punch right in my gut. He'd never spoken like that to me before.

I finally found the light switch and took a step back when I saw the hatred in his eyes.

"We didn't have plans tonight?" I said it as a question because maybe I'd forgotten something. I'd seen his texts come in and I'd meant to respond, but my hands were always busy and I just didn't get to it. I approached him despite the rage coming off him in waves.

"You said you'd make me dinner. But you got too carried away celebrating the biggest bakery in the Bay Area to come home." I didn't remember promising to make dinner and I'd missed the sarcasm dripping from his words the first time he said "biggest baker in the Bay Area." Suddenly I felt shame at my hubris in that interview. Shame I shouldn't have felt. I should have felt proud.

"You didn't mention all the help I gave you in that story. Not a single word about your boyfriend, who bankrolled your whole little hobby. Made it seem like you were self-made, that you did it all on your own. It's really so easy to forget me? Has this been your plan all along? Trick me into spending my hard-earned money on you and then leave me out to dry?"

I racked my brain for things I had talked about to the *Chronicle*. They hadn't asked where I'd gotten the money for anything. Money in San Francisco always seemed to appear as if by magic anyway. There was always a VC or a hedge fund or a rich daddy somewhere behind the scenes. In this case it was my rich boyfriend. But the reporter hadn't cared, hadn't asked.

"You've just been using me this entire time," he spat. His words socked me in the stomach with shame.

"Gray. I haven't used you for anything. You offered me the money. If you hadn't given it to me, I would have gotten a loan."

"With your credit history? With all your student debt? Don't think I haven't checked up on you. Don't think I don't know you never would have been able to do that without me." He was right and that made me even more ashamed. I wanted to run. I wanted to put as much distance between the two of us as possible. I turned and stumbled again over the shoes I'd just taken off and fell to the ground. He took a step forward and straddled me and then reached down to grab my hair. The shock of it hurt as much as the strands ripping loose from my scalp. He yanked me upright so he could stare into my eyes.

"You'd be nothing without me." His breath was hot on my face and smelled vaguely like liquor, but that was impossible because Gray didn't drink. He always called it toxic. Said it poisoned the mind, the body, and the soul.

"Say it. Repeat after me," he snarled.

But I couldn't open my mouth to speak. I couldn't manage to get the words out. He shook my entire body until my brain felt like it was jiggling in my skull.

"Say it, whore."

"I'd be nothing without you," I croaked.

"Louder."

"I'd be nothing without you." I finally met his eyes.

"You would." Then he let me go, the side of my head and my left eye catching on the corner of his beautiful Shaker coffee table. I could feel the blood start to pour over my eye. Gray picked me up again and carried me across the room. I wanted to scratch out his eyes, but I could hardly see and he was so much stronger than I was. Still, to this day, I'm ashamed for not fighting back. He carried me into his bedroom, opened the closet door, and threw me inside. Before I could even sit up, he slammed the door in front of me. It was pitch black. A key turned in the lock on the knob outside. A lock I never knew existed. I was trapped. That's when I finally summoned every ounce of strength I had left to bang on the door and scream, but I also knew no one would hear me. Gray owned the entire building anyway, so even if they heard no one would believe me. I screamed until my voice went hoarse and my jaw locked, until the blood had dried on my scalp and face.

Eventually I melted into the terror and blacked out from the pain.

When I woke up in the morning I was in Gray's bed, gently tucked into the blankets. And for the briefest of moments, I thought it was a bad dream. Because how could my sweet and loving, supportive, wonderful boyfriend have attacked me for no reason?

But as I opened my eyes a pain shot through my skull so intense I nearly passed back out. It wasn't a dream.

"I'm a terrible, broken man," I heard him whisper.

Gray's tone came as a surprise, retribution laced with a husky sadness. His cheeks were wet, tears dripping from his eyes. I wanted to murder him, gouge out his glassy pupils with my broken nails. All my rage from the night before came rushing back to me.

"Please forgive me. Please don't leave me. I made a mistake. So many mistakes. I . . . There's something I have to tell you."

"There's nothing you can tell me right now that will change anything," I managed, trying to sit up.

"Let me try. Please let me try." I went silent, mostly out of fear of what would happen if I didn't listen, if I tried to move. "There's a reason I don't drink. It's something my parents never approved of, but I used to experiment here and there with beer and liquor in high school and college with my friends. The problem was I loved it. I loved it so much because it made me finally feel light and fun and happy. I had a hard time with that when I was a kid. I was always working so hard to make my dad happy and live up to what he wanted a man to be. I never got to relax and let loose. And when I did it, when I drank, I got out of control. I was loose and happy until I wasn't. Until I got mad and I blacked out and I didn't remember anything in the morning. I turned into a monster. So I stopped. I made the decision that it was something I couldn't do. And I was so strong. It's been a couple years since I had anything to drink, but last night I went out with Marsden and I was crazy over the fact that you hadn't responded to my texts and he convinced me just to have one drink to relax. But I can't have just one drink. I had another and another and another. I was a disaster. And then Mars saw the article online and he started ribbing me about it. And he got in my head. He always does. He convinced me you were using me. Made fun of me. He was all like, 'Who is the breadwinner now?' And then I drank more, and I don't even really know what I did last night. I don't remember most of it. I passed out and when I woke up even though I barely remembered it I knew enough to come get you and when I saw you in that closet I wanted to die. I wanted to kill myself. I knew that I had done it, but it wasn't me. I swear to God, I would never hurt you. That wasn't me. It wasn't me. It wasn't me." He was trying to convince himself as much as me.

It made no sense and also so much sense. During our many bedtime conversations he'd told me all about Marsden, about how close they'd been their entire lives, about how Gray's family practically raised him when Marsden's mom died in childbirth having her sixth baby. How talented Marsden was at baseball and how Gray's own father paid for Marsden to go to the same fancy prep school as Gray, how Mr. Sommers helped charm the college baseball scouts so Marsden would get a scholarship to the same college as Gray. He'd once even admitted how jealous he was of the affection his own father gave to Marsden, how it made him feel small and how it was one of the things he would talk to Jesus about late into the night as a teenage boy.

I raised my hand to my throbbing head, dreading the moment when I would have to look at my face. I already knew one of my eyes was swollen shut.

I hated Gray for what he'd done, but there was something else inside me, a twinge of sympathy. Because didn't I, of all people, know how easy it was to get out of control when drinking? Hadn't I blacked out too many times to count in college and woken up filled with shame and regret, naked in some strange guy's bed? Hadn't I lost friends because I'd said something nasty or terrible that never would have come out of my mouth sober? Didn't this man deserve some empathy from me after everything he had given me and how he had supported me? Didn't he deserve a second chance, at least one more chance?

I wasn't there yet.

I rolled over and stared out at the multimillion-dollar view of the fog rolling gently over the Golden Gate, a view I would never be able to afford even if I was the best baker in the entire Bay Area. How ridiculous had I been? Thinking that any of this could be within reach on my own. I was a poor bastard girl raised on food stamps and hourly wages. Sure, I'd gotten into a fancy school, but that wasn't nearly enough to get ahead in this world. Real power, real success, real money, came from other money. Generational money. I never would have opened the bakery without Gray. I would have toiled away at the tech company for ten years to pay off my student loans and all the credit cards I maxed out in college. I would be nothing without him.

I wasn't ready to decide what to do about Gray yet. I needed rest and I needed the pain to disappear. But I also wasn't ready to walk out the door, which pretty much meant I'd made my choice.

Looking back, I know that now.

"Leave me alone," I managed. "Please."

"Forever?"

"Don't be dramatic. I need to think."

"I swear to you it will never happen again."

"No, it won't." I opened my eyes as wide as I could and set my lips in a stern line, despite the fact that it nearly killed me to do both of those things. When I fell the night before . . . no . . . when he threw me on the ground the night before . . . the inside of my lip had snagged on a tooth. It had left a nasty gash in my mouth and the tooth was loose. I knew it would fall out.

"I don't know what I'm going to decide. It will probably be that I never want to see you ever again." I so wanted him to believe that was a possibility. "But I can't make up my mind right now. I have to sleep. Maybe for an entire day, maybe for five. And that means I need you to do three things for me. I need you to call the shop and tell them I won't be in. Tell them I'm sick. Sound convincing. Then I need you to get me the strongest pain-killers you can. I don't want Advil. I want Vicodin. I don't care how you get it. And then I want you to leave. I want to sleep and I want to heal and I want to think. Can you do those things?"

"I'll do anything."

"Also food. Something soft. Soup. Do all of that. Leave the pills outside the door and knock when you have them and then go away."

It was the most assertive I'd ever been with him.

"I love you," he said then. He'd never said it before. No man had ever said it to me. In fact my own mother had never said it to me. The effect those words had on me was like nothing else. Maybe it was years of culture telling women that it was the ultimate form of validation, the most important thing for a young girl to strive for. Those three little words shattered me. Gray gave me an expectant look. He was a man unused to waiting for anything. And so that was the one thing I could do. I could make him wait.

"Leave," I repeated.

"It will never happen again, Rebecca." He had never called me Bex, which Lizzie called me, or Becky, which was what my mom had always called me. Not once had he used any of my nicknames and I always thought that was romantic. Now I know it was about control. He wanted to rename me himself. Naming something gave you power over it.

"No, it won't," I said, and closed my eyes. "You will never lay a hand on me like that again. And if you do I won't just break up with you. Grayson. Look at me." He cringed when our eyes met and he was forced to take in the extent of the damage he'd done to my face, a face that he had told me was how he imagined the first angels must have looked.

"If you ever hurt me again you will be digging yourself an early grave. Do you hear me?"

He swallowed hard and nodded before leaning down to kiss me on the forehead, then walked out of the room.

An hour later he brought me everything I asked for.

And you know by now that I didn't leave him. You can judge me for that all you want. I've already judged myself plenty. But when you've been raised like I was, without real love or affection, without any kind of safety net. When you were raised without hope for any kind of future and then all of a sudden something so much bigger and brighter seems within reach, you keep reaching. Or at least that's what I told myself. I also believed that I was a magnet for bad behavior, that maybe I deserved it because there was something deeply wrong with me. I'd been a curse for my mother. She'd never let me forget it.

Gray didn't hurt me again for a long time. At least not physically. He found other ways to destroy me over the years, but that was the last time he laid a hand on me until recently.

But he was much more devious and evil than I could ever imagine. Months ago, I discovered the one secret he desperately wanted to keep from me. And when I confronted him with what I'd found out, what he did was worse than that night he locked me in the closet, way worse.

I kept my promise. He did end up in an early grave.

CHAPTER TWELVE

LIZZIE

I dream about being back in college. It's a dream I have a lot, a few different variations of it. The buildings are always vaguely similar to the ones I spent four years in: Some are gray-stone imitations of European castles, others modern towers of glass donated by masters of the current universe. Even though I know this place, I never have any idea where I'm supposed to go or which classes I should be in. I'm aware that finals are coming soon and that I've never been to a single class. I know I will fail. Sweat pours down the back of my neck and tears sting my eyes. An intense dread settles into my stomach as I curse myself for being so careless. In my unconscious state I'm begging the registrar for a copy of my class schedule or I'm hunting down the one faceless classmate who I know has excellent notes for Victorian lit. My real friends and former boyfriends are rarely there, or if they are it's a cameo. They wave across the quad or smile at me in the hallway and then disappear. But in this dream I see Bex as I'm coming out of the registrar's office. My schedule is in my hand, but I can't read it. The words are blurry. In the dream she's a mixture of Rebecca and Bex. Her hair is long and blond and loose around her shoulders like it is today, but she's wearing ripped jeans that ride low on her hips and bare her perfectly toned belly, complete with a turquoise belly button ring, the same one I used to have after we pierced our belly buttons together at a place called Hole Lotta Fun. She's got on the purple halter top we bought at a street fair during spring break in Myrtle Beach, the one with shimmering beads and sequins that wink at me in the bright morning sun. Despite the hour, she's ready for a night out, a damn good time, and she reaches her hand out to me.

I shake my head. It's too early. I have to get to class. I have to find those notes. I have to study and pass the tests and get the degree and then the job and climb the ladder. I mumble all of this and she smiles ruefully at me.

"None of it really matters, Lizzie." Her voice echoes like it's coming out of an old radio speaker. She reaches out her hand again and I turn away.

As I walk across the quad, I hear her start to follow me, but I don't turn around. And then there's a bloodcurdling scream, the kind of scream that turns your blood to ice. I turn and Bex is gone.

When I open my eyes and look around the bedroom that isn't mine, it takes me a minute to orient myself in the beautiful suite in the middle of the desert, to remember that I did graduate from college, that I did so with honors. That I got a job that I loved in a city I never wanted to leave. That I got promoted and promoted again and that I got to do the kind of work that was meaningful and fulfilling.

Until I didn't. Until the goalposts moved and everything I'd worked for meant essentially nothing.

None of it really matters.

* * *

The Sommers ranch is about ninety minutes from the resort, and as I drive out to it, I can't help but imagine Bex on this same road driving home after she left my room just the other night. She had plenty of time. It would have taken her an hour and a half, maybe less, to get home, to find her husband, lure him out of his bed. Maybe she gave him something to drink with a sedative in it, because how could a woman as petite as Bex overpower a man who runs ultramarathons? But it's possible she gave him some milk laced with Valium and then lured him into the garage and shoved him in front of the spikes of some plow type of thing, shoved him so that his skin peeled away and spilled his guts all over the floor. My stomach curdles at the image, bringing a stinging bile up the back of my throat.

I need to think. Assess. This drive is as good a place to do it as any. The landscape changes as I get farther and farther into the red canyons. Alien rock formations rise high above the shrubs and dust, striated towers of orange, pink, and purple. It's beautiful and otherworldly, and I'm oddly calm even as I go through the gory details I know to be true and the possibilities that are playing out in my head.

Grayson was found by one of the farmworkers around seven in the morning. I know this from my discussion with Detective Walsh when he tried to pin me down on the last time I saw Rebecca. It was early when she left me, just after sunset, only about eight P.M. or so. Plenty of time to go back to her hotel room, get what she needed, pack up, and drive out here. I think about the text message I glimpsed on her phone when I picked it up thinking it was mine.

> You won't get away with this
> you fucking bitch

It came from G. Possibly Gray. But what exactly was she getting away with? According to Olivia, Bex was about to go behind her husband's back, her very controlling husband's back, and announce a major business deal that didn't involve him. A business deal she knew he didn't want her to accept. Had he found out about it? Did he know about her betrayal? Was that what set this all in motion? Did it cause a fight that ended with him bleeding out on his barn floor?

Murdering him would destroy everything Bex has worked so hard for.

Only if she doesn't get away with it, a little voice whispers in my head. *Are you helping her get away with it?*

A fine layer of dust settles on the rental car and the roads go from pavement to gravel to dirt. I know where I'm going. I spent a good deal of time last night figuring out how I would do this. The main entrance to the ranch is clearly going to be both sealed off and possibly crowded with cops and reporters if the police and media action at the hotel are any indication. But the property is huge, more than two hundred acres since it's technically still a working cattle ranch. I cross-referenced Google Maps and Bureau of Land Management records and then downloaded an app called OnX Hunt, which promised to be the most comprehensive property record locator for hunters who are trying to avoid hunting on private land. It showed privately owned land interspersed with government owned and public land. None of the boundaries were a perfectly closed circle and there was a public use easement right in the middle of the Sommers ranch, which meant there had to be a gate where the cattle were locked in on either side and could be moved across the public land when they needed to switch fields. I learned way more than I ever expected to learn about hunting, land ownership, Western ranches. It was weirdly fascinating.

Sure enough, Google Earth showed me a gate when I looked at it in the satellite view on my computer. Bingo.

That's where I'm heading. From the maps and the apps it looks like there will be a dirt road from that gate to the Sommers ranch house and the barn. I'm hoping it isn't occupied by the police at the moment. It's a risk. But I also have a gate code and two keys, which allows me to convince myself that what I'm doing isn't trespassing. I'm more than a little proud of this plan and the execution is giving me a bit of a thrill. I'm still good at this. I haven't felt this excited since I was nominated for a national magazine award for a piece about an underground railroad I uncovered, Catholic nuns rescuing young women from being sex trafficked. That was years ago, before the kids, but the memory of the reporting, the research and the flow of the writing, is as sharp as if it happened yesterday.

There's no cell service out here, but the GPS on my phone still works so I can follow the maps I've laid out for myself. And just as I expected, the fencing opens up, and there's a large metal gate on the side of the road. The gamble I'm making is that the gate code is the same for all the gates, since there's no way Bex could have known which one I'd be using. If it was Bex who left me the key. That's something else I need to consider. That all of this is bigger than Bex and bigger than Grayson. That this world Bex found herself in is much more dangerous than either of us knew.

I pull the car to the side of the road and suck in a deep breath as I remove the pale pink piece of paper from my bag. I had stared at the numbers long and hard last night and finally realized the code must be her first child's birthday. Alice, the beautiful redheaded piano prodigy. Further proof to me that Rebecca wouldn't put her children in danger. She loves them. They're a part of her. I lift the lid on the keypad and punch in the six digits. Three beeps. As the gate slides, I allow myself a smile at the small victory and return to the car, unsure how long it will stay open.

I shouldn't have worried. This fancy metal barrier is on a sensor and slides shut right behind me. Its efficiency makes me nervous that some kind of alarm has been sounded, that someone is watching me. But I calm my nerves by reminding myself this gate must be opened for the cattle on a regular basis. Also, who would be monitoring things right now? Possibly the police. Gray's dead. Rebecca's missing. There's probably a farm foreman but did they show up for work today? *None of it really matters.* Rebecca's words from my dream echo in my head again.

So what if they find me here? I've done nothing wrong. I'm just trying to help. I convince myself of this, but the important thing is that I've committed to this and I'm here. The only path is the one forward. I timed this well. The police are holding a press conference about Gray in the city right now, which means most of the people on this case will be more than an hour away.

I roll the windows down and bask in the high of my successful plan as I rumble along the rocky path through the pastures, hoping I'm not stripping all the paint off this rental car.

It's surreal being here, staring at this landscape that I've only glimpsed on Rebecca's social media on my small screen, like being an extra in a movie I've watched dozens of times while slightly high. Right over there is the massive gnarled tree where Gray and Rebecca stand with the kids during each of her pregnancy announcements, the existing children popping out from behind the trunk one by one until finally Bex emerges with a pregnant belly, again and again. The latest one of those videos has more than twenty-three million views.

Everyone always looked so exuberant and glowy in those videos. The last one filled me with the strangest emotions. Did I want another baby? I didn't. I sure as hell didn't. But was that somehow wrong? Should I want another one? Why did motherhood look so easy for her when it broke me on a daily basis?

Of course now I know it wasn't easy, but the images and the feelings those images and videos conjured inside me are impossible to shake.

There's the pasture where Gray and Rebecca renewed their vows a couple of years ago with a *Midsummer Night's Dream*–themed wedding ceremony and a dinner for fifty people at a long wooden table in a field. The children were all dressed as woodland fairies. Bex wore a crown of pink and white roses and peonies. They released thousands of fireflies into the night. Tripod, the three-legged goat, was the ring bearer. He had wings.

The ranch comes into view and it's bigger and more gorgeous than it appeared in pictures and videos. It's truly massive, set back against the red rock walls of the canyon. I know from my research that this part of the property is located in a small oasis. A creek flows beneath here, allowing for more trees and plants and the vegetable garden where Rebecca famously grows her organic heirloom tomatoes and the strawberries and blueberries she turns into perfect pies.

Everything around me feels so alive, so vividly real after years of scrolling through filtered images and staged moments. The ranch pulses with a raw, untamed energy.

I know from my research that the front gate to the ranch is on the other side of the property, at least a half mile away in the opposite direction. So far, I've encountered no one, a lucky accident for sure. It's time to ditch the car and move around on foot. It will be easier to avoid detection that way.

I park next to one of the rustic cabins beyond the wooden barn where Gray met his disturbing end. I can't even look at it right now. The entrance is cordoned off with police tape, though there's no officer stationed there. The lack of a more active investigation tells me something I already knew: The police believe they have their prime suspect.

They just have to find her.

I hurry down the perfectly manicured stone path to the wraparound front porch adorned with flowering annuals and hummingbird feeders. Adirondack rocking chairs dot the surface and I picture Bex out here rocking while nursing her twins, two babies at once, as natural as can be with a child hanging off each breast, more motherly than the Madonna herself. In this fantasy, a third child stands nearby sipping from a fresh-squeezed glass of lemonade they made from lemon trees in their garden. These images waft through my brain as if they're my own memories and not some parasocial creation or, more likely, something I saw on her account.

But the fantasy is punctured by more evidence of an investigation. Yellow police lines stretch across the porch, warning me away.

I hesitate for the first time. Am I really doing this? Am I writing myself into the story like this? Because once I open that door there's no turning back. I can walk away right now, get in the car, drive to the hotel, and go to the airport. I don't have to be here.

But then I think of Alice and Bex's other kids. I think of Bex too, not Bex now, but the Bex I met on the first day of college, the bright-eyed exuberant teenager who wanted to, as she said, grab the world by the balls and hang on until they fell off.

I duck under the tape and pull the key out of my pocket.

The air inside the house carries a faint scent of cedar and sage, mingling with the warmth of sunlit wood. The interior unfolds like a page from a designer magazine brought to life. Polished hardwood floors gleam under the soft glow of wrought iron lanterns hanging from exposed wooden beams overhead. The only evidence of an investigation are large dusty footprints marring the floors. It's as though even the police were scared of puncturing the perfection.

Bex's straw hat hangs by the door. It's such a staple of her uniform. Bex is rarely without it, even inside the house. It became so popular that some company created a Sommers Garden Hat and sold it on Amazon. Her lawyers, Olivia maybe, must have had it taken down because weeks later the same hat appeared on Bex's own website at double the price and sold out in three days.

The centerpiece of the living room is a grand stone fireplace, its hearth adorned with neatly stacked logs and an ornate wrought iron screen. Above it, a massive elk antler chandelier dangles from the vaulted ceiling, casting intricate shadows across the room. Plush leather armchairs and a weathered leather sofa beckon invitingly around a sturdy coffee table crafted from reclaimed barnwood.

From the living room, I wander into the kitchen. The space seamlessly blends modern convenience with rustic allure. Rough-hewn wooden cabinets line the walls, their rich grain glowing under the soft, ambient light filtering through large windows that frame sweeping views of the landscape.

It all looks and smells expensive up close, but somehow in the pictures and videos it looks simpler. It takes a lot of money to make life look this ruggedly homesteading chic and effortless.

A massive farmhouse sink sits beneath a window ledge adorned with fresh herbs growing in terra-cotta pots. The only sign of the absence of people is that the herbs are in need of watering. I turn on the tap and find a teacup to fill with water.

I glance uneasily at the gleaming freezer and think about the rumors that whoever killed Grayson sliced off a particular body part and put it in this appliance. The door is covered with more police tape. Looking closely, I can see the fingerprints marring its surface.

Despite the small signs of investigators milling around in here, it feels and looks like a soundstage. How many cleaners must Bex have in here on a regular basis to keep it looking like this with six children? My own house is consistently coated in sedimentary layers of dust, Legos, food, and sometimes even pee, since we happen to be potty training. Even when we had someone coming in to help us clean, the sanity lasted all of twenty minutes. Either Bex has the best-trained children in the world, or they never actually use this space. Something snags at the back of my mind as I think that. *What if they never truly use this space?* I suddenly remember a sponsor booth set up at the MomBomb conference. The woman manning it had accosted me as I walked by.

"Want a flyer? We have a QR code for a free three-hour rental," she'd shouted at me in an urgent tone.

Behind her was a massive banner with a photo of a pristine-looking kitchen and a well-coiffed woman baking brownies.

"Rental for what?" I'd asked politely.

"For your dream kitchen. We also offer dining rooms, kid rooms, and bathrooms for skincare and morning routine videos. Also nighttime routines. All the routines."

I had no idea what she was talking about. "You're renting rooms? By the hour?"

"We're renting the dream," she said again. *Dream* seemed to be their company's go-to noun.

"How much?" That seemed like the next-best question. How much did it cost to rent a dream?

"Oh, it varies. There are discounts if you need an entire day for a shoot and of course you can bring in your own photographers and videographers, but we also have a package where we can supply those for you. So all pricing is customized and you can sit down with one of our consultants right now if you like. We currently have properties in twenty-seven cities in fourteen states, but we are expanding every week. So many businesses are going remote that we are taking over old office space and creating the sets. Such a great idea, right?"

I still didn't fully grasp what was happening until she offered to show me their promo video on her iPad. That's when it hit me. They were renting houses and rooms for influencer backdrops.

If you didn't have the perfect kitchen or bathroom or child's bedroom to take your pictures and videos in, then this company would supply them for you. It was like Airbnb for influencer stages, or like a seedy motel that rented by the hour, but instead of getting illicit sex you got to pretend your life was just slightly more beautiful than it was in reality.

I wondered what it must feel like. Not to step into the fantasy, but to step out of it, to leave it behind at the end of the day and return to your unfiltered reality.

"We of course make small changes for every guest, so nothing is exactly the same. And we can book you on a monthly rotation so that you can shoot all your content once a month and be done with it. Where do you live?"

I didn't have words for what I was seeing. All those kitchens that I had coveted during hours of watching reels and stories on social media. No one owned them. Or someone did, but not the women in the videos. They were probably owned by some private equity firm based in the Cayman Islands, snatching up properties at auction and flipping them with new crown molding and posters that read, GRATEFUL.

Bex of course has enough money that she doesn't have to go the hourly rental route, but maybe she has the premium version. Maybe this is her soundstage. Maybe her real kitchen, her real dining room, her real TV room (if she has a TV, which she claims she never lets her children watch), are somewhere else.

I feel like Alice searching Wonderland for a hidden door. There is another key on this key chain. There's somewhere else Bex wants me to look. I walk down the hallway away from the pristine sitting room. The first door opens easily. It's a bathroom.

The second is a closet with all the standard hall closet things in it, kids' raincoats, umbrellas, shoes, hats. It's slightly more disordered than the rest of the house that I've seen and that fact gives me hope. The door at the end of the hallway is locked.

As I turn the key in the lock I wonder, for about the tenth time, why Bex is leading me on this wild goose chase instead of just calling me and telling me her side of the story. Wouldn't that be so much easier than all this subterfuge?

Maybe she knows me better than I think she does, knows my need to uncover things for myself, to report out a situation, to discover the proof rather than have it told to me.

I suddenly remember a conversation we had in college when I worked for the student newspaper. I was reporting out a story about the new restaurants opening up on the fringe of campus.

"Can't you just google them?" Bex had asked, irritated that I was missing a date party with Phi Delt to visit two of them.

"I could. But that's not the same. I want to talk to people in them. I want to meet the owners, taste the food, smell the smells. I need to see it all."

The same thing is true now. I need to see her life for myself.

She also must know that I don't trust her, not after all this time and all these years of silence. If she called right now and laid out her side of this story it would never be enough.

I open the door.

The hallway continues on the other side, practically a mirror image of what I've just seen except the sloppy and lived-in version of it. I almost giggle with joy. Here there are sneakers on the floor and greasy little handprints on the white walls. I step on a Lego and smile. Thank god. None of it is real. This is her real life.

This is all of our real lives. Every mother's life is coated in shit and Legos. It's so goddamn validating.

It's also proof that Rebecca's whole brand is a lie. But is that the right way of saying it? Aren't all celebrity brands manufactured? Bill Cosby pretended to be America's perfect dad for a generation. Ellen DeGeneres cosplayed as America's best friend. Apparently Dean Martin pretended to be a drunk even though he didn't like to drink because it made male fans like him more. What celebrity out there is actually portraying themselves on any screen? If I've learned anything over the past few days at MomBomb it's that these influencers are the next generation of celebrities and they're all working from a script.

I keep walking. Family pictures adorn the walls, the frames crooked, probably from getting knocked by flailing arms, lacrosse sticks, and soccer balls. There's another kitchen at the end of the hallway. It's nice and the appliances are high end, shiny, and clearly new, but it's normal-level cluttered, with actual things on the countertops like bottles of vitamins, a pill organizer, sandwich bags, water bottles. A tangle of device chargers is plugged into one of the outlets and a small notepad has a checklist of groceries that need to be ordered.

Have the police been back here? Did they also obtain a key to this shadow house? I imagine they've already searched the entire property. Yet, I see no signs of police activity, or that anything has been disturbed since Bex left to go to the conference.

Where the fuck are her kids? I wonder over and over again. It doesn't look like they took off in a hurry and I can't see any signs of a struggle. It's everyday normal-person cluttered in here, but not someone-just-kidnapped-six-people messy. I make my way up a set of stairs into another part of the house that I've never seen on Bex's Instagram. I peek behind every door. Mostly kids' rooms, one with cribs, one with a bunk bed. The shadow house must have other kid rooms that aren't actually slept in. Toys and books have been left out in these rooms. Inside one is a Casio keyboard and a double bed perfect for a twelve-year-old. This one must be Alice's room. That's the only one I walk into. There are unicorn stuffies on the bed, American Girl dolls primly lined up on the shelves, and framed pictures on the dresser. Alice holding one of her baby siblings, Alice and Bex in matching dresses. Alice on a stage at a piano recital. Gray isn't in any of these pictures. I had long wondered if he was the one taking them, all of the Bex photos and videos and all of the home-birth shots.

Now I know that was probably relegated to a professional photographer or videographer whose job was to make it look like everything was shot in the moment. I pick up the image of Bex and Alice. Their arms are wrapped around each other, and their smiles are wide. Nothing about it looks or feels staged. There's a genuine love there. I know it.

Bex would not put her kids in danger. Maybe that's one of the things she wants me to see here, to feel here. I put the photo down and move on. At the end of this hallway is Bex and Grayson's bedroom. It's neater than the kids' rooms, but still not perfect. The bed is made, which doesn't surprise me. Bex has always been a religious bed maker, even in college, when no one made their loft beds for an entire semester.

There's a fancy Peloton even though I know there's a complete home gym elsewhere on the property. I've seen videos of Gray and Bex working out together in there. At one point she sold a course on couples' core tightening. A chair in the corner has clothes thrown on top of it just like every other chair in every other bedroom all over the world.

I look at it all carefully, the wide-plank oak floors, the over-abundance of throw pillows on the bed.

This is probably her most personal space in the house. But I also have no idea what I'm searching for. I open the top drawer of her dresser and find your standard lingerie drawer. Everything in here is nude colored and exactly the same. Same flesh-colored bras and briefs. All of them utilitarian looking, which makes sense for life on a farm, but also reminds me that Bex was the person who first introduced me to what she referred to as "butt floss" in college. She once bought me a variety pack of thongs in every color of the rainbow. I still had one left until I had Ollie. The floss snapped unceremoniously the last time I tried to put it on. I don't want to rummage through her underwear. That seems a step beyond. In the back of the drawer, I see a small pearly pink case that I recognize from a similar one inside my own underwear drawer. A teeny-tiny discreet vibrator that I was convinced to buy on Instagram with an ad that gussied up masturbation as self-care. I wonder if Bex was influenced by the same one. Can an influencer still be influenced? I shut the drawer and turn to face the bed.

Those were my instructions. *Next to the bed.*

As I drift toward it, I hear a door creak open downstairs. Shit. I pause and listen hard because maybe I was mistaken about the sound, but no, there's a loud slam and heavy footsteps. Could be the cops, could be a farmworker. Could be anyone, really. Am I the only one Bex has left notes and keys for? Is this all some kind of sick scavenger hunt?

I glance one more time at the bedside table as I try to figure out where to go. The book on it. It's so familiar. Damn it! It's mine. It's the book I gave her! I know it is.

She kept it all these years. But why? And why is she reading it now? I grab it and the second book beneath it. I don't know why I want these things, but I do. They called to me somehow. Knowing what she's reading feels like a way to get into her head. We used to trade books back and forth every single week, devouring them the way most of the other students devoured movies and dumb TV shows. We had our own private book club of two and it felt like a special secret thing just for us. I put the books in my bag and duck into the en suite bathroom in case I need to hide from whoever is in the house. I lock the door behind me. The countertop is littered with skincare products, pill bottles, and even toothpaste stains. There's a massive claw-foot tub in the corner with a white linen shower curtain surrounding it. I climb inside and pull the curtain closed, my heart beating in the back of my throat. But as hard as I listen, I can't hear anything outside of this room. There's a window behind the tub. Having a beautiful view from the bath and shower has always felt like the epitome of luxury to me. I once stayed at a hotel in Paris on an assignment and the bathroom had a view of the Eiffel Tower that I still dream about. We have a window in the shower of our suburban house, but it looks out over the trash cans in our driveway and part of Marvin's backyard, which is more sad than luxurious.

This window looks out on the wide expanse of the ranch. I squint into the sun to see if there are any more vehicles on the property. A massive pickup truck is now in the main driveway, one of those trucks that is almost too big to be functional, the kind you hear about running over kids because the tires are literally taller than a six-year-old. I hear another door slam downstairs. The truck's owner is in the house banging around. I pull out my phone and think about who I should text because right now no one knows I'm here and if I went missing no one would know where to look for me. There's only one person any of this would make sense to.

> I'm in your house and I'm not alone.

Bex's phone has been going straight to voicemail and for all I know it's on the bottom of a lake somewhere, but I need there to be proof that I was here. I can't text Peter. The way I ended up in this bathtub on a ranch in the middle of nowhere is too confusing and he'll call me and freak out when I don't answer and then call the police because that's exactly what a rational husband would do. Who else can I text?

There is one other person.

I open my email app and scroll through to Olivia's last message, containing the information about Bex's deal. In her signature is a cell number. I have no idea if it will go to her or to a stable of assistants, but I have to try.

> I'm in Rebecca's house and someone just came in.

I see the three dots. I see them deciding to write back.

> Is it Rebecca?

It's a man, I think.

Is it Gray? lol

Olivia has a dark-ass sense of humor.

They're driving a massive white pickup truck. Sound familiar?

No

More dots.

Where are you in the house?

In her bedroom, hiding in the bathtub.

Do you want me to call the police? Because they may also arrest you for trespassing

She gave me the keys.

My phone rings and I quickly push it to voicemail.

I obviously can't talk.

When did you see Rebecca to get keys to her house?

> I didn't. She left me keys at the hotel. Or at least I think it was her.

A door slams downstairs. There's no more time for small talk with Olivia.

I press my back against the cool porcelain of the bathtub, my breath heaving in shallow gasps. Footsteps, slow and deliberate, echo down below. They move from room to room, methodically searching for something. Doors and drawers are opened and closed. The air chokes in my throat as the footsteps approach the staircase.

> I'm coming out there. It will take me an hour, but I'm coming. Get the hell out of that house and meet me at the front gate

I can't even make my fingers move to respond.

A creak on the stairs. They're coming up. I drop the phone into my bag and clutch the edge of the bathtub to push myself to stand. This massive window opens outward and there's no screen. We're above the garage so I could theoretically climb out and then try to find a way down. It seems almost too easy, but then it always seems too easy when someone just climbs out a window in a horror movie right when the ax murderer walks into the room. What if I get out there and there's no way off the garage roof? Also, I'm an uncoordinated, out-of-shape mother of two small children with no core muscles or pelvic floor. I'm not a ninja or a cat burglar.

I strain my ears to hear whether the footsteps are getting closer. Have they stopped? Are they listening to me? For me? Am I the reason they're here searching this house?

The bedroom door opens. They're just a wall away. I'm screwed. This is it. I hear the opening and closing of drawers. They're doing exactly what I just did, maybe looking for the same things. Maybe looking for evidence.

I hear the rustle of sheets. Are they climbing into the bed? No. Something hits the floor, knees maybe. There's a soft shuffling of someone crawling. They must be checking under the bed, a place I didn't think to look. I hold my breath for all the good that will do. Moments later I hear the footsteps again. Closer and closer. They're turning the knob, but it's locked. They jiggle it harder and harder.

As I inspect the window, my bag slips from my shoulder, all the contents clattering onto the bottom of the tub.

The jiggling stops. They're listening to me. Despair tugs at my gut and my limbs turn to liquid.

As I clumsily stuff everything back in, something flutters from inside the pages of one of the books. Two things. Polaroid pictures. They land close to the drain and I grab them and stuff them in my bag without pausing to see the images. I push open the window as slowly as I can, but it creaks anyway.

Someone bangs on the door, but they say nothing. What will it take to break it down?

Get the fuck out of the window, Lizzie. I push myself and go head-first through the frame, sort of crawling, sort of scrambling. I get stuck midway through, trying to hoist the lower part of my body up. This is so much more difficult than it looks in movies and I hate myself for even trying it, but there's no turning back now. I'm committed. I finally make it onto the roof. My brain spins as I pull myself into a crouch and look out over the horizon. I stay in that position, slowly inching toward the edge, keeping all four limbs firmly attached to the slate at all times. I pretend I'm a praying mantis in one of those nature shows my kids love to watch.

Nearby, a sturdy-looking trellis leans against the side of the house, its wooden frame weathered but still intact. I carefully maneuver toward it, testing its strength with a firm tug. Satisfied, I grip the rungs tightly and begin to descend, using the crossbars and thick vines for support.

The trellis groans softly under my weight but holds steady as I descend step by step. I keep my movements slow and deliberate, ensuring my footing on each rung and avoiding any sudden shifts that could dislodge the structure.

I reach the ground with a soft thud and land relieved and grateful.

I glance at the front door. It's slightly ajar, but I don't see anyone. I stare at the pickup truck and have the briefest moment of clarity. I whip out my cell phone and take a picture of the license plate. There's no reason to hesitate even a moment longer. I break out into a run for the car. I haven't run in about ten years and even then I was a half-hearted jogger at best. Adrenaline and terror both help, but by the time I make it to the rental car my chest is heaving. There's a fire in my lungs and a stitch in my side that feels like I'm being stabbed. I look up at the house in the distance and swear I see a face in the bathroom window I just climbed out of, but it has to be my mind playing tricks on me. It's too far for me to see anything. I'm paranoid.

I get behind the wheel and peel out toward the back entrance to the ranch. This car doesn't have four-wheel drive and it hates the speed I'm using. I hit something large and possibly sharp. I keep going, not worrying if it pierced the tire. With the gate in sight, I slam on the brakes and rush out, punching in the numbers. It beeps angrily back at me. Someone has changed the code. I'm trapped.

I try again. My fingers don't work. They're made of jelly. Maybe I've done it wrong. Do I hear an engine behind me?

The gate is once again pissed at me. I know my keypad at home locks you out for at least twenty minutes after three wrong tries. I can't fuck this up. I pull in a deep breath and concentrate. Alice's birthday. *One number at a time, Lizzie.* Go slow. Be deliberate.

The creak of the gate opening is the sweetest sound I've ever heard. I say a prayer to a god I haven't thought about since childhood and get back into the car and check the rearview mirror. No one is behind me. I've made it out.

I drive like the intruder I am, like someone who has just done something very wrong. I don't slow down until I've made it onto the properly paved road, and even then I go down to about five miles above the speed limit because the last thing I want is to get pulled over. My lungs still burn. I cough and can't stop coughing from all the dust I swallowed while I was running. I desperately need water and pull into the first gas station I see.

My wallet is drowning in junk at the bottom of my tote bag, and I fumble around for it. I haven't looked at my phone or responded to Olivia since I was in the house, and when I tap it, I see it's dead, and of course I haven't brought a charger.

My fingers brush the photographs next, and I pull them out to examine them. At first, I'm not sure exactly what I'm looking at but I recoil anyway. It takes a few moments for my mind to make sense of the two pictures together and once I do I know without a doubt they were meant for me to find. There's a reason they were in that particular book, my book.

I can't believe she still has this book. But my inscription to her is right there.

I hope you love this adventure as much as I do. Love you like a sister. Lizzie

It's a copy of *West with the Night,* which was one of my favorite books as a teenager. I happened on it at the library in high school. I loved it so much I never returned it and this is my copy from the Bucks County Free Library. The stamp is still right there in the back. I adored the biography of the first person to fly solo across the Atlantic from east to west because I loved the idea of a woman breaking all the rules of society and learning to fly a plane. I devoured Beryl Markham's sense of adventure and the freedom she gained as a pilot. I wanted to be her, and I knew Bex would feel the same way. I gave it to Bex on her twenty-first birthday. She finished it in one night and tried to give it back to me but I made her keep it because I loved that she loved it. That seemed to prove something about our friendship to me, that I had chosen her wisely.

Here it is now, and these horrible pictures were tucked inside of it.

Bex has always loved instant cameras. She liked the privacy of them, the fact that no one else would ever see the image if you didn't want them to. I wonder now if anyone has ever seen these photographs besides Bex and me.

Like most Polaroids these have a date in the lower right corner. The clearer of the two pictures, and obviously the more recent one, was taken a week before Grayson Sommers was murdered. It's a close-up of Bex's face, throat, and shoulder. Her left eye is heavily bruised and nearly swollen shut—the same eye Bex had heavily covered with makeup when I saw her. The bruises on her neck look like an actual handprint. Someone hurt her badly soon before her husband was murdered and she wanted me to know it.

The other picture is painfully similar to the first. It's also of Bex. Her face. Her beautiful face, bruised and battered. But she's different in this picture. It's the Bex that I knew. The one who just appeared in my dream. Younger. Not a trace of wrinkles or Botox or the battle scars of motherhood. There's something different about her eyes. I can't put my finger on it, but it's there. She looks so scared in this picture whereas in the other one she is simply resigned. There's blood matted in her hair. It was brassier then, or at least it looks that way in the faded photo. Goddamn that man. Because I have to assume it was Gray who did it. I look at the date last, though I know it's old. September 9. Fourteen years ago. There's something about that particular date that tugs at my brain. It's not her birthday, but it is a week before mine. And the year. It's the year before I met Peter, which means this was taken the week I went to San Francisco, the week that Bex ghosted me.

This is the reason.

This is the terrible reason.

I don't realize that I'm crying until a drop lands on the picture. I quickly wipe it away, but it still stains the delicate film.

Why didn't she tell me? I was right there. I was knocking on her door. I was running around the city looking for her. I was calling and texting her nonstop and the whole time I thought she'd ditched me, that she hated me, that she had blown me off for her new fancy boyfriend. But none of that was true.

Was she even the one who wrote that nasty email to me? Or was it Gray? It certainly didn't sound a bit like her but I'd been so pissed I accepted it at face value.

She kept this from me for a reason. Probably the same reason my mother hid it from all her friends for my entire childhood. My dad didn't flare up (as Mom called it) that often, but when he did it was bad, and she sent us up to our room and bore the brunt of it. Afterward he was apologetic and helpful around the house in a way he never was otherwise. He took us to the zoo and the mall. We got to order anything we wanted from the movie theater concession stand and we returned home on a sugar high with bloated bellies.

When Dad died the year before I left for college my mom was transformed. My quiet, fearful mother became a social butterfly. She took up swimming, met a nice woman named Roberta at the YMCA, and the two of them eventually moved in together and got very into river cruising. Robbie had money from a teacher's pension and a beach house. The first half of my mom's life became a footnote and she didn't want to talk about it. We're closer than ever now. She watches my kids once a week and they love sleeping over with her and Robbie, but we don't mention Dad and we never talk about the bruises.

I know it was shame that kept Bex from telling me then, but she *is* telling me now. She wants me to know, but what does she want me to do with the information?

She can't want me to publish these. If she kept this secret for this long, she can't want me to expose it like this. The abuse contributes to a motive for Bex killing Gray, especially if Gray was the one who hurt her. It also could be a plea for self-defense.

"I need more than this, Bex," I whisper.

The other book. It's only then that I remember there were two. There's no dust jacket on the other one, so I flip to the title page. *Grace Beyond the Diamond*. Oh god. It's an autobiography by Marsden Greer! And this book is also heavily highlighted and underlined, almost like she was researching him. There are exclamation marks in the margins and on one page someone, probably Bex, has very clearly scrawled the words *son of a bitch*. The underlined portions are mostly physical details about Marsden. Strangely, the fact that he had asthma as a kid. Another paragraph where he mentions he was slightly deaf in one ear until the fifth grade. A line about how his mother thought he was left-handed, but he switched preferences suddenly in kindergarten.

What the hell does it mean? Is she accusing Marsden of something? Could he have been the one who hurt her? The one who murdered Gray?

I pick up my phone. It's still dead. I need a charger. This gas station is also a small grocery store. I buy one of those ridiculously long hot-pink phone chargers they always seem to have in places like this, a large coffee, and a bag of Twizzlers.

I sip my coffee and gnaw on the red ropes while the phone charges in my idling car. I thumb through the pages of *West with the Night,* remembering all the reasons this book broke open my fifteen-year-old brain the first time I read it.

There are passages that I highlighted with my old yellow pen.

Life had a different shape; it had new branches and some of the old branches were dead. It had followed the constant pattern of discard and growth that all lives follow.

I could never tell where inspiration begins and impulse leaves off. I suppose the answer is in the outcome. If your hunch proves a good one, you were inspired; if it proves bad, you are guilty of yielding to thoughtless impulse.

These were things I thought were profound back then, and to be honest, they still feel that way now. But there are sentences that are underlined with faint blue ink too and I know that wasn't me. They were from Bex. One of them stops me hard.

The only disadvantage in surviving a dangerous experience lies in the fact that your story of it tends to be anticlimactic. You can never carry on right through the point where whatever it is that threatens your life actually takes it—and get anybody to believe you. The world is full of sceptics.

And then I see this:

There are all kinds of silences and each of them means a different thing.

Now I know what Bex's silence meant. And I know it's up to me to find a way to break it.

CHAPTER THIRTEEN

REBECCA

've been reading the news and scrolling enough social media to know what everyone is saying about me. Thousands of strangers, maybe hundreds of thousands, are convinced my children are in danger. Because of me.

But they know nothing.

They know nothing about our real lives.

I'd love people to stop and think for a second about what they actually know about my children because they think they know a lot.

They think they know everything.

There have always been haters out there online who are horrified at what I do for work, who scream from the comments sections that I'm a bad mother for exploiting my children's entire lives straight from the womb. Except no one realizes how little they really know about those six littles.

I'm not an idiot and I'm not a stage mom. I'm building a future for them. I'm ensuring they'll never depend on handouts or Goodwill or scholarships. I'm doing this all for them because my mother wasn't able to do it for me.

And I protect them in a way that no one notices.

I only use their middle names, except for Alice. I didn't make up that rule until after I'd already written about her. No one realizes that. I've never mentioned their birthdays. None of their faces are fully visible after their second birthdays but I bet no one has even noticed. I don't let them look at the camera, at any cameras in fact. They're always turned away. They could be anyone. They could be child actors. Maybe they're not even mine.

What does anyone actually know?

Nothing.

Despite how much money I've made over the past few years, it took a long time for me to hoard twenty thousand dollars in cash. All of my influencing payments go directly into different bank accounts that are managed by Olivia's team and disbursed to run my company. The ranch also bleeds money and a lot of what I make goes to keeping it up.

Gray's family money kept us flush for a while, but it began to run out about five years ago. The Sommers family had plowed through it, no pun intended, believing that money and power last forever. But oil wells run dry, stock markets crash, and real estate deals go belly-up. Nothing is a sure thing forever, but when you've been rich your entire life you don't believe that.

A few years ago, Gray started depending on my income more and more, and when that began happening, he kept a careful eye on it. But my husband did believe that I needed to pay various vendors and employees in cash, the photographers and the nannies. We also pay most of the farmworkers in cash for seasonal labor. So over the past year I've siphoned off the money I'm using right now. I didn't know what I would need it for, I just had the sense that I would need it. That we would need it, the kids and I.

So now we are all off the grid, paying cash for everything. We just aren't doing it together. My children are safe. They aren't even very far away. I know that much is true and they will stay safe no matter what happens to me.

I've been wearing a long dark wig, sunglasses, and a baseball cap whenever I leave this motel room, but that isn't often. I like the anonymity. After being so public for so long, being completely anonymous feels like stepping into a warm bath. So much so that I wonder if I can ever go back. I spent last night fantasizing about what it would be like if the kids and I could return to being nobodies, if we could completely step out of the public eye.

It will be impossible now, no matter what ends up happening. Things didn't go exactly to plan over the past few days. They got messy, horrifically messy. But I can't think about that now. The only thing to do is move forward.

Even if everything goes right from now on, we will never be nobodies again.

Lizzie found what I needed her to find. I know because I can access my texts and voicemails online even though I've kept my phone off so it won't ping a cell tower. She's so good at her job. Lizzie has always been a brilliant reporter. I don't know why she doesn't still report, why she stopped going behind the scenes, off the campaign trails. I loved her first-person pieces about riding campaign buses and that one story she did on the sex-trafficking ring brought me to tears.

I assume it has to do with becoming a mother. The juggle is real. I know that better than anyone, though I would never show myself dropping a single ball.

It's been a risk letting Lizzie discover all of this for herself. But one that's paid off so far. We'll have to see how today goes. Will she write about what she's found?

I still ask myself what would have happened if I'd just reached out to Lizzie right after Gray was violent that first time. If I'd called her straightaway and asked her to come a day sooner, to pick me up from Gray's place and take me home with her. What kept me from doing that? It's hard to access the exact emotion now, but I think it was my stupid pride. I threw away the most important friendship I'd ever had because I was embarrassed and ashamed, and losing Lizzie in that way, losing the only person who really knew me or cared about me, just yoked me even more to Grayson after that horrific night.

He did everything I asked of him that morning after he hurt me back in San Francisco all those years ago. I later found out he got the drugs from Marsden. Mars could get just about anything from his trainers. Gray told me he explained to everyone at the bakery that we'd gone off on a trip to celebrate. No one questioned it. No one ever questioned Gray about anything. I knocked myself out for days and every time I woke up I had a new bandage on my wounds and more food and drugs next to the bed. He took care of everything.

I loved the oblivion those pills gave me. I loved it too much and maybe Gray knew it because he kept bringing them as I slowly let him in more and more to care for me. And in that haze of care and healing I started to push it all down into the same black box I'd pushed all the terrible things from my past into.

Once the bruises healed, I finally looked at my phone again. Gray had handled all my incoming messages from work, and no one was any the wiser.

"What do you want to do about Lizzie?" Gray had asked me at one point during my stupor. I'd been so messed up, so out of it, that I'd forgotten she was coming.

"Is she still here?" I'd slurred and mumbled.

"She left days ago. She's been calling and texting."

He showed me several of her messages, holding the phone for me.

Fuck you. Seriously.

You know what, I'm done. Don't call me ever again.

"She's mad," I'd managed.

"You told me you didn't want to see her."

"I did?"

"Over and over again."

I had no idea if that was true, but it could have been. "Delete the messages," I said. I was high on the pills and still gutted with shame. That was it. It was almost too easy to erase six years of friendship, but there was no going back. What I had done was inexcusable. I had invited her to come see me, made her spend her hard-earned money, and then I hid from her like a goddamn

195

coward. I didn't deserve her friendship. She was so much better off without me. That's what I kept telling myself. And eventually I believed it.

Once I was healed, I spent most of my time in the bakery crafting my signature éclairs. I arrived there well before dawn almost every day.

I'd turn the music up as loud as I could bear and with practiced grace I combined eggs, flour, and butter, each ingredient an essential note. Whisked vigorously, the batter transformed into a silky sheen, and I could feel the heat of creation coursing through my veins. The anticipation of the finished product wrapped around me like a warm embrace, igniting a thrill deep within me. Once the choux pastry was perfectly piped onto the baking sheet, I slipped it into the oven. The gentle crackling and the rich, buttery scent were the only things that made me truly calm.

I filled each éclair with meticulous care, watching as the creamy custard oozed gently from the ends. The act of filling them was nearly sensual; my heart raced with the knowledge that I was creating pure joy. Baking was not merely a craft; it was my heartbeat, my passion, and the ultimate expression of love.

Baking healed me.

Gray apologized every day. He paid to fix my teeth. Not just the one that had fallen out, but all of the crooked ones that had been a mess for years. He bought me extravagant presents and eventually he did whisk me away on a surprise vacation to Hawaii, a place I had only ever seen in movies and magazines, and it was there that I began to soften to him again. He gave me all the safety and security I had always craved. He made life feel easy.

The bakery did well until it didn't. San Francisco was such a fickle city. They loved you one day and forgot you the next. Business eventually dwindled when some other shop across town began making some hybrid of an éclair, a cannoli, and a croissant that became all the rage on Facebook. An ecolissant. It sounded like an infectious disease, but it looked divine in pictures.

Then an Au Bon Pain opened next door and just sold the cheap version of both our stuff.

But it only made me try harder, work harder and longer. Gray hated it, but he never laid a hand on me again. Nor did he have a single sip of alcohol. He was on his very best behavior. So much so that the memories of that night eventually stopped haunting my dreams.

And when he proposed with his mother's vintage diamond ring encrusted with the most delicate tiny emeralds that perfectly matched the color of his eyes, I even cried when I said yes. I truly believed he would never hurt me again, that it was an accident, a onetime thing. And I still lived in fear of becoming my mother. I was massively in debt from school and always would be unless Gray paid it all off. I wanted a nice life. By then I felt like I deserved it and getting ahead in this world isn't based on merit.

Gray wanted babies right away. That was fine by me. I'd always wanted a gaggle of kids, the opposite of my solitary upbringing. But apparently it was not fine by my body. I couldn't get pregnant. I took the herbs and saw the acupuncturists. We used the apps that monitored my ovulation and the temperature of my uterus. Every month, there was the same result. I bawled when I bled, and Gray held me and rocked me like the baby I couldn't have. My doctors all said to wait a year to try IVF so we did the other things.

"You're under too much stress at work," Gray said over and over again. He wasn't wrong.

Each time my body failed I became more and more obsessed with trying to fix it. I was prediabetic, the doctor told me. My blood pressure and cholesterol were both high. My aura was off, a holistic specialist insisted.

When the lease on the bakery came up for renewal, we decided to let it go. I mourned, but I was also possessed with fixing whatever was broken in my body. I wouldn't work myself to death like Mom had. The desire to have a child took over my every waking moment and somehow I let my previous dream slip away. When Gray's dad had that stroke and turned the farm over to him, it all seemed perfect and simple and easy.

Our life out there would be beautiful and much simpler. We'd eat food grown on our land. Nothing processed. No chemicals and additives. My aura would heal.

I doubled down again on every possible noninvasive fertility treatment—pills, injections, acupuncture. Gray said we needed to pray, that prayer would fix whatever was wrong with me. We attended virtual prayer groups twice a week since we were so far out in the country, but we made the long drive into the city a couple of times a month to be with the congregation in person. I loved the community of it, the camaraderie. This is what had been missing from my childhood, a village to care for us, to support us and help us. So what if I didn't believe in God, if I could never truly believe; I wanted all of the other parts of it so badly that it didn't matter. When everyone placed their hands gently on my belly and told me I was in their nightly prayers I thanked them profusely.

I saw a new doctor out there, Dr. Carmichael. He was the man who had delivered Gray and he told me that it took my husband's mother more than a year to get pregnant with her first baby too.

"What you're going through is normal," he assured me. "And we are going to heal you." I asked about IVF.

"Not necessary," he insisted. "Artificial fecundation is a sin."

I didn't believe that was true, but I didn't push it. He promised me I would be pregnant soon. I felt so safe, so protected, so cared for. Gray doubled down on making sure I had everything I needed and eventually it all worked exactly the way everyone had promised it would. Who is to say what did the trick: the fertility treatments, the intrauterine insemination, the acupuncture, the lack of stress, or the constant prayer. I didn't care. Six months later I was pregnant, and I stayed pregnant. I know a lot of women who wouldn't agree, but I adored pregnancy. I felt whole for the first time in my life.

Alice was perfect and delicious and my everything. We stayed in bed together for entire days when Gray would travel for work, and it was the happiest I'd ever been. Everything I had been through, everything I had endured, was for her. I was so grateful to finally be a mother that I threw myself into it with the same furious intensity I had with my bakery. I made baby food from scratch. I sewed her little dresses. I rid our house of every possible toxin. I was a good mother. I was finally good.

It was Alice who found me after Gray came at me again, when he hit me so hard I passed out on the floor of our bathroom. I'd been unconscious for hours. That's when I saw the bruises on the top of her arm, thick purple lines made by a man's hand.

My sweet gangly colt of a daughter fetched me warm washcloths and wiped the blood from my face while I lay on the bathroom floor. I reached up to touch her arm.

"He grabbed me when I walked into the barn and startled him." She said it so simply. So resigned. I hated that she was resigned to his violence. But it turns out she wasn't.

"It will never happen again," I managed.

"No, it won't," she said. Only twelve and so wise. "It will not happen again."

"Where are the others?"

"Willow is here. Downstairs. The others are out in the fields with Kiki. I told everyone you're working."

I hated that she was lying for me.

It had to end. But I already knew that. Plans had already been made to get us all out from under his grip, but I worried it wouldn't be enough. I needed more help to be able to end things once and for all.

CHAPTER FOURTEEN

LIZZIE

I'm not okay.

It's the first question Olivia asks me when she meets me in the gas station parking lot. She was apparently close to the ranch, circling around and trying to find me. By the time I was able to power my phone on and see all of her messages she'd driven back out this way and now we're sitting in the front seat of my rental car.

"Are you okay?" she asks again, reaching over to pat my hand.

I shake my head. "Who the hell was in that house with me?"

"Well, they probably think the same about you. If they know you were in there at all. Let's not forget you were trespassing."

"I had a key."

"Semantics."

"I think they saw me."

"Describe the truck again."

"Pickup truck. Huge. Massive tires. Sparkling white."

"Sounds like the kind of asshole truck every asshole guy around here drives. I've always said I think the size of a man's truck must inversely correlate to his dick size."

Olivia manages to be wry and funny even in the worst of times and I can see why Bex must like her. Today she's in a yellow suit and somehow her hair now matches it perfectly again. I reach over to touch a strand. I can't help myself. She bats my hand away.

"Never touch a Black woman's hair. Where were you raised?"

"Sorry. Wasn't this purple before?"

"They're clip-ins. Just a little bit of flair to make my day more exciting. Don't underestimate flair. So what did you find in that big gorgeous monstrosity of a house?"

I hesitate, unsure how much to trust her. Does she know about the shadow house? She must. Maybe she even helped Bex plan and construct it. But I can't be sure. Instead, I turn the tables slightly and ask her a question.

"What do you know about Gray and Rebecca's relationship?"

She doesn't miss a beat with her answer. "I know that Gray Sommers was a bona fide asshole who wanted to control his wife and her business. I know that the ways he did that were toxic and often abusive. What do you know?"

Touché.

I gnaw on my lower lip as I pull the Polaroids from my bag.

"Asshole, indeed," I say.

I wait for surprise to flicker across Olivia's face as she glances at the photos, but it doesn't. She knew, or she assumed. But from the curiosity in her gaze, I don't think she's seen these before. I don't think anyone but Bex has seen these until now. Until me.

"One of these is much older," she says.

"Fourteen years."

"Where were they in the house? Just sitting around? Wouldn't the police have found them?"

"She left them for me." I explain about the book and how I gave it to Bex when we were in college, what it meant to the two of us. It was left out for me to find, I insist again. I tell her about the note.

"It seems like a stretch that you would stumble upon it."

"But I did." I know it seems like a stretch, but it also feels right. Bex knew I would come, and she knew I would gravitate toward that book and it was next to the bed. It's absurd, but I feel close to Bex again. Like we can once again crawl into each other's brains the way we did so easily when we were younger.

"Why did she leave that one, do you think? The older one? The recent picture, that I understand. She wanted us to know what he did to her less than two weeks ago, but the first one?"

Even remembering this now is so painful. "It was the last time we were supposed to see each other. I flew out to San Francisco for my birthday. We were going to spend the week together. But she ghosted me. I think she wanted me to know this was why."

Olivia only nods and then gazes out the windshield as if lost in thought.

"You should write about it. She would want you to write about it. About all of this."

"Would she?"

"Why else would she have left those for you to find?"

I shake my head. "It feels too personal."

"She's a victim, Lizzie. She needs a voice. She needs your voice. I won't tell you what to write or how to do your job. But she clearly trusts you." Olivia places a warm firm hand over mine and grips it tightly.

"She chose you. She wanted you here to help her escape Grayson. That was her plan. And she needs you now."

Olivia is charismatic and convincing, that's for sure. It's the charisma of a politician or one of those megachurch preachers.

"Where do you think she is?" I ask. Something tells me that this woman knows, but she definitely won't tell me. Still, I can try.

There's that stare into the distance again. "I honestly have no idea. She isn't answering my emails. Her phone is long gone, or she's been very careful to turn it off. I keep leaving voicemails and no response."

"Same. I keep leaving messages in the hopes that somehow she is listening to them. What about the kids?"

"They're safe." Olivia says this with a certainty I didn't expect.

"What do you know?"

She flinches and my reporter's instinct tells me that she's definitely about to lie to me. "I don't know any more than you know, but Rebecca would never let anything happen to those children. They're the reason she does all of the things that she does. They're her everything."

I play along and allow her the feigned ignorance. Often pieces of the truth will come out through the lies. "That doesn't mean they're not in danger though. That she isn't currently in danger. I mean, the man who was in the house with me . . . They were looking for something."

"You know it was a man?"

I think about the heavy thuds on the stairs, the groans and

muttering I heard in the hallway and the bedroom, the intense energy in the space since they walked into the house.

"I think so. Or I thought so at the time. I can't explain why."

"Okay. I've got no idea who it could have been. So many people work that ranch. Too many people have access."

"But to that part of the house?"

She shakes her head solemnly. "No. Not usually to there. But who knows who Gray gave access to over the years. Who knows what that man did and with who. He had his secrets. Lots of them. As you now know from seeing these pictures. That poor girl. I knew he was horrible. But I thought he was horrible with his words alone. He was always telling her she was worthless and stupid, that she was nothing but trash even though she was the one keeping the family afloat, making enough money that he could invest in a bunch of worthless start-ups and still pretend to be a cowboy. He needed that money, but he hated her for making it. She told me plenty of times that he threatened to leave her and take those kids, even though it was an empty threat. No one gets divorced out here. The church looks down on it and judges are wicked to women who ask for one. So many of these women get trapped in these marriages when they're practically teenagers. Rebecca's exit plan was to have so much money that she could tell them all to screw off."

"But her plan didn't work out."

"That one didn't work out. But focus on the present. We have to pivot. What do you say? About what I said. About writing the truth about Rebecca?"

"I need to think about it," I respond carefully.

"You want to go somewhere to think? Right now?"

"Right now?"

"Get some food. Clear our heads. Go somewhere that we can talk and lay out what we know that isn't your rental car. There's a halfway decent watering hole down the road. And by down the road I mean about twenty miles away."

"It's early for a drink."

"It's never too early in the desert, and besides they have a rib eye that will knock your teeth out and their drinks are all watered down because they pretend they don't believe in overindulgence here."

What a strange woman Olivia is. And convincing. I agree. I'm hungry and spent and I want to get out of my dusty rental car to eat some red meat and sip on a watered-down lager.

It isn't until we get settled in a booth at a place literally called the Rib Eye that I remember I took a picture of the license plate of the truck that was in the driveway. I pull it up on my phone to show Olivia.

"Is this familiar?"

She squints and then puts on a pair of massive yellow reading glasses. I wonder if she has them in every color to match every suit and every piece of hair flair. If so, the dedication to the vibe is impressive. "I'm not in the habit of memorizing license plates," she says. "So I've got nothing for ya. You're a reporter though. Don't you know someone who can search these kinds of things?"

I do actually. Or I did. A friend from a long time ago who used to work for the NYPD who now works in private security.

"It's harder than you think. I doubt it." For some reason I still don't want to show Olivia all of my cards because I'm pretty sure she isn't showing me all of hers.

"In the meantime, I think you should get writing. Get Rebecca's story out there. Create a safe space for her to return to." Olivia helps herself to a Twizzler from the pack I brought inside with me.

Her phone rings. The ringtone is Wagner's "Ride of the Valkyries."

"Inside joke," she murmurs about the tune, and looks at her screen before pushing a button to send it to voicemail and beckoning the waiter over to our table. She orders a steak that is "so rare it is bleeding out on my plate," and a cup of chili.

"You have to get the chili." I do. I match her order except I ask for less gore.

Once the waiter is out of earshot I ask if I can turn on my recorder.

"No recording. But you can write some notes. Let's talk on background for a bit."

"I did what you said. I spoke to some of the women at the conference. And one of them told me that there were dangerous men, powerful men, supporting Gray, men who could be after Rebecca now. What do you know about that?"

Olivia nibbles on the end of the Twizzler and then perches it between two fingers as if it's a lit cigarette.

"There probably are. No . . . no. That's not right. There definitely are. You don't know much about this part of the country, do you, Lizzie?"

I want to say, of course I do. I'm not one of those East Coast snobs who doesn't "get" the rest of the country, who refers to everything west of Philadelphia as flyover country. But if we're being honest here, that's exactly what I am. I grew up in the

Philly burbs, went to college in the city, moved to New York, and haven't left the tristate area except for vacations for my entire adult life. I know more about the UK from being with Peter than I do about anything between California and Ohio.

So I admit what I don't know and ask her to explain it to me. Sometimes you need to know exactly when to show your ignorance. Male reporters are terrible at it.

"You all like to think of Silicon Valley when you think of tech. But all those tech companies need you to be the product. They need content. They need users. And this is where they get both. This place is ground zero for it. It's Valhalla for influencing and digital creating. It's where the mommy blogs began and where they all died to give birth to the influencers. It's why I chose to move here from Los Angeles. I saw something in this desert. Everyone I worked with in Hollywood thought I was a fucking moron, but I saw what was coming. My dad worked in the entertainment business in the nineties."

"What did he do?"

"He was the assistant, the right-hand man, to this big shot music producer who built boy bands. There was a lot of traveling and the head honcho always wanted Dad around so I got home-schooled on the road and the studios paid for it. We'd go all over the country auditioning teenage boys, plucking out the cutest ones with a modicum of talent and nice hair and clear skin. Made them dance and prance and show their hairless little chests. Made them millionaires. You remember that one music video of the band SweetBoyz, the one where they're all puppets, marionettes, bouncing around on the stage? That's how I always think of my dad's boss. That motherfucker was the puppeteer. He was pulling all the strings."

"Where is he now?"

"Prison. Embezzlement. He was a greedy bastard. But brilliant. It would have been any other little girl's dream, getting so much access to those bands. But those dudes always seemed so silly to me. It wasn't until I was a little older and my dad wasn't doing so well anymore that he sat me down and explained what they had done with those boys, how those teams had molded them to be exactly what teenage girls, and even horny moms, wanted. That's when I understood. I wanted to do what his boss did. It felt like the perfect combination of business and art. So I got a dual degree in management and accounting from UCLA. I got in-state tuition, which I needed because by 2002 we didn't have that much money. My dad's job ended when the big guy went to prison. Pop's cancer treatments were expensive. I started working at different accounting firms and then at talent agencies. Got my law degree at night. I think some people felt sorry for me. They used to see me sitting in the wings at those concerts and in the hotel lobbies while my dad scurried around getting shit done."

Her hands are flying all over the place, intensely animated. She loves telling her story to me. Most people do. It's one of the things I learned when I became a journalist. Get someone talking about themselves and 99 percent of them won't shut up until you ask them to.

"I realized early on that social media was going to be the future of media. And then I found the women here. They were bloggers at first. Their churches encourage women to stay home and have as many kids as possible, but they also encourage journaling and they loved the idea of the blogging. It showcased the lifestyle in a way they liked. It was a way to bring new people in. Come for the beautiful pictures of four blond children pulling eggs out of a chicken's ass and stay to find out how to save your eternal soul. Plus the girls are gorgeous."

I take note of the fact that she calls them girls and not women.

"They're all blond and blue-eyed with skin so tight you could bounce a quarter off of it because they've never had a drink or a smoke in their lives. You don't smoke, do you?"

I shake my head, because no one smokes anymore, but I do miss it in times like this.

"I don't either, but I could go for one now. I miss it every day when I have my first sip of coffee or a shitty beer. The men here are usually gorgeous too, but so fucking thick, and the kids . . . oh my god, the kids. You could go to a dozen casting calls in the Valley and never see angels like these. They're obedient and beautiful. A talent manager's dream.

"The culture out here definitely pushes women hard to be a certain way. The quest for perfection at all costs is intense. They'd do it without a camera so why not give them one—I moved here and I offered up my services. Accounting at first. There was a lot of money coming in from banner ads and sponsored posts. And then management when the bigger brands and deals started waking up to how influential the girls were. It was similar to what my dad's boss had done with the bands. He found the kids who had something special. They didn't have to have too much talent, in fact real talent could be a pain in the ass. They just needed an 'it' factor. Everything else can be manufactured. And over the years that's what I've done for these ladies. I find the ones who have something and we work together to nurture their careers."

"How long have you worked with Bex?"

"A long time. Seven years now. She was one of my first. We figured a lot of this out together. And she really has it. That 'it' factor. She's an incredible baker, but she was shy about showing it off at first. I convinced her to amp that up. To be proud of it. I also launched Tripod's Instagram. That stinky-ass goat pays the mortgage for the whole farm."

"Gray's family seemed so rich. Why are there all these debts and mortgages?"

"Gray's granddaddy made that money. He had eleven kids and Gray's own daddy had eight. That's a lot of slivers of pie to dole out even if you've got a lot of pie. And then a bunch of them made some shitty investments. Gray's been in financial free fall since they got married, but he hid it for a few more years afterward. When they first moved out to the ranch, he had big plans to breed bison like a millennial Ted Turner. Thought he was gonna make a bison-cow hybrid called the beefalo. But bison are ornery and nasty. They break out of every fence. They rip up your land and they'll try to kill you every chance they get. No vet wants to touch them, and the farmers out here have no experience with them. It was a disaster. Also, they're never camera-ready. Rebecca actually took to the farming pretty well. She was raising chickens by hand while she was raising those babies and was making some dough from her egg money alone. And then those chickens made her a star on Instagram. We got more and more of them. Henfluencing is a real banger. The chicken phase was incredibly lucrative for her. That's when we decided to start selling merch. Her wicker egg-collecting basket was the first thing we tried on the product side, and it was a massive hit. From there we expanded into clothes and linens and kitchenware. We figured out how to do one media day a week to streamline the production process. Rebecca became a real vibe real fast.

"And she has something else too. She's not from here, so she wasn't afraid to push the boundaries, to want something bigger than what this tiny world could offer her. More and more of the women out here are seeing that now, but they didn't then. She's truly a star. Always has been."

"It's insane," I blurt out. "They're all pushing this arcadian fantasy of homemaking and living off the land, the anti-girlbosses, when they're all building capitalist empires."

"It's genius, right?" Olivia claps her hands like an excited child. "She gives the people what they want. They all do. Don't you fall down rabbit holes of bread baking and closet organizing and baby swaddling? No one is immune to it. You all can't get enough."

"How do the husbands feel about this? Do they hate it?" I think about how the tables have turned with Peter and me since he lost his job. He's grateful that I have mine, but I know he bristles at the fact that I've become the sole breadwinner. He can't seem to help it even though he has the feminist soul of a man raised on the Spice Girls. How must these "manly" and painfully masculine men feel about their wives' success?

"Not all of them hate it. In fact, plenty of the hubbies like the cash. Money is always nice. But when it's women making the money they get power. They want things. They question things.

The husbands don't like that and the men who control these towns and the churches, they don't like it either."

"How did they feel about Rebecca?"

"Loved her until they hated her. She got too big. She had so much influence, such a big audience. People actually moved out here saying they wanted what @BarefootMamaLove had. They said that to the real estate agents. They showed up at the church services. They bought into the lifestyle. At first it was great. It really set Gray up to be a star in the church and the community."

"Did Gray want to be a star?" I keep thinking about the cipher on the edges of Rebecca's pictures.

"He wanted to be important. His dad was an important man around here. He was a big deal in the state, and everyone loved him. Gray wanted that kind of love, that kind of admiration. Politics always appealed to him. Rebecca told me that early on. I could always tell he was desperate to prove himself, desperate to show he was more than his family's money, especially when it was gone. You can smell that on a person."

"What's it smell like?" It's half a joke.

"Expensive cologne." She doesn't miss a beat. Our steaks arrive, Olivia's as bloody as she requested. When she slices through the flank with exquisite precision, the blood pools around the muscle. Some of it drips off Olivia's lips as she continues.

"With Gray's swagger and cheekbones he could have run for office without her, but throw in a pretty blond wife and six perfect children and he was gonna have it made. But he got itchy when she got bigger and bigger. He never wanted her to expand. None of them did."

"Them?"

"Gray's family. The church elders. The local political party. They wanted to keep her where she was at. Make her even smaller if they could. Keep her in a box, a glass box where she couldn't grow."

"And that's not what she wanted. Or what you want?"

"Hell no. That woman is a star and she deserves to shine."

"And there are probably people out there, out here," I say as I wave my hand toward the desert outside, "who don't want that?"

"That's exactly right."

I take it all in. All of this information about a world I have uneasily consumed on Instagram and YouTube. A world that looked beautiful and aspirational. A world that made me feel bad about my own messy life. We pause the conversation to gnaw on our steaks. Mine is delicious and exactly what I needed. I have the feeling that Olivia is good at giving people exactly what they need when they need it.

There are people who want to silence and control Bex. But she also had every reason to want to get rid of her husband. I'll be leaving here with more questions than answers.

Olivia's phone goes off again with that ridiculous ringtone.

"I'm going to have to call them back pretty quick. Always on duty. Go back to your hotel. Get writing. Your room is paid for there as long as you need to stay. I've made sure of it. Call me if you need me for anything."

I finally get a glimpse of her screen to see who is calling. "Veronica."

One of the Smith triplets? Is Veronica Smith a client?

"Who do you think killed Gray?" I flat out ask her as she signs the bill, leaving a 50 percent tip.

"Not Rebecca," she says with intense certainty. "And that's all that matters."

"Is it?"

"Yes, it is." She stands. "Goodbye, Lizzie. I'll see you soon."

Before she can reach the exit she pivots on her heel and doubles back. "Can I have another Twizzler?"

"Um, sure."

"Also one more question: What do you want?"

"What do you mean?"

"When this is all over what do you want?" I continue to stare at her dumbly. No one ever asks me what I want anymore.

"I want Rebecca and her kids to be safe. I want to know that she didn't do it. I want justice."

"Right. Of course. All those things. But what do you want for you?"

It's such an odd and seemingly inappropriate question given the circumstances.

"I want to write again, to report out real stories again." It erupts out of my mouth like it was waiting in there this entire time. "But it feels impossible."

Olivia gives a satisfied nod. "Elizabeth, I'm a gay Black woman living in God's chosen countryside. We make our own success. Nothing is impossible. You can do anything you put your mind to."

She's deadly serious. "Okay. Good to know your dreams. I like knowing people's dreams." With that she strolls out the door, Twizzler dangling from between her fingers.

Who the hell is this woman and what kind of a game is she playing with all of us?

Rebecca Sommers's Picture-Perfect Life Was Far from Perfect
By Elizabeth Matthews

Like many of you, I've been watching Rebecca Sommers's Instagram and YouTube channels with a sort of morbid curiosity over the years. She was beautiful. Her family was beautiful. It all seemed so perfect. But nothing is perfect. No marriage, no parent-child relationship, no friendship. I was friends with Rebecca a long time ago, back in college. I called her Bex then. We all did.

Bex was a force of nature. So smart, so driven. Insanely ambitious but always up for a good time. When we lost touch almost fifteen years ago, I was devastated, and reconnecting recently meant a lot to me. But in reconnecting I learned something about Rebecca's seemingly picture-perfect marriage to Grayson Sommers that I am only sharing now because I think we all need to understand that what we saw on our screens was not Rebecca's reality...

CHAPTER FIFTEEN

REBECCA

When you have kids you're never truly alone, but it's still possible to be painfully lonely.

Once I became a mother my loneliest moments came in the middle of the night, after I'd gotten a colicky baby to bed, after I'd rocked them for hours and hours, bounced up and down on my toes until my calves burned because the babies liked the vertical sensation better than the side to side.

I'd crawl back into my bed, next to a sweaty toddler who refused to sleep alone, and stare up at the ceiling fan as Gray snored blissfully next to me. Even though he didn't drink he took prescription pills to sleep. Not that I think he would have gotten up with the babies anyway.

"I'm terrible with them," he said any time he tried to do anything. Pure weaponized incompetence.

Sleep always eluded me, and I felt more alone than I ever had in my entire life.

Back then our church leaders encouraged us new mothers to keep journals and even start blogs where we wrote about our life with our children. "Show the world your joy. Connect with other women going through what you are bearing," the pastor said. It was easy to start pretty soon after I had my first, Alice. Took about five minutes in the dead of night to create a blog on Word-Press and the confessional nature of it was addicting at first. I kept going when the others came along. I couldn't tell the truth exactly, but I could write a version of it that made what I was doing as a mother feel right and good. I *was* serving out my purpose. I could complain about the colic, but I could also post pictures of my gorgeous babies, and other women would comment and tell me I was doing a good job, that the kids were perfect, that I was perfect. It was the validation I didn't know I needed.

My first truly viral post was about natural birth. I delivered Alice in the hospital, which made sense given everything we had been through to get pregnant with her. I wasn't taking any chances.

I even had an epidural, which Gray thought was unnecessary, but I'd insisted after being in labor for forty-seven excruciating hours. I'll always remember that gauzy, hazy tingle in my lower half, the way I was completely present for Alice's birth, but not in agony. I'll always remember it because it never happened again.

Gray told me I was weak for not doing it the natural way. *As weak as you are when you can't fall asleep without an Ambien?* I wanted to snap, but I didn't.

"Drugs don't agree with you. Remember how hard it was for you to wean off them back in San Francisco?" Gray had said. It was the only time he ever mentioned the incident from back then. And it felt like a warning of sorts.

Our ranch was quite far from the hospital, and when Willow came along, Gray insisted we could manage just as well at home with the same midwife who had delivered him and maybe some help from Dr. Carmichael if we needed it. Who was I to disagree? I had been blessed again, or so I believed. Our lives were filled with abundance.

Gray filmed the birth on my phone. I don't even remember him doing it. I didn't ask him to. I don't remember anything. I became a wild animal in those moments as Willow began to rip her way through my unmedicated body. I howled like a beast and scratched at the wooden floor so hard that I will always be able to see the marks. I barely made it into the water where I had planned to give birth.

"It's normal," the midwife assured me. This was the pain of the sacrificial mother, the pain all women must go through in order to be purified for motherhood. But I had already been "purified." I had Alice. I had been a mother for two years.

In the midst of it all Gray filmed me as I screamed in horror. Then out came the baby. Everything went black. I didn't find the video until much, much later. We took so many pictures of Willow, and of Alice holding her, that the video of the birth was buried deep in my photo stream. I only discovered it when I was pregnant again. I was looking for the last picture I'd taken when Willow was still in my belly. I wanted to show it to her to prepare her for the new baby.

By that point I had been blogging regularly about our life on the ranch. I didn't think I would love it as much as I did. And for all Gray's swagger about how he wanted to get back to the land and get his hands dirty he never seemed entirely comfortable with the hard work of farm life. He liked it when things went right, but 90 percent of things go wrong on a farm. And that's if you're lucky. I was always stepping in to find solutions to our problems. When the bison broke out of the paddock I found us steel fencing. When all of the chickens caught a virus and stopped laying, I figured out how to get them inoculated. You would hardly know that Gray grew up on the ranch. The more time we spent there the more he seemed like a bumbling city boy. But I didn't write about that. I would never. I blogged about the beauty of it all. I wrote about mothering the babies, about my devotion to our church and our community. Though I remained skeptical of God, I did believe that it was the power of prayer that ultimately delivered my children to me.

I watched the video of me screaming in pain and thought, *Wow, other mothers should see this.* Until I had babies, I hadn't seen a woman give birth.

I edited the video slightly. I didn't include the worst of it—no one needed to see that—and I added some soothing music. I simply put a shine on it. It would be easier to digest that way. I also wanted to pretend that the next birth would be simple and beautiful because Gray again forbade me from going to the hospital. He told me I would be a failure as a mother if I couldn't make it through childbirth without drugs. He said so many things to me, and I began to believe them. I convinced myself I was doing a service by sharing the video, but I also wanted that same thrill I always got when I showed off my work of mothering. I wanted people to tell me I was strong. That I was capable. I wanted the assurance that I could do this again.

I hit POST.

It had millions of views within days. And most of the commenters seemed to love what I was doing. They wrote that they longed for a life like mine, that living on a ranch was their fantasy while they toiled away at their desks from nine to five. When the next babies came the attention only amplified. My audience loved babies. They loved me. I wasn't lonely anymore. I had all these new friends.

That feeling didn't last, but it was a high for a long time. I started baking again. It had always been my salvation, but now it was more than that. It was almost an addiction. Éclairs, croissants, peasant bread. I made Oreos from scratch one day and then ketchup the next. The attention was addicting, but it was also lucrative. Sponsors reached out to me by sliding into my DMs. They wanted to know if I would wear their dresses, use their frying pans, try their natural nipple balms. I said yes, yes, and yes. Gray didn't need to know. By then he was on the road so much. He had a couple of start-ups going, had invested in real estate in the dodgy part of the city, and was already considering a run for office. The ranch bled money. My husband was by no means a real cowboy. He could ride a horse, but he passed out the first time he had to castrate a bull calf. And having a staff was expensive. By the time Gray realized what I was doing he was grateful for the infusion of cash. He even agreed to be in some of my posts and reels, but only if he got approval of them first. He was so vain.

He did like doing workout videos together because he had invested in a bunch of fitness and creatine supplements. He was fine doing anything he considered "manly."

That's when Olivia showed up on my doorstep. Out of the blue.

She grinned like a wolf when I opened the door. "I'm gonna change your life."

CHAPTER SIXTEEN

LIZZIE

C ome to a secret dinner," she whispers in my ear.

I turn my head to look behind me, but the woman is standing directly in the sun, and I can't make out who she is at first. My eyes stare at the perfectly tanned and toned legs that seem to go on and on and then the modest but stylish one-piece bathing suit in blue gingham. Finally, the halo of blue-black hair rippling in the wind comes into focus.

Veronica Smith in the flesh.

She's here.

The article I wrote for *Modern Woman* about Bex and what she's been through got the most traffic of anything we've published in two years. There's no way Alana is letting me out of here. And after what I've seen and my talk with Olivia, I'm committed. I'm in.

This time I wrote the truth as best I could. Occasionally my own emotions got the best of me, and I had to rein them in. We published both of the photographs, the old and the new. Obviously, we couldn't say that it was Grayson who hurt Bex. I have no proof, but I also have no doubt.

The Internet is deeply divided over the photos. There's currently a SAVE BAREFOOT MAMA campaign running, complete with memes and GIFs. No one is clear on what exactly Bex can still be saved from. The damage has been done. Grayson Sommers is dead. The same "citizen journalists" who castigated her only twenty-four hours earlier are now desperate to get to the bottom of the abuse. They're trying Gray Sommers in absentia, combing through a decade of visuals on Bex's accounts looking for more evidence. They claim they see a bruise here, a scratch there. One believes they have cracked a secret code within her captions where Bex was consistently crying out for help.

There's a second camp too, one filled with defenders of Grayson. They claim the images are doctored; that Bex is a delusional narcissist, desperate for attention; that she probably hurt herself just to make Grayson look bad.

The cops called me this morning. They want to talk and now I think I need a lawyer so I told them I'd be there tomorrow morning with our *Modern Woman* attorney on conference call. I may also ask Olivia to join me. I touched base with Peter to check on the kids and was reassured but also slightly put out that everyone seemed to be faring so well without me.

For the next couple of hours, I'm letting myself soak in the good life. It would be a travesty for a lovely pool to go to waste, even given the circumstances. Yes, everything that's happened in the past five days has been horrific. But frankly it's also the first vacation I've been on without kids in years and even with all the drama it's still easier than keeping my kids from pooping in the pool before drowning.

I braved the precarious swinging rope bridge this morning with my laptop in tow and I've been working from a chaise on the mesa for a few hours. I could get used to this, though I miss Peter and the kids. I haven't sat alone by a pool since our honeymoon. As soon as I got myself settled, a waiter brought me a complimentary papaya smoothie. Just because. A cool towel scented with eucalyptus was draped on the back of my neck. Every so often someone appeared to ask what I needed, what would make me more comfortable, how could I feel more zen. After years of ignoring my own needs, being cared for feels like the ultimate gift.

I'm typing away with my earbuds in, munching on lightly buttered zucchini flowers, when I hear the sultry whisper. For the past twenty-four hours I've pored over all of Smith's media channels.

Knowing she could also be working with Olivia has made her even more interesting to me. And if she truly was having an affair with Gray that could be my next story. In fact, she could also very well be a suspect in this case. If he hurt Bex maybe he hurt her too. Or maybe she wanted revenge because he refused to leave Bex. Maybe she has nothing to do with this at all, but it's something to pursue while I have no other leads.

And reading about her is addictive anyway. So is watching her. I can't stop. Like Bex, she has "it," even if the content of her videos isn't necessarily my cup of tea. She's sweet as pie one minute and militant and controlling the next. She's a drill sergeant dressed like a picnic table. She's obsessed with carrot-and-stick parenting, a form of discipline that seems to border on abuse, but her audience adores it. They want to know everything about her life and her parenting techniques for her four boys—Jaxon, Callum, Finn, and Revy. They want a constant rundown of her days, and most of all, they want to know how to land a man like Marsden.

Her voice from all the videos now rings in my ears. She lives in my brain.

"Hey, guys, and welcome back to my channel! Today, I'm going to be giving some tips for the ladies on how to attract a masculine man—a provider man," she says in one clip.

"Thank god I didn't waste my twenties chasing career success and instead devoted them to raising babies and caring for my man. My life is truly filled with purpose," she insists in another.

"Let me tell you the six habits that turn my momming game up to eleven. I rise before the sun is up. I work out hard daily and do it first thing in the morning. Working out gives me vibrant energy that coffee cannot re-create and puts me in a positive headspace with my kids. Every supermama needs a superpower. Endorphins are mine," she explained as she tried to sell me a workbook to better organize my entire life called *Mom So Hard*.

One video rolled into the next and into the next. Before I knew it, I'd lost two hours and I desperately wanted to be the kind of woman who could wake up at five in the morning and do burpees. I had to genuinely admire her dedication to running her household with the iron fist of a *Fortune* 500 CEO. I admittedly run mine more like an illegal day care overseen by Oompa Loompas.

"Excuse me?" I say to Veronica now, popping out an earbud.

"Come to dinner tonight? A few of us have organized something. Since the conference isn't really happening anymore we decided to make the most of the time. I'm Veronica, by the way. We met in the lobby on the first day."

"I remember," I say, and sit up properly. When I do, she sits down next to my legs, perching beside me like we're old friends.

"My family owns this place, you know."

"The Sensoria?"

"Yup. Always has. I learned to swim in that pool and got potty trained in one of the suites." She laughs at the silliness of it.

"I thought it used to belong to a Spanish countess." I remember the fact from my tour when I arrived.

"My great-grandmother," she says. "And then it went to her son and then my dad. But he died without a boy. Only three daughters, heaven forbid, so what happens next with the property is totally up in the air. It'll probably go to one of our husbands."

"Can't it just go to you?"

"Probably not."

"That's annoying."

She shrugs as if to say, *Of course it's annoying, but it's also a fact of life and how dare I question it.*

"So, what do you say? Secret dinner." She drops her voice conspiratorially and rubs her palms together as she says *secret* and then delivers a husky laugh.

"I guess. When? Where?"

"All excellent questions." She crosses her legs and tips her face up to the sun. "We're setting it up at sunset out in the desert. Over there." She gestures toward the expanse. "Behind Devil's Staircase. Invite only."

"Devil's Staircase?"

"That rock formation. Look at the horizon, slightly to the left. The rock that looks like a spiral staircase. Do you see it?"

I squint into the distance and can sort of make it out.

"Why Devil's Staircase? It looks like it's going up. Wouldn't the devil be . . . you know . . . in the other direction?" As if I'm some sort of scriptural expert.

"It also goes down. Straight down into the gorge on the other side. Straight into hell." She says this with a wide smile. I remember her vacant expression from Marsden's statement about Gray. The way he squeezed her leg. In person she's the opposite of that stiff woman. She's electric.

"So I just walk out into the desert and look for a table or something?"

"Be on the patio at five. We have dune buggies."

"Can I write about it?"

"Not about the dinner. It's a safe space for everyone, but I'm dying to get you next to me at dinner. I'd love to talk to you about some things."

"I'll see you at five."

"Looking forward to it." She gives a beauty queen wave and sashays away. She's even more of an enigma than Olivia Jackson.

* * *

I study the other women waiting for the dune buggies to take us out to the ominous Devil's Staircase. What had I expected? All women like Veronica? All of the tradwives? This mix is more eclectic than that. Every single variety of influencer is present. Trads, Hens, Fitness, Bosses.

I see the pregnant panelist who had been onstage that first day, @B0ssBabe$$$.

Her real name is Amy Weisberg, according to her badge, which everyone is still inexplicably wearing. I vaguely remember what she said on the stage: "I am a multi-hyphenate human who goes with the flows of the moon to show up authentically for myself and my community." I wonder if she always speaks in code, and I sidle up to her and introduce myself.

"When do you head home?" she asks.

"Soon," I say vaguely.

"It feels like we're all trapped. Stuck here while we wait for flights back."

I'd heard this from a few of the women. There had been a big basketball tournament in the city this week, along with some college graduations, so no one has been able to switch to earlier flights. Everyone is in a holding pattern at this hotel. No conference to occupy their time, but still plenty of networking to be done.

"I'm a reporter, actually. I was covering MomBomb and now I'm working on some pieces about Grayson Sommers." Why lie. Why pretend. Amy flinches at his name.

"Right. You wrote that piece for *Modern Woman*. I read it twice. It's awful. What he did to her. I can't get those images of her out of my mind. You were brave for writing that. Wherever Rebecca is . . . I hope she saw it."

I don't say that I hope so too. That it *was* the point, or some of the point at least, of me writing it.

"I thought tonight's dinner was going to be off the record though," Amy says nervously, rubbing circles around her belly. "I love talking to press. Don't get me wrong, always be branding, but I don't want to be involved in the Grayson Sommers story. I'm sure you can understand . . . the optics."

"I'm not working tonight," I assure her, now afraid that I've made a miscalculation coming here at all. "Please don't worry. I'm here as a guest." That's a half-truth. Is anyone ever not working these days? Aren't we always on? Isn't she searching for content here in the desert? Someone will probably be live streaming this dune buggy ride. Someone is probably live streaming us right now.

I see Veronica's sisters, Betty and Skipper. So strange that I feel like I know them intimately despite never speaking to them.

Betty is much less militant than Veronica in her videos. She's a silly mom who loves pranking her kids and making slime. Making slime seems to be a whole influencer category unto itself. Skipper does mostly unboxing videos where she and her kids open dozens and dozens of boxes of toys a week. Where does she keep it all? The three of them live in massive houses, but still. The Barbies alone look like they'd take up the back of a Mack truck.

I look around for Katie, the easygoing woman I sat next to on day one at the conference, but she's nowhere to be found. She must have found a way out, must have gotten a flight. Or maybe she's a local. We hadn't gotten into too many personal details. I just liked her straightforward, no-bullshit vibe and view on this world, and I wish I'd gotten more of it. She'd make a fun dinner companion and maybe a good source.

Cricket's still here too. I wonder how Chad feels about that. Chad is probably not very happy. I'll bet babysitting his kids is driving him crazy. She gives me a wide smile before strapping herself into the first vehicle that arrives to whisk us all away. I've never been in one of these. It's a glorified golf cart with massive wheels and seat belts that go over your head and strap across the chest like on a roller coaster.

"Would you like some goggles?" a hotel employee asks. "To protect your eye makeup." I see everyone strapping goggles to their faces. Who knows what sand does to false lashes. No one wants to be the first to find out.

"Wait for me," a voice calls out. Through the sandy haze I see a petite brunette jogging toward us. She's in jeans and a T-shirt, her face free of makeup. Katie.

I wave for her to take the empty seat next to me. She collapses into it, breathless.

"I haven't seen you around," I say. "I thought you'd left."

"No. Still here. Just busy . . . I've been hunkered down in my room, but then I heard about this dinner." She shrugs. "I want to talk to as many of these women as possible. My app is going into beta and I want them to try it out."

"Did Veronica invite you today too?"

"Yeah. At the last minute. I was kind of shocked. Maybe she messed up."

I doubt Veronica messes anything up. Whoever is here is meant to be here.

The parade of dune buggies sets off in single file across the sand and then up the smooth rocks, across the vast expanse to Devil's Staircase as the sun winks on the horizon.

Distances are deceptive in the desert. The drive is longer than I expected. It's dark by the time we arrive nearly an hour later. We're on a plateau of flat rock on the edge of the spiral. As Veronica had explained we're at a midway point. The stairs ascend to the stars and then continue down the rock face into the vast canyon below. Dinner is served on a flat outcropping in between the two. We're on a plateau of purgatory.

There are at least ten vehicles, each carrying four women. Perhaps this isn't as exclusive as Veronica had made it seem. The entire expanse is lit by tiki torches and fairy lights that must be plugged into some electric generator. Two long tables with ten seats on either side are waiting for us. As I step out of the cart a handsome man in too-tight black pants and a white button-down shirt that hugs his intensely toned physique holds out a black bag.

"Your phone, please."

"Excuse me?"

"Your phone. We'll be keeping them for the duration of the dinner."

I feel naked the second my device is gone. Naked and slightly anxious. There should be a German word for that, I think, for the anxiety you feel when your phone is out of reach.

Music plays. A soothing but slightly ominous symphony and I'm reminded of Olivia's ringtone. Will she be here tonight? I received a single text from her after I published my latest piece and all it contained was a thumbs-up emoji.

Another handsome young man who looks barely out of college approaches with a tray of canapes.

"The waiters are very good-looking," I say to Katie.

"So handsome," she agrees. "Veronica's family is a big donor to the university here. They're probably undergrads."

"I feel slightly filthy ogling them like this."

"Maybe that's the point of them being so good-looking," Katie says. "To remind us to be good. That seems like Veronica. Dangling temptation right in front of you." I wonder how well Katie knows Veronica, but then, as if we've conjured her, our host for the evening appears from behind a massive boulder. No dress on tonight. Instead she's clad in all black. Still slightly retro, but more of an early sixties vibe than the fifties. She's got on snug black pedal pushers and a black turtleneck. Her hair is pulled into a high and tight ponytail and she's wearing large tortoise-framed reading glasses. She could be going to a beat poetry reading, about to slam some Ginsberg. I see her approach her sisters' clique of ladies with hugs and kisses on the cheek.

"Will there be booze here?" I ask Katie.

"Doubtful. Veronica definitely doesn't drink and her house, her rules, but someone here probably has some of that chocolate with magic mushrooms in it. They all started on psilocybin last year for depression and anxiety. Trying to be perfect all the time probably breaks them. But I think the drugs just make them even weirder."

"Drugs are allowed?"

Katie shrugs. "As long as their doctors prescribe it. I also think it keeps them docile. Like sheep."

"So Veronica's father is the owner of the hotel?"

"Was. Died last year. Now the board is figuring out what to do with it. God forbid they give it to his three successful, competent daughters. Did you just find all this out? I thought everyone knew. The Smith family is probably the richest in the state. But her dad had three girls. Imagine his disappointment that he had no one to leave this empire to."

"I suppose he was delighted then when Veronica married Marsden."

"That's an understatement." Katie scoffs as she flags down a waiter for another appetizer. "It was practically an arranged marriage. Probably planned from the womb. She was pretty much a child bride from what I know. Veronica definitely didn't have much of a say in it. They're super conservative. It was one of those stay-at-home-daughter situations where the girls are groomed for nothing but marriage."

"Stay-at-home daughter?"

"Like they're wedded to their fathers and trained to do all the wifely things until they can be passed on to a man. Veronica has been married to Marsden since she was seventeen. Never even went to college."

"Wow. So you're from here. You know all the gossip."

"I'm not from here at all. I grew up in Southern California. I work here. It's been about ten years now. And I live here."

"So the app isn't a full-time job?"

"Oh god, no. It's a hobby. For now. A very expensive hobby. But I hope . . . we always hope, right?"

"What do you do? For work?"

"I'm a nanny," she says.

"Is there even a market for that out here?" I think about what Bex told me about her own childcare situation, how she had help but never talked about it.

"Huge market. You just need to be discreet. But I've been with the same employer this whole time. We have an understanding." I think I see her grimace, but the tiki torches are casting all kinds of strange shadows over everything so I can't be sure.

"Do you like the family?"

"I love the kids like they're my own." Nothing about the parents.

Before we can chat more, Veronica strides over to us. She reaches out a perfectly manicured finger to pluck a stray hair off Katie's jacket and flicks it into the wind.

"How'd you like the ride out? Gorgeous, right?"

"It is," I agree. "Why'd you take our phones?" I ask pointedly.

Veronica wags a finger like a stern mother. "Because you don't need them. Be present. Enjoy the moment." She floats away, somehow graceful in the teetering heels despite the slippery surface of the rocks.

Of course, there are place cards for where we should be sitting, like a wedding. How did Veronica manage to pull off something so elaborate in about twenty-four hours when I can't even get four moms over to my house to split a bottle of wine with a month's notice?

Katie huffs in indignation when Veronica strides away. "Bitch."

"Why did you come if you hate her?"

She hesitates. "I wanted to network, but I also wanted to see . . ."

"See what?"

"Just see . . . I don't know. Yeah, it's good for work, but I also want to know what Veronica is up to with this dinner." Her sigh is exhausted and defeated, and I wonder if she wishes she hadn't gotten on that dune buggy. A part of me wishes I hadn't come. We're stuck out here now, for god knows how long, doing god knows what. It's like when you agree to one of those all-you-can-drink boat parties that are lovely for the first hour or so, but then you're stuck on a boat and you can't get off and you can't drink any more watered-down gin and tonics because there's only one bathroom.

That reminds me. A bathroom. Are we supposed to go pop a squat behind the Devil's Staircase?

The wind is picking up. There's sand in it so it's rough when it whips past my cheeks and then blows over one of the tiki torches, sending a gaggle of women in long calico skirts scurrying away lest they ignite.

"We should get started," Veronica calls out. The handsome waiters turn into sheepdogs, gently herding all of us into smaller and smaller circles. I shiver, wishing I'd brought a sweater to cover my bare shoulders. The desert is colder and darker at night than I ever imagined. But Veronica has thought of this. She's thought of everything. Portable heaters are wheeled out from somewhere. They surround the tables as we sit in front of small cards bearing our names in beautiful cursive script. Katie and I are nowhere near each other and I'm sad we can't continue our conversation. I get the feeling there's something going on with her. Some other reason she's here.

I'm seated between two of the women in the long calico skirts. They look handmade, possibly out of rags. That means they're probably expensive. The shabbier the material these days, the higher the price tag. They both smile sweetly at me, and I feel like I'm flanked by matching Anne Shirley bookends. Veronica is directly across from me.

The wind is only getting worse. A fine layer of sand now coats the table in front of us. A dozen straw hats have already been lost to the elements. I watched them whisk away on the current of the breeze and then waft over the edge of the steep cliff, which is much too close for my comfort.

"I'm so happy you're all here." Veronica has to yell to be heard. We should abandon this endeavor sooner rather than later. Where are the dune buggies? Did they leave us here or are they waiting just around the rocks? Will Veronica abort this event or see it through no matter what the desert chooses to do to us?

"It's getting brisk out here. But that's normal right after sunset. The wind will calm down, I promise you. And we've faced worse, right, ladies? We don't head inside at the first sign of discomfort." It's reminiscent of her Instagram messaging, plow through the pain, toughen up your spirit through prayer and CrossFit.

This elicits a cheer. We all want to be told that we're strong. That we're capable and can do hard things. I want it too. When was the last time someone gave me actual praise or complimented my work ethic or mothering?

"Two rules for this evening. You know how much I love my rules." The crowd giggles. "A couple of subjects will be off-limits. We can't talk about our kids, and we can't talk about social media or the work we are doing."

"Then what will we talk about?" one woman shouts over the wind. Joking, but not joking.

"Ourselves. Our dreams. Our chosen paths. Our audiences might never know the real us, but we should share that with each other. I've been praying a lot. Telling God that I want more connection. I've been asking for inspiration. I know that I am meant to spread my wings. It's what the Good Lord desires for me and I am ready to follow his directions. If I were in control of my own destiny, perhaps I could remain working in our home forever, but that is not what God is calling me to do."

I'm trying to translate in my head. If it were up to her, Veronica would be content to be a housewife and stay-at-home mom forever, but God wants more for her? It's God who is controlling her ambition? That's quite a handy way around the patriarchy.

She's still going, in the careful cadence of a megachurch preacher. In another life she could have been one of those preachers. She's that compelling.

One of the things I learned from my dive down the Smith triplets rabbit hole is that Veronica doesn't just dole out advice on her social media. She is also selling it. She sells courses for $49.99 on how to run your household like a business. She has an entire line of vitamins for the "modern mother who needs more energy to do the Lord's bidding." She's a rich woman who is minting more money and cloaking it inside the coziness of God's plan for her. What a brilliant scam.

"I'm made for more and so are all of you. That's what we are here to discuss tonight. What are you made for?"

It's a question that shouldn't feel so uncomfortable and I don't enjoy the swirl of emotions it brings up inside me.

A second tiki torch tumbles over in the wind, but Veronica merely throws back her raven mane and laughs into the gale.

"You've got this. You are all queens. We are all queens. Queens of the desert." She extends both her arms wide and twirls around in a circle. I feel like she's gonna sell me a time-share or indoctrinate me into a cult. And maybe I'll say yes.

"Great things rarely come from sitting in comfort zones!"

The waiters push through the weather to bring out our first course, an arugula salad in hand-thrown pottery that's so lumpy and strange it looks like it could have been made by ten-year-olds. We're all silent at first. Are we all so used to talking about our kids and our work? What else is there? My husband? My marriage? I don't have a single hobby to speak of. I'm either parenting or working. It's who I am.

It's who most women I know are. Men have hobbies; women struggle to take a shower.

Everyone around me is pushing their arugula around on their plates. I'm glad to know I'm not alone in not knowing what to say.

"What is God calling you to do?" the woman to my right asks me. Before I can answer, a crack of lightning illuminates the sky. We should have noticed the black and purple clouds blotting out the stars, but we were so focused on being praised as queens. Only seconds later comes a boom of thunder so intense I feel it in my bones. The wind whips over the table, taking with it flower arrangements in crystal vases, the napkins, and the plates. Three tiki torches tumble over, sending us into blurry darkness. One torch picks up speed as it rolls over the rock, only stopping when it slams into the leg of one of the tables. The flames appear to leap from the lantern to the white cloth, which lights up with a furious vengeance. That's when the rain comes. Sharp staccato streams of water, which will hopefully calm the flames, but are also making the rock slippery as we all clamber for safety. None of us can see. The edge is so near, the canyon so deep. Anyone could topple down the Devil's Staircase at a moment's notice. A scream comes out of the darkness and then another one.

Everyone panics until the plateau is illuminated in twin beams of headlights. The dune buggies have arrived. We may be saved. We may not.

"Get in," Veronica yells out. Her tranquility finally punctured. Someone grabs my arm. I look behind me. Katie.

"Flash floods come on fast out here. We've got to go," she shouts into the wind. The tablescape is still burning despite the torrent of rain. I can barely see as the raindrops sting my eyes, but I make my way to the waiting vehicles. We're all pushing to reach them. It's an unruly scrum of soaking-wet women desperate for escape.

I make it into one of the vehicles. There's no roof to protect us. As soon as the four seats are taken the driver steps on the gas and we're off. Rain and sand mix to coat us in mud.

Another scream punctures the darkness.

"Help me," a voice yells into the void. "Help!"

"We have to stop. We have to go back," I scream at the driver. He doesn't seem to hear me. Or maybe he does and keeps going anyway. I'm pinned to the back of my seat from the velocity of the cart. We're sliding all over the place. I remember how deep the canyon was on the edge of the plateau. One wrong turn and that's where we'll be.

One of the tires snags on a jagged rock and my side of the vehicle flies off the ground. Blood rushes through my skull and I'm close to blacking out. I reach over for Katie, though I can barely make her out through the rain. Her head is bowed. I think she's praying.

My eyes keep searching the horizon for the hotel, but there's nothing. We must be going in the wrong direction. What had the woman told me during my tour? There's a hundred miles of open desert this way. No one will ever find us.

I find Katie's hand. Our fingers are slippery, but we try to hold on until finally the outline of the hotel appears in front of us. It's a mere shadow in the darkness, almost a mirage. The power must have gone out during one of the lightning strikes. But still, we're safe.

We reach the circular driveway and workers rush toward us with plush towels.

"Someone is hurt back there." I'm hysterical and I don't know if anyone is listening to me as they swarm me with warm towels that smell vaguely of eucalyptus.

Finally one hotel employee responds, "We'll take care of it. Don't worry. Please don't worry."

But how will they get there? Out the massive windows I can see headlights from the other vehicles making their way back here. Another slash of lightning. The thunder fast after it. It's close. So close. I can smell singed earth.

The lobby is lit with an abundance of candles, most of them lavender- and cedar-scented ones from the gift shop.

"The generators will kick in soon," the young woman behind the desk says calmly. "Any minute now."

Katie is frantic, her eyes darting around the room. "The elevators are out?" she says.

"They are. But you can use the stairs."

She makes a mad dash for the fire door. Before I can think about what I'm doing, I follow her, curious about why she's so desperate to get upstairs. An employee chases after me and thrusts a flashlight into my hand. Only then do I realize that I don't have my phone. It's still in that black bag. Probably still out on the rocks or dropped down into the chasm. Lost forever.

I can just make out Katie's footsteps in the stairwell. She's only one floor above me. I take the stairs two at a time with the same energy I used to sprint out of Rebecca's house just yesterday. The door to the second floor slams in my face as I reach it. Once it's open I see Katie rushing down the hall, squatting and opening her arms to a small figure hunched in the hallway. By the time I reach them, Katie's clutching the person; they're rocking back and forth and Katie is soothing them.

"It's okay. It's okay. You're safe. You're fine."

I hear the distinct cries of a child.

Katie doesn't notice that I'm here, she's so focused on comforting the little creature in her arms. I kneel down next to them.

"What can I do?"

I have to repeat myself a couple of times before Katie squints into the glare of the flashlight. The look on her face is one of horror and fear. She doesn't want me here. And when the little girl lifts her head I can see why.

I gasp as I look into Rebecca's daughter's pale white face, streaked with tears. "Alice?"

CHAPTER SEVENTEEN

REBECCA

It was less than a year ago that I realized my husband had betrayed me in the worst possible way.

He never thought I would find out. What kind of sick son of a bitch keeps that sort of secret from his wife? One who loves control and power, that's who. One who has lost both of those things and knows it.

I'll back up a little. There's a whole universe in which I might never have found out what he had done—had been doing for over a decade. It's maybe a little ironic that I learned about it because of my influencing job, because I've been desperate to keep us all afloat since he lost so much of his family's money.

About a year or so ago, I got a big sponsorship from Genealogy Genius, one of those DNA testing kits that have been all the rage for a few years, the kind that promise to tell you all sorts of personalized genetic insights like whether you have celiac disease or type two diabetes or if cilantro tastes like soap and mosquitoes like to bite you. Genealogy Genius could also show you where your ancestors likely came from and maybe match you with relatives you didn't know you had. The deal was a big one and I had to promise to test my entire family. I didn't like that. I'm protective of my children and their identities. I said no at first and then they doubled the price tag. We needed the cash to keep things going.

I figured maybe I would do one test with just me and maybe Alice and it would be up to me what information I would reveal to my followers. I could always make something up. No one needed any of our real data. Besides, who knew what the tests would turn up. Maybe I'd finally learn something about my long-lost father that my mother never spoke about.

To fulfill my deal, I had to at least send the tests back to the lab. Alice and I both spit into a little test tube and swabbed our cheeks with giant Q-tips. I still wonder what would have happened if I hadn't tested her. I never would have known what Gray had done.

My phone pinged with a text when the results came in. First, I scrolled through the ancestry overview. Irish, German, Dutch, Polish, 2 whole percent of Neanderthal DNA! Then the health traits. Nothing that surprising. My finger wavered over the button that would list potential DNA relatives. I understood that it would only list relatives who had also done this particular testing kit, but it was a massive company with reach all over the world. It wasn't crazy to think that my own missing father, or someone related to him, could have spit into a tube to unlock their genetic mysteries for $99.

I clicked on my genetic relatives first. A handful of second and third cousins with last names I recognized from my mom's side of the family. They shared approximately 3.3 percent and 2.5 percent of my DNA. No surprises. No long-lost dad and brothers and sisters. I allowed myself a brief moment to feel the disappointment I hadn't been expecting. Then I clicked through Alice's results.

Alice's ancestors were mostly the same. She was a pan-European mutt. No weird genetic variants that could predispose her to rare cancers. I almost didn't scroll through the relatives' DNA section. What could it possibly tell me that I didn't already know?

Turns out it would shatter my entire world.

My child, my little Alice, had relatives listed in the company's database who didn't make any sense, namely Marsden Greer's children. His wife, Veronica, had gotten the same sponsorship deal from the testing company so she had also tested her kids at the same time. Alice's test claimed that Marsden's kids were directly related to my child. They shared 25 precent of their DNA.

It wasn't possible. The lab must have gotten something messed up. All of us influencers were probably being tested at the same time and they mixed up someone's spit. It was probably bogus. Still, the chance that it wasn't clawed at my brain like a wild animal.

I needed to know more. First, I made sure that Alice's test wouldn't be made public like Veronica's kids' results were. I didn't want Veronica or Marsden to see what I saw when I logged onto that website. Then I tested Willow and waited two agonizing weeks for the results, the whole time questioning everything I thought I knew about my world. Same thing. Same half-siblings.

As I stared at the cheerful web page that identified my children's DNA connections, the room seemed to collapse inward. My thoughts spiraled, savage and unrelenting. I ignored James's cries when he woke from his nap as I tried to make my brain understand how this was possible.

The first thought that flitted through my head was that this had something to do with Gray's dad. He had practically raised Marsden, after all. Maybe he did it for selfish reasons. Maybe years ago he'd had an affair with Marsden's mom and they all kept it a secret. I had lived out in the desert long enough to know that even though everyone projects an absurd amount of piety, there is plenty of scandal happening behind closed doors.

Gray's dad must have had an affair with Marsden's mom. But that would make our children cousins, not siblings. The math didn't work.

I tested the other kids. The same connections appeared. It soon became clear to me that there was only one explanation for it.

Marsden Greer was their father.

Anxiety fed on my flesh. None of it made sense. I thought back to all those years of fertility treatments, the half dozen doctors I visited who couldn't figure out what was wrong with me. Was it polyps? No. Something wrong with my ovaries? Nope. Hormonal imbalance? Uterine scarring? Nope. Nope.

"Maybe we should check your husband?" one of them finally said. But Gray would have none of that. He was fine. He was virile.

He wouldn't allow it, and because he paid for all the tests and treatments out of pocket, I let him make those decisions. I was desperate to keep going and I began to believe him that the problem truly was all the stress I was under at work at the bakery. When we moved, I let him choose our new doctor, Dr. Carmichael. He'd been his own mom's doctor, had even delivered him and his siblings along with the midwife. Dr. Carmichael was also a powerful leader in the church. I trusted him. I respected him.

Confused and furious after receiving all the test results, I became a madwoman, desperate for more information to prove all of it wrong. At first, I wanted to call Dr. Carmichael, but something told me not to. Something told me to figure this out for myself.

I found a way to break into Gray's email. It wasn't nearly as hard as I'd expected it would be. His password was my birthday written out in long form. Going back through years and years of messages, I finally found what I was looking for.

Gray was infertile. He had been shooting blanks all those years. There was absolutely nothing wrong with me. Gray had a genetic condition that rendered him completely infertile. He'd gotten the sperm testing after all and kept it from me. There was an email where Dr. Carmichael suggested a sperm donor, at which Gray balked. A stranger contributing half of his children's DNA? Absolutely not. Carmichael suggested that someone close to Gray could be an option. His brother. He even suggested Gray's own ailing father. I threw up a little in my mouth when I read that email.

Gray's dad fathering his own grandchildren!

Who the hell did these men think they were, playing God, having all these conversations behind my back as if I didn't matter, as if I didn't even exist?

But no. That was wrong. I existed as the vessel to carry these children. And after that it was my job and duty to raise them and keep them safe. But having any authority over how they lived their lives or who they became? That was well outside my swim lane. The emails made it clear that I didn't need to know anything about what they were doing. Dr. Carmichael assured Gray there was a way he could mix another man's sperm with his own in a centrifuge and that the healthy sperm could help Gray's. I screamed then. I covered my face with my pillow and screamed for another hour.

It was bullshit pseudoscience and a massive lie designed to make Gray feel like less of a failure.

Gray was many things, many terrible things. He had hurt me physically that one terrible time all those years ago, back in San Francisco. But he had managed to redeem himself for a while after that. It was when I started making money to support us that he got mean again. That's when he began verbally cutting me to the bone. He'd told me I was worthless, that I would be nothing without his help, without his money. He had even dangled my failure to have children in front of me more than once, saying I never would have been able to conceive if it weren't for him and Dr. Carmichael. But he was projecting his own weaknesses on me. I'd rationalized all of this away by reminding myself of the financial stress he was under. And every time he was wicked to me, he found a way to make up for it. He would flip a switch and be gentle and kind for months on end, helping with the kids even though I could tell they drove him insane and he hated being with them for more than an hour at a time. He'd buy me presents we couldn't afford. He'd build a new porch swing so I could watch the sunset from my favorite spot in the house. I grew so used to the highs and the lows that they seemed normal to me. I was such a fool. It got harder to rationalize the more recent abuses. He never touched me hard enough to leave marks, but on two occasions he slipped something into my drink that made me practically comatose. He told the kids and the staff that "Mommy needed a little break," while he kept me practically paralyzed with drugs and taunted me during my few waking moments by telling me he'd take my children away from me and have me committed to a mental hospital.

He'd open my social media and read me the most hateful comments on my posts, things I'd learned years ago never to read.

"You're a fraud."

"Your kids must hate you."

The first time I came out of my drugged haze, I truly believed I was simply exhausted. Six kids! A multimedia business! A fucking farm to run! But the second time he did it, I knew in my bones something was wrong, and I stopped accepting food and drinks from him.

I kept going through my husband's emails, slowly piecing together the extent of the deceptions. Gray eventually relented and gave in to Dr. Carmichael, who was very persuasive.

"You'll never have children any other way," the good doctor wrote. "And how will that look?"

So Gray turned to the man he respected the most, the one whom he loved like a brother, and he asked him the most egregious of favors. This didn't take place on email. I would have been even more surprised if it did, so I never saw the exact exchange with Marsden. I had to imagine it.

In my mind I conjured Marsden's initial hesitation but puffed-up pride that Gray would be forced to even ask him for such a thing. I pictured Marsden enjoying the power this gave him over my husband, over the real son of the man he idolized as his father figure. At some point he must have agreed because appointments were made and when I looked at my own calendar I saw they lined up with my IUI schedule. IUI was explained to me very carefully when we first started out. It was a process where the doctor washes a sperm sample and then uses a thin catheter to inject millions of healthy sperm into the uterus at the time of ovulation. It was different from IVF. We wouldn't be creating an embryo, which was what the church considered a sin.

Dr. Carmichael simply substituted Marsden's sperm for my husband's, and I was kept completely in the dark.

I never questioned Alice's strawberry-blond hair, which came from neither of our families. Genetics can be so strange, I thought. And I'd never met my mother's parents or my own father, so what did I know? I never questioned anything about my perfect, gorgeous babies. I felt blessed. I felt saved. Gray and the church elders made sure of that. They attributed our little miracles to prayer and the fact that we lived our lives in service to Jesus Christ. We were good. We were chosen.

Once I got my first baby, I felt that same new comfort of protection like the time Gray rescued me from my apartment after the break-in. I was cared for.

Looking back, it explains so much. Why Marsden was the first person to visit us after the birth. After all the births. He literally wanted to see the fruit of his loins.

Why Gray was eventually so insistent on the home births

with only Dr. Carmichael and a midwife present. He wanted to keep all our medical information as private as possible. He didn't want a record at the hospital of the children's blood types because it could prove he wasn't their father.

It also explained why Marsden took such an intense interest in our kids when he had absolutely zero interest in me. I don't think Marsden ever asked me a single question about myself or even truly looked me in the eye.

Thousands of lies and half-truths. We have six children and none of them are biologically related to my husband.

And five of them are related to Marsden. Because James, our bonus baby, was a surprise. We didn't do any IUI fertility treatments to have James. At the time he was a miracle.

Once I learned the truth about what Gray and Marsden and Dr. Carmichael had done, I remembered Gray's intense surprise that I was able to get pregnant with James. But he must have attributed it to God's grace. He must have believed that he was cured. But he still never touched that baby if he could help it. We slept in separate bedrooms by then. Had perfunctory sex once a month. It was after James that we started the #WhoopieWith-YourSchmoopie challenge to make it seem like we were doing it all the time. I think we maybe slept together one or two times, but Grayson was into it because it made him seem like a stud and the church was very keen on promoting marital relations.

When I got pregnant with James, I just assumed that so many healthy births had somehow healed me of the problems that had plagued me for so long. I didn't think about the timing of the MomBomb 2019 conference and a night I spent with a certain single dad.

My children may not belong to my husband, but they *are* mine. That became even more true after the revelations. Those children were mine and mine alone. Marsden was nothing. He was a means to an end. An anonymous sperm donor. As I read those emails, as I looked at the genetic results, I made the decision that I would take complete control of their lives. I would finally be the mother they needed, the one who took agency over their futures, because they deserved better.

It was then that I finally said yes to all the deals I had turned down because Gray didn't approve of them. He didn't want me to do a cookbook or release a magazine with my face on it or star in a television show. He was fine with the money coming in if it wasn't obvious that I was running the show, if it was contained on the small screens of people's phones. Then we could all still pretend it was just a lucrative hobby. He wouldn't have to feel less than for not making as much money as I did. Once I made big deals with major media brands, all the figures would be public. People would *know* what I was worth.

I told Olivia we could finally go big. I channeled the energy I'd had fourteen years earlier when I wanted to be the biggest bakery franchise in the Bay Area. It was okay to want it all. It was okay to think outside the box. Gray's lies and obfuscations gave me the permission I needed to go against him.

I didn't confront him right away. I made all my plans first and I told no one but Olivia. I had to tell someone, and she was my best option. I had no real friends, no family to speak of. I longed to confide in Lizzie, but she was gone. I spoke to her in my head sometimes. Long conversations where I bared my soul and begged her for forgiveness.

My children's paternity wasn't the only thing I discovered in Gray's emails.

I discovered filthy love letters he sent to Veronica, hundreds of them over the years.

I remember the first time I saw you in church. I couldn't stop staring at your shiny braids. I wanted to yank on them, use them to pull you into me, wrap them around my hands as I devoured your luscious lips.

But now I need to pay for my sins. For coveting you all those years ago.

Now I want you to own me. I want you to possess me. Pin me down. Make me squirm. Tell me when I'm allowed to orgasm.

I tried to remember when Veronica moved to town and did the math. My stomach twisted and curled. She must have been ten when Gray first saw her in church. That was one of the tamest emails.

He'd sent them late at night, probably while lying in bed next to me.

I'd seen him scrolling her Instagram feed hungrily when he thought I wasn't watching. He was obsessed with his friend's wife. Gray had always wanted what Marsden had and vice versa.

I never expected Gray to cheat on me, but I wouldn't have put it past him and frankly I didn't care. His interest in sex with me had waned over the years. I had looked at his computer's browser history once before because I was curious about what kind of porn he watched. There were two extremes. The most boring vanilla sex MILF videos with women old enough to be his grandmother, and then intense female dominatrix videos where men were tied to a bed and degraded and humiliated verbally, but never touched. This all tracked with his emails to Veronica.

I was less upset about the affair than maybe I should have been. My marriage was over the second I found out about the paternity of the kids. Let Veronica have him. Let Marsden and Gray fight over her.

I also found what he had written to Lizzie all those years ago when I lay bruised and battered in his bed. He'd written to her from my email account but he had bcc'd himself.

Dear Lizzie,

You shouldn't have come out here. I didn't even ask you to come. I should have been more firm about the fact that I think we've grown apart and I don't want to see you. Get on with your own life. You're obsessed with me and it has to stop. I'm a little scared of you.

Rebecca

He had sent this and deleted it from my email. I never knew. I'd assumed Lizzie never got back in touch with me after her nasty texts because I'd ghosted her, but now I knew that I'd done so much more than that.

Gray, writing as me, had eviscerated her and made sure that our friendship and shared history were completely destroyed. He made sure that she would never want to be in my life again. He made sure that he would be the only person I could turn to.

There didn't seem to be a deep enough well of hate for what

I felt for my husband. I didn't just want him out of my life, I wanted to destroy him. But doing that would destroy my children. I had to be careful. I just needed to be able to leave him, not an easy task when every judge in the state drags a woman through the mud for requesting a divorce.

I knew three things: I needed Gray out of the way, I needed to keep my business, and I never wanted my children to know what their father had done. No one could ever know their connection to Marsden. So I had to make sure that both men would remain silent. No matter what.

I waited until all my potential deals were in place. Olivia was outstanding at brokering them. That's when I contacted Lizzie. I knew there was a chance she would say no, but I also hoped that I could get her back, that one day we could return to what we were. And I needed her. I needed her platform and her voice. I needed her empathy if I was going to do what needed to be done to escape from Gray.

It was only after I reached out to Lizzie, only after I signed all those contracts and all those deals, that I could confront Gray and Marsden about what I knew. It was the one part of my plan that I could not control, but it had to be done if I wanted their silence.

I had to proceed carefully. So carefully. Every detail had to be meticulously planned out or I would lose everything. Didn't I know how easily the world would turn against a woman defending herself? I needed all the ammunition. I needed their confessions.

I invited Marsden to breakfast in a public place, as public as possible because I worried what he might do to me in private.

He strode to our secluded table in the back of the small bistro I'd chosen in the city, oozing arrogance. At our wedding he stood next to Gray as the best man and gave a speech that was mostly about himself. Hours later he cupped my backside on my way to the bathroom and slurred into my ear, his breath hot and nauseating, "Let me know when you're ready for a real man." I think about that every time I see him, about his hand squeezing so hard it left a bruise. I'd had to explain that bruise to Gray by telling him I'd bumped into the side of a table. "Oops, I'm so clumsy." I knew even then that I could not come between Gray and Marsden.

He didn't marry Veronica until a few years later. He'd become a star by then, traveling the country with the ball team. I remember the first time he brought Veronica to our house. She was an actual teenager, just seventeen at the time, and she hardly spoke or met my eyes. She seemed terrified until I asked if she wanted to hold baby Willow. Her eyes lit up then. "I'm dying to have a baby girl," she gushed and cooed over the baby.

"How did you and Marsden meet?" I tried to start a conversation with her while the men were out throwing darts in the barn after dinner.

She cast her eyes away from me. "I didn't have a choice," she whispered.

"What?" I said, louder than I should have.

"I mean. I've always known him. Gray too. We grew up going to the same church. My daddy has had his eye on Marsden for a while. He knew he would be the perfect son-in-law."

Veronica's family was conservative, much more than we were. We were heathens compared to them. I knew plenty of those kind of people out here. The father chose his daughter's groom. She didn't have much of a say in it. The men came back in then and Veronica and I didn't speak any more. She started her own Instagram account where she cheered at Marsden's ball games, doted on his every play, and then she became a mom influencer just like me. I think she saw me as competition then because she always seemed like she was avoiding me. Little did I know she was probably carrying on with Gray behind my back.

"To what do I owe this honor, Your Highness?" Marsden smirked at me as he sat down.

"Just a catch-up." I smiled my thirty-six-thousand-dollar smile. That's the way I always think about it, because that's what it cost to fix the damage of not having proper dental care or braces as a child and replacing the tooth my husband had knocked out of my mouth. What I have now are veneers. My back teeth are mostly capped. My teeth were the only thing about my appearance that Gray criticized early on. He pointed out my snaggletooth, the grayish, crooked canine that I should have dealt with years earlier but had no money for. It ached all the time and even my top-notch dental care from the tech company I worked at right after college didn't cover what it would take to fix it. It's one of the reasons I rarely smiled with teeth for about twenty years. Now I do it as often as possible. And even though I had no reason to be happy or joyful, or generous or kind, I kept beaming at Marsden. I needed to catch him completely off guard.

"Should we order mimosas?" I studied the menu.

"Naughty girl. I thought you didn't drink."

I winked at him conspiratorially. "I won't tell if you won't."

He waved over the waiter and ordered absurdly expensive

drinks. I knew I would hardly taste mine and I'd be careful to only have a few sips. I needed all my faculties for what I was about to do.

Marsden ordered food for both of us. Matching egg white omelets. We were both apparently watching our figures. I let him gulp down his drink and tipped mine into a planter when he wasn't looking, so he would keep refilling the glasses from the pitcher on the table. We made small talk, or rather he did. It was the thick of baseball season but he was on the bench with an injury, something to do with his shoulder, so he wasn't traveling with the team, and according to him, that was the reason "they truly suck balls this season." But I knew the truth. I knew he was probably done for in the majors. We all knew it. It was part of the rumor mill. That's why he was branching out, trying to build some dumb app, investing in real estate just like Gray had and probably doing it as badly as my husband.

His chair inched slowly around the table as we nibbled on our respective eggs. By the time the waiter asked if we wanted dessert he was close enough I could hear him chew. He'd finished off most of the drinks himself, but he didn't know that.

"Should we be bad?" I giggled, pretending I was as squiffy as he was. "Should we order the chocolate cake?"

He placed his hand on my bare thigh then and it took every ounce of resolve inside me not to pull away like I'd been burned.

"I've been waiting a long time to be bad with you."

We ordered the cake. I got an espresso. He got a whiskey despite the early hour.

"So are you going to tell me why we're really here?" he asked, leaning in even closer.

"I am." I looked him straight in the eye, as sober as I'd ever been.

"Does it involve going somewhere after this?"

"I want to talk about my children first," I finally said as I hit the record button on my phone in my lap.

"Get them on the record," Olivia instructed when we made our plans. "Make them admit it. Then we can use it against them. We can get them to do whatever we want. The emails might not be enough."

"What about your kids?" Marsden mumbled.

"Well, maybe I should call them our children." That was the line I'd practiced over and over in my head. And I knew it would be the one time I said it in my entire life, because my children were not his. No matter what. No matter if Rider was left-handed like him, no matter that Alice had his strawberry-blond hair, that Willow had asthma that was likely genetic.

All the swagger melted out of him then. His face went from a ruddy pink to the color of wet concrete.

"What did Gray tell you?"

"Nothing. But I know the truth and I want you to tell me how you did it."

I thought his hubris would shine through then, that he would be happy and drunk enough to brag, but he clammed up. He stood to leave. I was desperate.

"I'm here to make a deal," I said. "I don't want you in their lives. I don't want Gray in their lives. I never want anyone to find out about this for as long as they live. Do you hear me?"

His eyes narrowed into slits. I could see the gears turning slowly behind them. What my husband, Marsden, and Dr. Carmichael did was illegal, unethical, and entirely immoral. They deserved to rot in jail for the rest of their lives. They deserved worse for how they had violated my body and my children's bodies. But I didn't want any of it to be public. I couldn't let it be my children's legacy.

I reached out to grab his arm. "I'll tell Veronica," I croaked in a strangled voice. I hated myself for sounding so desperate. He had barely said a word. I had played all my cards for nothing. I had no confession.

Marsden plastered a massive smile on his face, and I cringed when I noticed his dimples looked exactly like Alice's. Would I ever be able to look at my children and not see this vile man? He glanced around the room and then pulled out his wallet to drop money on the table. Another power move.

He whispered so only I could hear it. "Don't fuck with me, Rebecca. I'll destroy you."

I knew that he meant it. I knew I had to find a way to destroy him first. The clock was ticking.

* * *

I confronted Gray next. The children were off at an annual checkup in the city that I had hastily scheduled and asked Kiki to take them to.

It was a Thursday, but I told Stacy not to come. Media day would have to wait.

Gray and I had breakfast together, something we hadn't done in years, just the two of us alone. It was almost nice. Or at least it looked that way. He made me pancakes like he did when I was first pregnant with Alice, smothered in thick butter made right there on our farm. I wanted him to be calm when I confronted him. I even considered leading him up to our bedroom to use sex to lull him into submission, but every time I looked up at him I choked back bile so thick I worried I would gag and give myself away.

I had to scare him, catch him off guard.

So I lied.

"I'm pregnant," I told him through a perfect smile. My eyes never left his. What would he do? What would he think? He had accepted James as his own, but another one?

"Are you sure?" he stuttered.

"Positive." I placed my hand angelically on my belly. "Why do you look so surprised, Gray?" When our eyes met, I allowed my gaze to harden.

So did his. I felt the anger radiating off him. He knew he was being played, but he didn't know the game.

"Have you been to Dr. Carmichael to confirm?"

I shook my head. "I've decided to see a new doctor. Someone Olivia recommended."

"I don't think that's a good idea," he managed.

"I wanted to see a woman," I added for good measure, feeling like a cat dangling a mouse between its claws.

"You should see Dr. Carmichael to be sure."

"Is there anything you want to tell me, Grayson?"

"What do you think you know?" he snarled.

I suppose that standoff could have gone on all day. But I didn't let it. "You and Dr. Carmichael did a terrible thing. You allowed that old man to trick me. You both manipulated me." Gray stood suddenly, so quickly that his chair clattered to the floor, but I didn't let it stop me.

"Our children. Our beautiful children. They aren't yours."

"They are mine," he roared.

"They're Marsden's." The angrier he became the calmer I felt. I was the eye in the center of a hurricane. Unflappable.

And Gray was erratic. "I'm the reason they are here. Whatever you think you know is a disgusting lie. Did this come from Marsden? Have the two of you been talking?"

I laughed right in Gray's face. My husband despised being laughed at. That was enough to light the fuse. He crossed the distance between us in seconds. Before I could utter another word he struck me with his open palm flat across my cheek and left eye. As I fell to the floor he kicked me swiftly in the stomach. Before I could recover, his hands were on my shoulders, pulling me upright and then tightening around my neck.

"Those children are mine," he hissed. Flashbacks to the last time he hurt me physically were inevitable. I had prepared myself for it this time, but it didn't hurt any less. He was also sober now and that felt different. He had no excuse except for his anger and his terrible deeds. He could never apologize his way out of this. We were finished and he knew it.

His grip tightened, but I didn't drop my gaze from his. I was no longer an awestruck young woman desperate for love and affection.

I let him continue to squeeze, let him think he was draining the life from me, before finally mustering every ounce of strength I had left and slamming my knee upward directly into his balls. I choked and gasped as he backed away, reached behind me for the butcher knife I'd used to slice the sausage from the roll just that morning.

"Get the fuck out of my house, Grayson. I will stab you and watch you bleed to death on this floor. I'll watch you cry for your mother. Get out and never come back." I thought he might charge me again, but he backed off. He still didn't know exactly what I knew or how I knew it. The ball was in my court, and I know he would have kept squeezing my windpipe until the life drained out of me if I hadn't been strong enough to kick him. I lunged forward, allowing the tip of the blade to nick his freshly ironed plaid shirt. Blood peeped out from the small tear. He turned then and walked through the door, out to the barn. I managed to crawl through the kitchen and up the stairs to my bathroom.

Only then did I collapse into the darkness. And I still didn't have a confession.

CHAPTER EIGHTEEN

LIZZIE

When the lights come on in the hotel hallway they blind all three of us and we recoil against the wall.

It can't be. This fragile, scared child crying in front of me on the floor cannot be Rebecca's daughter.

"Kiki," she moans into Katie's chest. "I'm sorry."

"Shhhhhh, shhhhh," Katie keeps soothing her. "It's fine. It's okay. You're safe."

"I walked out to the ice machine. Same as we did earlier. It hurt so much. I just needed more ice for my ear. It hurt so bad. I thought I left the door open, but it must have slammed behind me and then everything went dark and I was trapped out here. I didn't know what to do. You told me not to leave, so I stayed right here. I did the best I could."

"You did great. Great, you hear me? You are brave and I never should have left you."

Only now does Katie look at me.

"Kiki?" I ask her.

She's resigned to giving me an explanation. I can tell. "Alice couldn't do a 't' sound for the longest time when she was a baby. Katie became Kiki when she was about two and it stuck with the littlest ones."

"You're Bex's nanny?" I ask. Katie nods.

"You lied to me." At that she shakes her head furiously.

"I didn't. Absolutely not. There were some things I didn't tell you, but I never lied. You made assumptions."

"Why are you here? Why is Alice here?"

Katie's eyes dart left and right down the hallway, but we're still alone. We won't be for long now that the elevators are up and running. All the other guests will be returning to their rooms. Or hopefully all of them. I can still hear that scream out at the canyon, the woman calling for help.

"Let's get inside the room. Let's get Alice to bed." Katie whispers something in the little girl's ear that I can't hear and helps her to her feet, pulls a room key out of her pocket. The door opens easily, as if the blackout had never happened.

"Why is she here?"

"She has an ear infection," Katie says.

"But why was she here alone?" I know my tone is filled with judgment, but I can't help it.

Alice chimes in. "I'm twelve. I stay alone all the time. I watch the littles sometimes too."

"She does," Katie says. "And it was just going to be a couple of hours. I had no way of knowing the hotel would lose power and I thought I needed to be out there. I wanted to see what Veronica was up to tonight. I don't trust her. I still shouldn't have left Alice." She turns to the girl. "I shouldn't have left you and I won't do it again. How is the ear?"

Now that I know Alice is listening to us so intently, I don't want to alarm her. I table the rest of the questions running through my head for the moment. Where are Rebecca's other children? Why is Katie, or Kiki, or whatever her name is, at this conference? Was her app all a front? Does she know where Rebecca is right now? Has she been leaving me these cryptic messages? The keys? And why doesn't she trust Veronica?

"I want my mom," Alice wails, cupping her hand over her left ear. "But she's not answering the phone."

And one of my questions has been answered. They know exactly where Rebecca is, or at least they've been in touch with her.

Katie shoots me a pleading look that seems to say, *Just wait. I know you have questions.*

A knot of dread settles in my stomach. "Can I get you some ice, sweetie?" I ask Alice. She nods and buries her head in Katie's lap, then turns and looks at me with one glassy eye. She's shaking and I don't know if it's the pain or if I'm scaring her. "Who are you?" she whispers.

She doesn't know me, but I feel like I know her so well. I've seen images of her as a tiny baby, as a chubby toddler, on her first day of homeschool, on family vacations. I've watched her grow up, not because I was once close friends with her mother but because her childhood has been broadcast to millions of people.

My fingers twitch for my missing phone as I walk down the hall to the ice machine. Then I think again about the scream back in the desert, the cry for help. I take a detour to the lobby to try to get information. It's full now, women huddling under damp towels and blankets on every available couch. Something is different, slightly off. It takes me a beat to realize that it's because no one is on their phones, no one's head is bowed, tapping away on a screen. They're all staring off into the distance, dazed and a little lost.

I don't see Veronica anywhere. Instead, I walk up to Cricket and sink onto the couch next to her. Her eyes are red, and her nose is running.

"Did everyone make it back?" It seems like a better question than, *Did someone fall to their death over the side of that terrible cliff?*

"Betty fell," she finally says.

"Betty Smith? Veronica's sister?"

"She slipped. She was so close to the edge." Her teeth are chattering, but it's not from the cold. She's terrified. "No one could see her. It was so dark. I thought she was gone." I exhale slightly, because it's now clear that while this story might not have a happy ending, at least it probably doesn't have a tragic one.

"Where is she now?"

"They found her. Thank God. But she still hasn't woken up. An ambulance got here and took her to the hospital."

"Did Veronica go with her?"

"She came back with us. Said she had to go upstairs to get their insurance information."

I curse Veronica for taking us all out into the desert and into that thunderstorm. What was the point? What was she trying to accomplish? I look around for anyone who might have my phone and then despise myself for being so concerned about the device when someone is fighting for their life in the hospital.

"I'm in room one ten," I say to Cricket. "I need to run upstairs for a little bit, but stop by if you need me." She nods without say-ing a word.

I do stop in my room before returning to Katie's. I want to check my email since it's my lifeline to the outside world, but there are only a couple of messages from Alana, desperate for my next story. I shoot Peter a quick note to let him know about my phone being gone, and that I'm all right. Then I compose an email to Bex. Fury flows through my veins as I write.

WHERE THE HELL ARE YOU?

CHAPTER NINETEEN

REBECCA

The knock on the door comes after the thunderstorm is finally over. I hadn't been asleep exactly, but I was lying in my bed, waiting for Kiki to call and update me about Alice. My baby. My poor baby. I should have gotten her that ear-tube surgery I read about online ages ago, but Gray hated doctors, especially specialists in the city.

Now I know he was probably wary of Alice having any kind of tests in a lab.

If it's not too late we'll do it now, as soon as possible. We'll do all the things we couldn't do because of him.

I haven't gotten any phone calls or updates from Kiki about the infection, but the cell service is always spotty out here and the motel's Wi-Fi has been out for hours.

I peel the curtain slightly aside and glance out the window to see the sweet old man from the front desk. He brought me banana bread from his wife yesterday. They're both at least eighty and I doubt they recognize me, so I haven't been as cautious as I planned. I'll be out of here soon, hopefully. Lizzie's article paved the way. God bless her and god bless Kiki for everything she's doing. Maybe she likes me more than I think she does. Maybe she's actually a friend. I love her and Juan Carlos, her partner. They've kept my children safe this week at Juan's mother's house. I owe them everything.

I open the motel door for the owner with a smile.

His eyes dart from side to side before he's shoved to the ground. I reach out for him and when I step outside the room I see Marsden. He sneers down at the man. "You never saw me here. Don't bother to call the police. They won't help you. You know who I am, you know the power I have in this state. You'll forget this ever happened if you know what's good for you." I look pleadingly at the man, but he can't meet my eyes. I know he'll do exactly what Marsden says. He scurries away on his hands and knees. Marsden turns to me.

"Get in my truck now, Rebecca. Don't make a scene."

I try to inch back into the room, but he grips my arm and growls into my ear. "I know where your children are."

The words take a second to penetrate my brain, but when they do, they crush me. What choice do I have? I get in.

We drive into the darkness. He doesn't speak to me, merely glowers in my direction. We're a two-hour drive from the ranch and we're heading that way, but who knows where he's taking me. We could be going anywhere.

"How do you know where my children are? Have you hurt my kids, Marsden?" I scream. "What the hell have you done?" He doesn't answer, merely smirks. He likes this.

Maybe I despise him even more than I hate my husband. In some ways I think he turned Gray into the monster he became. Or rather, they did it to each other. It was a chain reaction. All the men out here perpetuated a toxic cycle, generation after generation. It was Gray's father and grandfather too. It was Dr. Carmichael and the church elders. They all fed both of those young boys a pack of lies about how the world worked. How power and control worked. What they deserved and how they should do anything to get it.

Marsden's words from the restaurant echo in my head now. *I'll destroy you.*

He will. This man murdered my husband in cold blood. I know, because I watched it happen.

CHAPTER TWENTY

LIZZIE

have to calm myself down before I get back to Katie's room. There's a child there, one who is scared and desperate for her mother, and I can't let my panic infect her.

The door is slightly ajar. Katie's been waiting for me, even though I imagine I'm the last person she wants to see. Her room is a suite like mine. Of course, Bex probably got it comped. Katie is sitting on the couch sipping a tumbler of brown liquid. She lifts a finger to her lips to warn me to be quiet and motions to the closed bedroom door. I put the bucket of ice dumbly on the counter. She walks over and takes out a couple of cubes to drop in her glass and then offers me my own. When I nod, she motions that we should go out to the balcony.

We're on the second floor, so there's no infinity pool here. The rain is gone as quickly as it came. The violence of the storm a fading memory.

It's almost as if it never happened.

I take a long sip from my glass. It's straight-up whiskey, not my drink of choice, but I want it anyway.

"So, Kiki."

"You can call me Katie," she says.

"Where's Bex?"

"I don't know."

I snort and take another sip as she keeps talking.

"Look. I don't know where she is right now. She's been in a motel over in Krieger for the past few days. But she's not answering the phone. It's been twelve hours since I talked to her, and she never goes that long without talking to the kids. I called the front desk. They said she's not there anymore." Katie bites down on her bottom lip. "I'm worried."

"Where are the other kids? Are they all in the bedroom?" I joke, and nod to the back of the suite.

"Just Alice. She gets ear infections and she wanted a good night's sleep away from the others. They're with my husband and his mother. She lives about a hundred miles away."

"Have they been there the whole time?"

She nods.

"So you knew that Bex was going to murder her husband? You knew and you took her children and hid them?" My voice rises and Katie shushes me again.

"Please don't wake Alice up. She just fell asleep. She needs rest. The infections keep getting worse. We think she's losing some of her hearing in her right ear. And if she does, well . . . who knows what that would mean for her future. She's an incredibly talented musician."

"You didn't answer me."

"Rebecca didn't kill him."

"How do you know?"

"Because she told me she didn't."

"Why do you believe her?"

"Because she's never lied to me."

"Doesn't she lie to everyone?"

"Not to me."

The way she says it, I know she believes it even if it's not true. I switch gears slightly.

"How long have you been with the family?"

"A long time. Since Willow was born. Rebecca wasn't well afterward. Depression and anxiety. There were days she couldn't get out of bed at all. The birth was hard. She tore, badly. Lost a ton of blood. At least that's what she told me later. Gray didn't want to bring anyone in the house to help with Alice and the baby, but he didn't have a choice. Someone had to watch over them while Rebecca healed and I was dating JC at the time—he's the ranch foreman, Juan Carlos. He suggested to Gray that I just hang out with Alice. That's how he put it and it seemed acceptable. I wasn't going to be a nanny exactly. I was just a body hanging out with the children. Gray allowed it. I loved her from the very beginning."

"Bex?" The whiskey is getting to me. But Katie offers up a feeble laugh.

"Alice. Rebecca took longer. But we eventually got there. We've been through a lot together. Both of us."

I wait for her to continue, but she stays quiet. How could Bex hide this beautiful woman and all the care and love she gave her children from her audience of millions? Why didn't she just reveal she had help? Would anyone attack her for that? Why flatten Katie's work and her labor? Why pretend she doesn't exist? I'm

273

almost bold enough to ask it when Katie picks up the landline and punches in some numbers.

"It's going straight to voicemail. It's off." I know she's talking about Rebecca's phone.

"I've been calling her for days and no answer," I say.

"She isn't using that phone. She has a prepaid one. I was texting with her right before we left for the dinner."

"When did you take the kids?"

She hesitates before answering.

"They've been at Juan's mom's house since two days before the conference. But it isn't what you think. She had a plan to get away from him, and Gray wasn't going to like it. She wanted the kids to be far away from him and the house when she made her announcement. And he agreed because he couldn't take care of them on his own while she was gone and I made up something about how I couldn't sleep over. I knew what Rebecca had planned for this conference. I know all about you, Lizzie. I know all about your past with Rebecca. So I'm gonna trust you here because I also know we're working for the same things. We want Rebecca to be safe. We want those kids to be safe. She entrusted the kids to us because she was about to announce her big deal and she knew Gray was going to lose it. That's the only reason. But then the night before she was set to make the announcement . . . Well, you know what happened."

"I don't know what happened," I snap.

"That's not what I meant. Look, I don't know what happened either. Something went very wrong that night. I just don't know what it was. But I trust Rebecca. Maybe I shouldn't. Maybe I'm being naïve and maybe I'm just hoping she didn't do it because I don't want those kids to have a dead father and a psychopath mother, but I've practically lived in that house for a decade. I've watched Gray and Rebecca. He's terrible. It's gotten so much worse the bigger and more successful she's gotten."

"How long has he been hitting her?" I know Katie is taken aback by the bluntness of the question and that's what I want, to catch her off guard. But she recovers quickly.

"I don't think it's been like that. At least not until recently. It's emotional. It's the control. He's always tried to keep her small. He belittles every accomplishment, tells her anyone could do what she does, that she's silly, that she's stupid. He blames her for everything that goes wrong on that ranch when all the problems are due to his terrible investments and crap management. He isolates her from everyone. She has no friends except for me, and I don't even know if she'd consider me one. He's rotten to the core."

"How is he with the kids?"

"Mostly ignores them."

"But he did hurt her physically recently. Did you see that?"

"I was with the kids at the doctor for most of the day, but when I got back, I helped her bandage it all up. The kids saw the damage. It was horrible."

"She trusts you."

"Like I said, we've been through a lot. JC nearly got deported a few years ago. Rebecca's been paying for his attorneys. She's been funding development for my app. She's good people. I wouldn't blame her if she murdered Gray, but she didn't."

A moan, so loud we can hear it outside, comes from the other room.

"Alice will need some more medicine soon. This damn infection. She should have gotten tubes as a toddler, but Gray kept ignoring the problem and every time Rebecca wanted to travel to see a specialist he found some way to stop them. I brought her here so we could be closer to the hospital if we needed it, even if that would have completely blown Rebecca's cover. You should go back to your room."

"You've been giving me the clues. You gave me the keys."

She nods slowly. "It was me."

"And that's why you're still here at the hotel? You've been watching me."

"I've been back and forth between home and here. But I'm not just here for you. Rebecca wanted me to keep an eye on Veronica. She doesn't trust her or Marsden."

"Why?"

"I don't know all the details. But I trust her gut."

"Why did you go to that dinner out there? Why leave Alice?"

"I wanted to talk to you, figure out what you're writing next. Also keep an eye on Veronica."

Another moan.

"You should go."

"Give me Rebecca's new number."

Katie reluctantly picks up a piece of paper and writes the digits down.

I stand and stare out into the distance. I want to go home and hold my own children. Grab them tight and devour them. Never let them go.

I head toward the door, but Katie stops me halfway.

"Be careful, Lizzie. I'm getting out of here with Alice before sunrise and I'm not coming back. I don't know who murdered Grayson Sommers, but whoever did it wants us to believe it was Rebecca and I imagine they're desperate right now. Be careful."

I'm cross-eyed with exhaustion as I make my way to the elevator to reach my room. I don't even see Veronica Smith until she's right in front of me, blocking my path.

"Thank god you're okay," she says in a sultry purr. "I've been checking on everyone. And I have to give you this."

She rifles through the leather bag slung over her shoulder. "Is this your phone? I only have two left."

I snatch it from her greedily.

"How's your sister?" I ask.

"Awake, thank god. I'm heading over there now."

I glance behind me, curious if she knows which room I just came out of, hoping she doesn't. I don't want her to know where Katie is, where Alice is.

"What a night," she says, then sighs and rubs her temples. "That didn't go as I planned."

I manage a strangled laugh, but a chill runs down my spine as our eyes lock.

"I really wanted to spend some time with you tonight, Lizzie. I was hoping we could talk more."

"Maybe tomorrow." I glance nervously around her. I want to leave.

"I'll be here. I'll find you."

I have no doubt about that.

"See you then." I'm walking away, running almost, but suddenly she's right there at my heels. I can feel her breathing down my neck.

"I need to tell you something, Lizzie. I read your story. And it's terrible what Gray did to his wife, how he treated her all those years. I've watched it. Grayson Sommers was a true son of a bitch and he deserved everything he got."

CHAPTER TWENTY-ONE

REBECCA

I can't control myself any longer. I reach over and grab the wheel, yank it as hard as I can to the right, sending us flying off the road and into the soft dirt shoulder. Marsden's elbow crashes into my lip.

"You'll pay for that."

He slams the brakes so hard I can hear the bones in the back of my neck crack when my head whips forward.

Marsden opens the driver's-side door and runs over to me, but I have just enough time to do what I need to do. I reach into my back pocket for the burner phone Olivia bought me at Walmart, and without taking it out, I press the button that will dial the last number I called.

Kiki.

I keep it open and tuck it smoothly in the back of my underwear, sliding it down as far as it will go in the hopes he won't see it. I only need a minute, maybe less. It's the only way I can tell anyone what's happening to me.

Before I know what he's doing I'm being dragged out of the car.

"Where the hell are we going? Are you taking me home to the ranch? Marsden, answer me."

Those were the only three things I needed to reveal before the phone fell into the dirt and I kicked it under the truck.

My hands are pinned behind my back with a zip tie. Marsden shoves me back into the passenger seat and binds my ankles and then replaces my seat belt. I don't know why he didn't just throw me in the bed of his truck, other than I think he wants to toy with me as we continue the drive.

When we're back on the road he can't stop talking.

"Your children deserve a mother who can truly take care of them. It's clear that you can't do it. It has been for some time. Gray knew it, I think. He prayed about it. The whole church was praying about it. Your children need role models who are strong in their faith, strong in their morals. You've never been strong. Veronica is a strong woman. That's where your children will be. My wife will keep them safe. She knows how to raise morally sound children of God. Thank god Gray chose Veronica and me as their godparents. It will make all of this so much easier."

"Oh my god." I gasp, my thoughts running in panicked circles. He's right. I'd fought Gray on that decision years ago, but I also didn't have a good substitute for his best friend and his best friend's wife. I had no family, no friends I was in touch with. I'd agreed, thinking it was such a long shot. Both of us wouldn't go at the same time. It wasn't possible. But I had planned to switch it. I had the new document all drawn up and ready. It said that the kids would go to Kiki and Juan Carlos if anything were to ever happen to us.

I'd planned to make Gray sign it using the confessions I'd hoped to get out of him. But obviously that didn't happen and the document remains unsigned. Mars and Veronica will get our children if something terrible happens to me tonight.

"It's so fitting," he says. "I'll get to raise all of my children under one roof. It's what the Lord always intended. We just didn't know it at the time. But he works in mysterious ways and he always provides exactly what we need. They'll miss you, I'm sure. But they'll forget. Kids do. And Veronica will be such a wonderful mother. The mother they deserve."

What does Veronica know about any of this? Was she complicit in Marsden offering my husband his sperm? As a mother, I can't believe she could let me go through what I did. I bite down hard on my lip to keep myself from screaming because I can't have him hit me again. I need to be as present as possible, as strong as possible, to deal with whatever comes next, because the only way this man is taking my children from me is over my dead body and I won't let that happen.

I have to control myself. I know that, but somehow the words slip out. Maybe they'll catch him off guard. "I'm surprised you feel that way after what happened with her and Gray."

He nearly drives off the road then. I knew it would screw with him. It did that night in the barn, the night when he murdered his best friend in cold blood. When I watched him kill Gray, when my plan led to my husband's murder.

It was my fault. I put the two of them together in the barn that night. I needed their confessions. I needed them on tape. The emails weren't enough. Emails can be faked. Words can't.

So I planned for Gray and Marsden to meet out there the

night I spent with Lizzie at the conference. I wanted them to think they were alone so they could have it out. I'd placed the cameras in there so I could record their entire conversation. I needed to have it all on the record that Grayson and Marsden colluded to trick me. And once I had that proof I could properly make my escape. I'd tell them I'd go public. I'd ruin them. Ruin Dr. Carmichael. Ruin the church. But I would only do it if they didn't let me and the kids go.

That's all I wanted—freedom.

The planning had been exhausting, but planning was my full-time job as a mother and content creator. I was used to it. I tried to think of the recording I was hoping to capture as just another piece of content. How could I get it perfectly?

Men never talk on the phone. I just sent Marsden a text from Gray's phone and then deleted it. I made a dummy email account for Marsden and emailed my husband. I knew there wouldn't be much back-and-forth after they agreed to meet up, but I kept an eye on it.

The barn is their favorite place to hang out together. Both of them hate being in the house with the kids crawling all over them for much longer than an hour or so. In the barn there's a dartboard where Mars and Gray have been playing the same game for a decade, the score constantly updated in scratch marks on the wall with a bowie knife kept out there for that specific reason. They smoke cigars when they play, something I've always ignored, but I gag when I go out to milk the cows for at least a week afterward because the stench of cigar smoke never truly goes away.

In the hours leading up to their rendezvous I sent Marsden the real reason I wanted them to get together. An ironclad contract for him relinquishing all parental rights to my children. I also sent over the DNA tests and the disgusting emails my husband had sent to Veronica. I made it clear that I would publicly destroy both of them. All I wanted was his silence and my babies.

I got Marsden's text right after I left Lizzie's room.

> You won't get away with this you fucking bitch.

They came from G, or Marsden Greer. I kept him in my contacts as that because I hated seeing his stupid name. I could abide by just the one letter on the few occasions we communicated.

I ignored it. He and Gray would have plenty to talk about in the barn and that's exactly what I wanted.

That's when I went to Dan's. I was wound so tight. I needed a release. I needed comfort. It was quick.

I was back in my suite when I watched the live video feed from our barn. I knew they'd meet after ten P.M. because Marsden wouldn't come over until the baseball game was finished. I'd spent a lot of money to set up a surveillance camera and microphone in the rafters that no one would detect. It was all too easy to order on the Internet. Home security systems are now at the level of CIA espionage tools. It all operated over Wi-Fi and streamed to my phone. It was the audio I cared about the most. I wanted them to have it out about what they had both done. I wanted proof in their own words.

I sat in my room and saw it all on my phone the same exact way my nine million followers have watched my family and me for a decade. Because of that none of it felt real at first.

I watched as Marsden came into the barn drunk and seething with rage. Gray was confused and caught off guard from the very start. He'd been tossing darts. He had no idea what Marsden knew. He just stood there smoking a Cuban.

When Mars came in Gray offered him a cigar, but his friend smacked it out of his hand.

I'd wanted them to discuss the children and the horrible thing they'd done. I wanted all the details revealed. But I'd made a mistake trying to catch Mars off guard with the emails Gray sent to his wife. I'd meant to drive a rift between the two of them from the start, but it became Marsden's singular focus. I could hear the two of them so clearly I felt like I was in the barn with them.

"Did you think I wouldn't find out about the pervy emails you've been sending my wife?" Marsden shouted. "I knew you wanted her, but I didn't think you had the balls to try to do it. You really think she'd go for it? You think she'd choose a limp dick like you over a man like me?"

"What are you talking about, man?"

Gray denying it only infuriated Marsden more.

That's when Marsden punched him right in the jaw. Gray attempted to fight back. He grabbed the bowie knife from where it hung on the wall over the dartboard and slashed at Mars's face, but he missed. They ripped at each other's clothes. At one point Gray's shirt just sort of fell off his body.

The bird's-eye view from the camera perched in the rafters was like watching amateur ultimate fighters go at each other.

It seemed evenly matched at first, but that was impossible. Marsden was a professional athlete and I always suspected that he took things to enhance his performance on the field.

They wrestled. Gray gouged at Marsden's eyes, begging for the two of them to stop and to talk. He denied ever being with Veronica, apologized for the emails, said they were all a dumb joke.

Marsden delivered a kick directly to Gray's left kneecap, causing him to buckle to the floor.

Gray was howling in agony, screaming out for help over and over again as I watched.

I thought back to my husband's crumpled face and his apology fourteen years ago when he beat me and locked me in that closet in San Francisco.

I'm a terrible, broken man, he had said then. I heard it so clearly so many years later.

"Terrible. Broken. Yes, you fucking are," I whispered to the screen.

I could have called the police and an ambulance to go rescue him. I just sat there.

I didn't kill my husband, but I didn't save him either.

I watched.

I had hoped it was almost over. But then Mars clocked Gray one last time on the side of the temple. Blood streamed out of my husband's skull. Marsden looked up then. He must have seen the tiny red light on the camera above him. He grabbed at a wrench lying on the barn floor and hurled it into the rafters with the exactness of a major league pitcher. The screen went dark.

I waited an hour after watching the screen go black. I sat in silence in my room before trying Marsden's phone. Straight to voicemail. Then Gray's. Same thing. I called Olivia. I had no one else to turn to. She stayed cool as hell the whole time even though

I was hysterical. She picked me up, said we had to get out to the barn, had to know what we were dealing with. But she never seemed surprised. That stuck with me afterward. Why wasn't she more shocked when I called her?

Only Gray's car was left in the driveway when we arrived shortly after midnight. For a moment I held out hope that he might have survived, that Marsden had relented and dropped him off at the nearest ER.

I nearly slipped on the blood seeping across the barn floor. Marsden had turned off the lights when he left and I could barely make out Grayson's limp body propped like a scarecrow on the blades of the brand-new shiny piece of farm equipment that sat in the corner of our barn. Two of the blades sliced cleanly through his lower back, filleting him wide open. It was a gift from the machinery company, a potential sponsor of mine. They were willing to pay $30K for one picture of the kids and me riding on it. More if Gray did some reels with it. It never even left the barn.

"We need to leave," Olivia whispered. "Now."

"I'll call the police," I stuttered as I stumbled closer to Gray. My legs gave way as I tripped over the large wood ax we usually kept in the corner. The one I used when I was pretending to chop wood in videos on my Instagram and in one intensely viral Tik-Tok. Its blade is always dull because no one actually uses it, but that night it was covered in splatters of nearly black blood.

I squinted into the dim light and realized what the ax was used for, what was chopped off of Gray's body as a souvenir. My stomach retched again.

"Let's go," Olivia said more forcefully.

"No. The police. I have the video of Marsden killing him," I said. "Before it went dark. Before he climbed up there and took it down. It recorded into the cloud. We can go to the cops with it right now. He beat the hell out of him. I watched it. And afterward he must have done this. It wasn't enough to break open his skull. He had to destroy him. He's a monster." I imagined Marsden throwing Gray's limp body onto the blades after the camera went dark. It wasn't sympathy for my husband that I was feeling, not exactly. It was mostly rage and fear at Marsden.

"We're not going to the cops just yet," she said evenly. "Let's make a plan first. Play offense instead of defense. I don't think the police will let you get away with calling Marsden the only monster here. You ordered that camera with your credit card days ago. You put it there. Didn't you bring them together tonight? The cops will figure that out. This is messy, Rebecca. You could lose everything if you don't play your cards right. We can't let Grayson be the only victim here. He hurt you and the world needs to know that. We have to get your story out first. We have to be patient, and we have to pivot slightly. It's the only way to save everything we've worked so hard for."

I wavered. Screw the deals, screw the money, I screamed. I just wanted my kids and me to be safe. I worried that I'd lit a powder keg under Marsden. He could find a way to kill us to protect himself.

"You can have the money *and* be safe," Olivia kept assuring me. "Trust me."

So, I did. I went back into the house and left the Polaroids for Lizzie to find. I'd planned to show her anyway when I finally had the chance to explain why I'd abandoned her years ago. I had them ready. I just had to find a way to get her in my house so she could see my reality. I wanted her to see how I lived so she could tell my whole story.

Olivia grabbed me by the shoulders and looked directly into my eyes. "You are going to be fine. Better than fine. We just have to pivot. Shift the plans. Do you trust me?"

I trusted her more than I had ever trusted anyone in my entire life, probably even Lizzie. Olivia had helped me realize dreams I didn't even know that I had and she had been my key to a future of stability and happiness far away from my husband. "A man is never the plan," she'd told me the first time we met. "You are the plan." But as I gazed into her eyes I saw a glint of something devious that I knew I had overlooked for all these years. A chill ran down my spine, but I nodded. "I trust you."

We left Gray's body for the farmworkers to find in the morning. By the time they called the police I was nowhere to be found.

* * *

As Marsden drives me through the inky black night, I run through Gray's last moments again in my mind. Was he still alive when Marsden impaled him on those blades? When he came at him with the ax?

The gate to our house comes into view now. Marsden strokes my leg with his long fingers, the same shape as the ones my daughter uses to play the piano so beautifully.

He sneers over at me with pure evil in his gaze, shearing away my remaining hope for escape. "Time to go home, Rebecca Sommers. For good."

CHAPTER TWENTY-TWO

LIZZIE

could have been asleep for a couple of hours or a couple of days. That's how hard I crashed after leaving Katie's room. The room is pitch black when a banging on my door startles me awake. Sharp, fast cracks on the wood. Each of them resonates through the room like a gunshot.

"Coming." I rub my eyes and glance at my phone. It's filled with notifications. I'd silenced it so I could sleep. I reach for it in a panic now as I open the door.

Katie is standing there in flannel pajamas with puppies on them, her hair disheveled and sticking out every which way around her head.

"Rebecca's in trouble."

"We already knew that."

"No. Real trouble. She's in danger right now!"

"What's going on?"

Katie pulls out her phone.

"When did you get that back?"

"Veronica dropped it off after you left. Listen to this." Katie puts it on speaker, then plays me a voicemail.

It's static at first and then there's a creaking sound, maybe a car door opening, and a woman's scream.

"Where the hell are we going? Are you taking me home to the ranch? Marsden, answer me."

It's Bex.

"Get the hell off of me, Marsden," she yells so clearly that it feels like it's meant for us. A primitive male grunt and then a yelp. He's hurting her. Wherever they are, he's definitely hurting her. I picture it in my head.

A crack of flesh hitting flesh. A whimper.

More rustling, more movement.

And then nothing but static. A car engine revs up. I feel useless.

Katie turns off the message. "That's it. Static and then it cuts off. Phone might have gone out of service. He might have found it." Her focus is contagious, but so is her fear. It itches and claws at my skin.

"That was Marsden."

"What tipped you off? Was it the fact that she screamed 'Marsden'?"

"Do you really think now is the time for sarcasm?"

"We need to find Rebecca," Katie practically shouts.

"How? She could be anywhere."

"They're going to the ranch. She said it for a reason. She wanted us to know. We have to get out there."

"Okay, let's call the police." I pick up my phone, but Katie stops me.

"Absolutely not. They're all in bed with Marsden the same way they were with Gray. Even more so because he gets everyone season tickets and passes to the World Series. The things he gets away with in this county are unreal. At least five DUIs that I know about. If they go to that ranch and Marsden has Rebecca there, they'll probably help him finish her off."

"What about your husband? Is he close?"

"Not close enough. He's at his mama's and they have the kids. He shouldn't leave them alone with her. His mother isn't very mobile and she can't pick up the little one. I can't leave Alice and I certainly can't bring her with me."

"So it's me. I have to go."

Katie is wringing her hands. "I don't know who else."

"What about Olivia? How close does she live to the ranch?"

"I tried her."

"Let's try her again."

Olivia answers on the second ring and doesn't sound like she's been sleeping at all.

"How can I help you, Lizzie?"

"It's Bex. Marsden kidnapped her. We think they're heading to the ranch. Can you get out there?" I hear movement, maybe a woman's whisper behind her. A door shuts.

"How do you know?"

I explain about the voicemail. I explain about Alice being here with Katie. Olivia is surprised by some of it, but not all, and I wonder how much she knows about where Bex and her children have been for the past few days, how much she's been keeping from me. How much she's lied to me. But there isn't time to ask it now.

"I'm closer to the hotel than the ranch. I'll pick you up on the way."

"Me?"

"I'm not going out there alone, Lizzie."

I know she's right. I can't send her out there alone. But can I go? Can I put myself in danger like that? I'm a mother. I can't do that to my own children.

"We'll be safe together," Olivia assures me. "I'm not going in without some ammunition."

She doesn't say any more before she hangs up and I know she's on her way. I do have a choice here. I don't have to go. I can leave right now. I think about Nora and Ollie. Both asleep in their beds at the beach house, safe with my mom, Robbie, and Peter. I think about Rebecca's children. Also safe for now, but probably terrified.

I think about Bex. I still love her. After all of this I still love her like a sister. She's responsible for so much of who I am today. She was my only real witness to the time when I became an adult.

"Go back to Alice," I tell Katie. "I'll get ready for Olivia. I'm going out there."

CHAPTER TWENTY-THREE

REBECCA

Marsden doesn't like my jeans and dirty blouse streaked in blood. He wants me to look a certain way. We're in my bedroom now. My feet are free, but my hands are still bound, my mouth gagged so I can't speak and I can hardly breathe. He nudges me where he wants me to go with the sharp tip of the bowie knife that Gray always kept in the barn. He's drawn blood with every single poke.

He opens the door to my closet and begins rummaging through my long flowery dresses. I watch as he slides his hand down the front of his jeans and gently strokes himself. Whatever he's going to do to me will bring him an intense amount of pleasure and I wonder how he'll violate me before he finishes this. Unfortunately, I want to draw it out as long as possible in the hopes that my call to Kiki went through. I'll need to take whatever he doles out in case it keeps me alive even a moment longer.

He finally selects what he wants me to wear. It's one of my least favorite dresses because it's one of the least practical. It's so long that I trip on it every time I wear it. The lace at the neck and the wrists is scratchy and gives me a rash. But my audience loves it. Every time I wear it while I'm milking the cows or gathering the eggs they tell me I'm elegant and beautiful, a model of femininity.

There's no way to get the dress on me without unbinding my hands. He does it, but pins my arms behind my back as he drops it over my head.

"Be a good girl now."

He lowers his head and kisses each of my breasts before the material flutters down over them. He bites down softly on one nipple, like a child searching for milk. I stare daggers down at the growing bald spot on the back of his head and picture myself clawing the skin of his skull with my fingernails.

When he's done taunting me, he marches me into the bathroom.

"Put on your face," Mars sneers. His beady eyes flick up and down me hungrily. "I want you perfect."

I'm shaking as I use a washcloth to remove the splatters of blood and then swipe on foundation, lipstick, mascara. Through it all I'm plotting how I can possibly use anything in here as a weapon. Organic hairspray in his pupils? Mascara wand up the nose?

It takes about ten minutes for me to get enough makeup on that he gives me a satisfied grunt. He reaches down and places his meaty fingers beneath my dress, runs his hands up the sides of my thighs. I prepare myself for the worst, but instead he just holds my legs in his viselike grip and stares at our two faces side by side in the mirror.

"I see both of us every time I look at them," he says, and I know he means our children. If I survive this, will I ever be able to stop seeing him in their eyes and their smiles? I hope so. I'll do everything in my power to forget. But first I have to escape. We stand like that for another thirty seconds, my breath hitching with his every movement, certain he is about to have his way with me against the marble countertop, but he eventually grabs another washcloth off the hook next to the sink, wets it, and then runs it up the sides of my legs and then down my arms, erasing all his fingerprints. He dons a pair of leather work gloves and pushes me out of the bathroom, then out of the bedroom and down the stairs, wiping his prints away as he goes.

Outside the full moon is so bright it might as well be morning. Marsden wants us to walk side by side and he loops his arm through mine as if we're on an after-dinner stroll on our first date. The intimacy is almost worse than the violence.

He isn't going to rape me. I realize that now. He wants to. He wants to so badly. I can feel his desire pulsing through him. But that would leave too much evidence and that's not part of his plan.

"What are you going to do?" I finally ask. He'll want to tell me. It will make him feel powerful and smart to outline his plan.

"You're not well, Rebecca. You haven't been for a long time. You've been able to hide it from your audience, but not from your husband. Gray has been confiding in me. Told me you've been so depressed you've taken to your bed for weeks at a time, while he had to care for the children. He told me you even threatened to hurt them. He told me over and over again that he might need them to come live with Veronica and me while you went away for help. I felt so bad for him. But I was also worried for him and for you. He says you've lashed out at him, that you've been violent and psychotic, that he was afraid of you. I told Veronica I didn't believe it until that night. That terrible night when you murdered your husband right in his own barn."

He says these lies calmly and evenly, as if they are facts. And maybe in his brain they are. The same way he convinced himself of an all-powerful god who will grant his every wish, he has convinced himself that I killed Gray.

"You can't take it anymore," he continues explaining as he pushes open the massive barn door. "You have to repent. You'll take your own life here in the same barn where you attacked Gray. You called me to confess everything earlier today."

Now I finally pivot and stare directly into his eyes. He's smirking as he pulls out his phone and opens a recording. Only then do I actually want to die. It's my voice, there's no mistaking it. I'd thought it would be harder to doctor a spoken confession than written words. I'd been so wrong.

"I killed Grayson. The voices told me I had to do it. I couldn't get them to stop screaming at me. But I can't handle the shame and the guilt. My children will be better off without me. If I end my life here then maybe Gray and I can be together forever in the afterlife. Please forgive me, Lord."

It's me. But it's not me. I've never said those words.

"You don't talk that much in your videos, but you talk enough. Veronica and her sisters didn't learn how to use AI all on their own. I've picked up some things here and there. Digital voice creation is almost too easy these days."

I follow Marsden's gaze as he looks up at the rafters in the barn. A shaft of moonlight comes through the door illuminating a noose resting on the edge of the ledge where we keep the hay.

He prods me up the ladder.

"Don't make this hurt more than it has to. I don't want there to be any marks on your body, but if there are, the police won't investigate them. They won't question much here. I've made sure of that. So climb on up, darling. Be a good girl. Do as Daddy says."

I climb and I curse myself for letting this beast get the best of me. I curse the god I don't believe in for trapping my children in this impossible situation. I also know that I will not go down without a fight. He's climbing right behind me, but I reach the ledge first, and when I look out from that vantage point I can see something in the moonlight, a figure just outside the door.

Is it possible? Is someone truly coming to save me?

I stand up and allow Marsden to place the heavy rope around my neck.

"It will be easier if you take the first step," he growls. "But I'll push you if I have to."

"You'll burn in hell for this." I want to believe in a fiery inferno in a way that I've never wanted to before.

"I've been chosen by God, Rebecca. Never forget that." He leans over and I think he wants to kiss me on the mouth.

"You're right, Marsden," I spit, trying to buy some time. "You've been chosen." I'm hoping whoever is out there beyond the barn door isn't alone. I'm hoping they brought backup with them. I'm hoping they have a plan because I'm out of options. I take a step closer to the edge. Marsden is right there with me, watching me teeter.

"You've been chosen to die tonight."

I pull in a deep breath, and as I step away from the edge I muster all the strength I have, all my rage, all the burning love for my kids, and I kick Marsden right in the gut and send him over the edge as I go flying through the air, the noose tightening around my neck.

CHAPTER TWENTY-FOUR

LIZZIE

O livia has a gun. I hope she knows how to use it. We parked at the front gate of the ranch and walked the half mile in on foot, not knowing what we'd find here, if we would find anything, but hoping that if we did, we weren't too late.

She met me at the hotel, and we covered the distance to the ranch in an hour, speeding the whole way, slowing down only twice.

"I know where the speed traps are," she told me. What else does she know?

When I saw the light on in Rebecca's bathroom I nearly ran to the house. We weren't too late. But Olivia stopped me.

"Wait a second. We have to assess."

She pulled the handgun out from a holster beneath her crisp black blazer. She'd reached me so quickly, I wondered if she slept in a full suit. When I looked at the gun with disdain, she rolled her eyes and whispered, "Everyone is armed in this state, Lizzie."

That's when the front door to the house opens and we duck down behind the hedges. In the moonlight I can easily make them out, strolling casually arm in arm, like two lovers out to get some fresh air.

"She's with Marsden." I let out a strangled cry. "They look like they're together. Like they're romantic. Did they plan this whole thing? Did they kill Gray together?" Olivia shushes me by placing a finger over my lips. The two figures glow in the moonlight as they finish their stroll and disappear into the barn.

Olivia pulls me forward until we can peek in through a small dusty window on the side of the building. I don't see them at first, but finally they come into focus. Two figures about to kiss in the hayloft. My stomach twists with disgust. Only then do I see the rope around her neck. It's too late. She's flying over the edge.

But so is he. She kicked him straight in the gut with enough force to send him tumbling down two stories. It isn't that far to fall, but he was also caught off guard and he doesn't have time to get his feet under him. Marsden lands directly on his spine with a shrill scream and then silence. Bex is hanging above us, her legs dangling, twitching as she gasps for air.

Olivia moves like lightning. She's up in the loft, hacking at the rope with some kind of knife.

"Lizzie," she screams. "You'll have to break her fall." I look up to see Rebecca wiggling. She has both hands slipped under the noose. A few fingers are the only thing that saved her from breaking her neck when she swung, but the noose is still suffocating her and she can't hold on for much longer. I've never moved so fast without thinking in my entire life. I push two bales of hay under her and I climb on top of them the best I can until I can nearly touch her toes.

"I'm cutting her down," Olivia yells.

"Bex, I'm right here. I'm here. I'm going to catch you. I've got you."

And I do. When Olivia gets the rope cut Bex tumbles down and we both topple over, but I'm able to break her fall and we both roll onto the hay. It isn't soft, but it's also not the polished concrete floor that Marsden snapped his spine against.

Olivia is standing over him as he starts to come around. His neck is twisted at an impossible angle and it's clear his back is broken, but his eyes flutter open. She calmly and wordlessly places the gun in his hand and then into his mouth. She looks back at Bex, her expression asking the question for her. *Do you want to do this? Do you want to kill him?*

"You do it," she whispers. And with a single click Olivia pushes Marsden Greer's finger on the trigger of the gun and splatters his brains against the beautiful moonlit barn walls.

DET. WALSH: *Why do you think your husband murdered Grayson Sommers?*

V. SMITH GREER: *He was obsessed with him. Always had been. Since we were all kids. They were always competing for things. In sports, for girls. Who could kiss a girl first? Who could lose their virginity first? Who could get better grades? It was never ending. But . . . I never thought . . . I mean, Marsden wouldn't . . . I didn't think he would ever do what he did.*

DET. WALSH: *Can I get you a tissue?*

V. SMITH GREER: *That would be wonderful.*

DET. WALSH: *I know this must be difficult. We can continue this later on.*

V. SMITH GREER: *It's okay. I want to help you as best I can. My husband was obsessed with Grayson. It was unhealthy. He was so jealous of him and his family. Of how much Grayson had growing up. But Grayson was also obsessed with Marsden.*

And then there were rumors. I don't know if you heard them. About me.

DET. WALSH: *About you and Grayson Sommers being . . .*

V. SMITH GREER: *Being intimate, yes.*

DET. WALSH: *We did find the pictures of you under his bed. Did you know he took those?*

V. SMITH GREER: *I had no idea. He took all of them when I wasn't paying attention. The close-ups of my entire body. It was just so disgusting and inappropriate.*

I would never have cheated on my husband. I loved him with all my heart. Grayson sent me so many emails over the years. So many inappropriate things and I never responded. But my husband found them. And that must have set him off.

But I should have known. This is my fault.

DET. WALSH: *None of this is your fault.*

V. SMITH GREER: *It is. I'm Marsden's wife. We were bound by God. I should have known. I should have talked to the church. I should have gotten him all the help he needed before this happened. You watched the recording from the security cameras in that barn. He was crazy with jealousy when he killed Grayson, when he bashed his head in. And then he must have thrown him on those blades.*

DET. WALSH: *And do you think he killed himself in that barn because he felt guilty?*

V. SMITH GREER: *I don't think he could live with the guilt. In the end he truly was a God-fearing man.*

DET. WALSH: *Do you know whose gun it was?*

V. SMITH GREER: *Definitely one of his. He had dozens of unlicensed firearms. Was always worried the government was gonna take his rights away so he stocked up. You understand.*

DET. WALSH: *Oh, I do.*

V. SMITH GREER: *I recognized the gun right away. It was his favorite.*

DET. WALSH: *Is there anything else you want to tell me? Please take another tissue.*

V. SMITH GREER: *Both of those men who died in that barn could have been good men, but they had problems the Lord could not help them with. I only hope they will find some peace and freedom in the next life. We all deserve peace and freedom.*

EPILOGUE

REBECCA

I t isn't my dream wedding, but it's also not the worst day of my life. Far from it, actually. I didn't think I'd end up having as much fun as I did the second time around.

When Olivia suggested that Dan and I get engaged just a year after Gray's death I told her she was crazy. But she laid out all the reasons that it was a good idea so rationally I couldn't say no.

There were the optics of it all. The redemption narrative, the clean slate. And then there was the money. So much money for both the big day and its aftermath.

Let's be honest, I have rarely said no to her when she's wanted me to pivot.

Everyone loves a happy ending and what's happier for a widow with six children than a wedding?

In America? Nothing.

Nothing except a new baby. And that's coming in about six and a half months. But no one knows yet. The pregnancy reveal will be epic. Dan is psyched that I'm pregnant again. This time I know exactly who the father is. It's the same one as my bonus baby, but I'll never tell Dan that. I still don't know if I'll ever reveal what Dr. Carmichael did or if I'll let the secret die with those two men in the barn. Besides me, only Olivia knows, and she'll never tell. She promised me that.

Olivia sold the exclusive photos and videos of the wedding for more than a million bucks. The entire thing is sponsored and bringing in at least double that from vendors. There are more than three hundred guests, including every major influencer to ever attend MomBomb. We're thinking of starting our own conference, so it was a nice way to test the waters. It's been the perfect relaunch for my brand. The first issue of my magazine hits stands next week. The TV crew will start filming us at the new ranch and new bakery in the first quarter of next year. Our hotel is still a few years out, but the designs are in the works.

Dan doesn't mind letting me be the boss. He's from New York originally, so women being in charge is second nature to him. He was psyched to quit being a foot doctor and start being a full-time stay-at-home dad. His kids are the sweetest and they seem to genuinely like living out in the country with my brood. I suppose we *are* the modern-day Brady Bunch. Our audience has been eating it up.

We're expecting another wave of attention when Lizzie's book publishes next month. Olivia brokered that seven-figure deal too. It was enough that Lizzie could quit that magazine and launch a new career in true-crime writing, a niche she says she never knew she'd be into, but now she loves. I gave her everything she needed to write my entire story.

We open it with the first time that Gray hurt me and how ashamed I was, how that shame kept me yoked to him and brought me to the ranch. We talk about how I kept it solvent all those years, how I became the farmer, the mother, the homesteader, and the influencer despite everything Gray put me through.

I catch Lizzie's eye as she finishes her matron of honor toast.

"There were years when I didn't know if I would ever get to talk to Bex again, if we would ever get to laugh the way we did when we were naïve eighteen-year-olds searching the couch cushions for change to buy a pizza. But we found our way back together, and I think that makes our bond even more special. There should be a German word for choosing your friends again as a fully formed adult. But because there isn't one, I want to share this poem that Bex sent to me a few months ago. It's from Lyndsay Rush."

Why shouldn't I let love consume me and hold you in the
    center of my happiest days?
I believe the best is yet to come . . .

I'm bawling by the time she's finished.

Veronica whistles loudly by placing two fingers in her mouth. She's wearing a very Olivia-like red pantsuit and she's been mugging for all the cameras after acting as our wedding officiant. That was also Olivia's idea. She has Ronnie, that's what Veronica calls herself now, auditioning next week for the *Real Housewives of the Wild West*. She wants to get her all the exposure she can, even though she's a shoo-in. Veronica was ready-made to be a newly empowered widow influencer. She's embraced it with all the gusto she first embraced being a tradwife. Now she's live streaming her dates and she might outstrip me in terms of followers. Good for her.

I still don't like Veronica, but I think I understand her a little better. She felt as trapped by Marsden as I did by Gray. She's sworn up and down to me that she never had an affair with my husband. She told me and the police that he emailed her and stalked her for years, but she ignored it until Marsden confronted her.

Olivia is dying for us to be friends. She thinks Veronica should be a regular on my new show. I told her I'd think about it.

I know I don't question Olivia as much as I should. I know she does things behind the scenes that I don't want to know about. But I also know that I have never felt as safe and secure and strong as I do right now. That's all due to her. She helped all of us understand exactly what we were worth.

Olivia knew it was time for a rebrand for both Veronica and me, and she made that happen for both of us. The submissive, idyllic prairie daydream moment has ended. The audience, according to Olivia's data and research, is now craving realness, vulnerability, and connection.

My hand shakes a little from holding the glass aloft for so long. The nerves in my fingers will never be the same. I tore a bunch of tendons trying to keep myself from suffocating as I strained against the noose that Marsden tied around my neck. I honestly didn't think I'd make it when I jumped, but I had to try. I needed my kids to know I fought for them.

Mars and Gray might have had the local police in their back pockets, but Olivia got the FBI involved in the investigation after that night. She gave them what we called the "security footage" from the barn when Marsden murdered Gray, before the camera went dark. It was still saved. The agents wanted to know why I didn't turn it over earlier, but I said I was afraid for my life and for the lives of my children. I showed them evidence of Grayson's and Marsden's connections with the local police. I said that I was waiting to figure out how I could keep all of us safe and I didn't feel like I could come forward until Marsden finally killed himself in our barn. They accepted it. Maybe Olivia had a hand in that too.

Kiki is sitting with Alice at the piano bench as my daughter begins a beautiful piece she composed herself for the occasion. We had her second eardrum surgery a month ago, and she's doing great and heading off to the special music boarding school in the fall. Kiki beams at her. She quit six months ago to work on her app full-time. Olivia got her the venture funding that she needed, and it looks like it will be a massive success. Our new ranch is much closer to the city and the big kids are in a good school nearby. The littles have a small army of babysitters to support me. I don't hide them from my feed. My entire audience knows them by name. Same as they used to know the names of our chickens and Tripod (RIP to that nasty bastard). Shouldn't we fetishize women's labor more than barnyard animals?

* * *

Lizzie walks over to me now and wraps an arm around my slightly rounded stomach. She leans down and kisses my belly, making sure first that no one is watching. "Hi, Baby Elizabeth," she says.

"Is it okay that I'm naming her after you?" I ask for about the zillionth time. Our friendship isn't what it was fifteen years ago. Like she said, we chose each other again as fully formed adults. It's stronger now that it's been broken and put back together bit by bit.

"I'm honored."

Her handsome husband, Peter, is beaming at her. His own novel is finally finished. It's about a cowboy from the Wild West who somehow manages to travel forward in time to present-day New York City and becomes the hottest thing going on Tinder. It was Olivia's idea and she also brokered his deal. We'll see if it's any good. It probably doesn't have to be all that good to sell. Infamy is contagious.

I know that better than anyone. We were initially worried that I'd lose some followers, lose some deals, but it hasn't happened. Everyone loves drama and scandal and redemption. I was able to give them all three. Now that all the dust has settled, I still give them the same kind of idyllic baking and ranching and mothering content just with a blended family and more help. It turns out my audience didn't want me barefoot and pregnant and silent. They just wanted to watch something beautiful and aspirational. Now I'm a lot more interesting to them as an entrepreneur and a survivor. I might even run for the congressional seat Gray had his eyes on. Who knows what the future holds. I'm a household name now and I plan to keep it that way.

There's a new right way to be authentic.

EPILOGUE

LIZZIE

I deleted my Instagram account after everything that happened. I didn't want to scroll or be scrolled. Once you've been on a tour of the sausage factory you don't really want to eat another hot dog.

When I sold the book, my publisher was annoyed by my decision to delete my Instagram account. They were worried that I wouldn't be able to promote myself and the book, but Olivia stepped in. She promised we'd sell the book on Bex's platforms and no one had to worry about me doing anything but writing it.

"You deserve this," Olivia reminds me all the time. "We make our own success."

But the truth is that Olivia has made us all a success. Me, Bex, Veronica, and countless other women. She truly doesn't kiss and tell. We never know what she's doing behind the scenes or with who, and I don't think we want to.

I'm slightly terrified of her. Everyone seems to be. Even Bex and Veronica.

Veronica is truly something else. We did hours of interviews for my book and I still don't feel like I know her at all. When we started out talking about how she viewed Marsden and Gray's toxic history together, I couldn't stop asking her questions.

"It was unhealthy," she told me. "Ever since they were kids. Marsden wanted what Gray had. His family's money and his power. He never felt like he was good enough even after he became a pro athlete. He always coveted Gray's life. The two of them pushed each other harder and harder. Who could be the bigger man? Who could have the more perfect-seeming life?"

It was a big thread in my book, the toxic jealousy between those two men. We hear so much about catfights and jealousy between women. It was refreshing to write it the other way around.

Veronica is hard for me to like, but once I knew her whole story, I had to have compassion for her. She was practically promised to Marsden from the age of twelve and married off before her eighteenth birthday. She went from her father's home to her husband's and she never got a chance to be herself. Until now.

Now the Smith triplets own the Sensoria outright. Olivia made that happen too. Veronica says she'll never get married again and I believe her. If I'd endured half a lifetime of Marsden Greer, I'd swear off men too.

"Nice toast," Veronica says now, as she sidles up to me at the bar.

"Thanks. It only took me twenty years to get to be Bex's matron of honor."

"They seem happy." She nods to Dan and Bex. He's massaging her shoulders and she's leaning into his chest. "But you never know who is happy and who isn't. Right?"

It's true. I think I'm happy now, genuinely happy. I feel useful and successful. I feel validated in a way I haven't in years. Peter and I are slowly emerging from the haze of early parenthood and a season of career instability. The money helps. It always helps and anyone who says it doesn't is lying to you.

"I think I have your next book," Veronica says.

"Is it about you?" I ask.

"It's about all of us."

"I'm listening."

"What did Bex tell you about Dr. Carmichael?"

The name rings a bell. He was her ob-gyn, I think. He did her fertility treatments. I say as much.

"He was my doctor too. He treats all of us. Or treated. I stopped seeing him. I desperately wanted a daughter, you know. Every time I got pregnant I hoped and I prayed that it would be a girl. A couple of times it was! I knew it from the early tests. But I miscarried each of those times. Each time was after a visit to Dr. Carmichael. That always seemed to satisfy Marsden. He wanted all boys. And I can't help but wonder what kind of role Dr. Carmichael played in helping my husband get exactly what he wanted. In helping all of the men out here get exactly what they wanted."

My jaw drops. I can't even comprehend what she's saying. Is she insinuating that Dr. Carmichael made her miscarry her girl babies?

She nods like she can read my mind and whispers, "He's sick. Someone needs to take that bastard down. You should ask Rebecca about him. He did things to her too. I know it. Olivia told me. We'll keep you in the book-writing business as long as you want. The prairie is filled with secrets."

"To be honest, it's more of a desert out here than a prairie." I've always wanted to say this, ever since I saw the first #Prairie-Life hashtag pop up in every rural area in America. "Prairies are typically in the Midwest."

"This place is whatever we want it to be," Veronica snipes back. "Think about the book idea. Olivia told me to mention it to you."

Olivia has made a fortune off of both these women, and off of me. Yet, she blends seamlessly into the background of it all.

I don't know why I'm so scared to push Olivia more about what she knew about Grayson's murder and when she knew it, who told her what details. There's still something that doesn't add up for me and I know it has to do with how she manipulated both Bex and Veronica behind the scenes throughout the entire situation, how maybe she even played them off each other when it was beneficial for the outcome. She's managed to turn the horrific deaths of two prominent men in this state into a windfall for all of us. She truly does make her own success every single day. I'll push her for answers eventually. I keep promising myself that I will.

I watch Olivia now. She's helping Bex's littlest one walk through the garden. I wonder when these kids will decide who they want to be or how they want to brand themselves. How long until they have their own YouTube channels and TikTok accounts?

I wonder if Olivia will still be around when they make those choices. If she'll be their managers too. I gaze over at her as she holds both the toddler's chubby hands over his head, helping him walk as Stacy films the two of them in the distance.

Ever the puppet master. Always pulling the strings.

EPILOGUE

VERONICA

'd been told I was nothing and that I didn't matter for so long that now I can easily be anyone and anything.

Everyone is lying to you. Never forget it. But here's the truth: Grayson Sommers would still be alive if it weren't for me.

I knew Marsden was meeting Gray that night when he went to his barn, and I knew exactly why. My brain works like a computer playing three-dimensional chess. It's such a shame I wasn't allowed to keep going with school, but to be honest, who needs college these days? You can learn everything you need to know about everything on YouTube, especially when you're a teenage girl sitting at home alone, barely homeschooled by your exhausted and beaten-down mother. I had so much time on my hands and the world at my fingertips.

Working outside the home was never going to be an option for me growing up. Not only was it not an option, but it was strictly forbidden for the women in my family. I was trained to serve the men around me and told that in order to be holy and to belong to God I had to follow the rules and not question anything. If I disobeyed, I would burn in hell and be cast out of my family. I believed it. Took it all to heart, let it settle into my bones as fact. But once I became a teenager something didn't sit right. I wanted more. So much more, and all the lies I'd been told about how small and insignificant I was made me that much more desperate to break free.

But it's harder than you think to just leave. I was a child with no money or power of my own. Despite the fact that my family owns one of the fanciest hotels in the state, despite the fact that they were rich as hell, I'd never been allowed on a plane. They kept my world as small as possible.

When my dad forced me to marry Marsden, I didn't think it would get any better, but I knew my husband would be easier to manipulate than my father. My father was dying to give his hotel to Marsden one day because he couldn't imagine having to give it to one of his daughters.

If I couldn't work outside the home, I would make the best of it. I'd be the best damn mother I could be. I became the CEO of our household and ran it like a business. I did it because I loved the control and also because I didn't want my boys to grow up like Marsden and Gray, as entitled little shits who believe they're masters of the universe. I wanted them to see who was boss even if it had to be in my house. They saw me in charge of things and they respect the hell out of me.

I've been reading Marsden's emails and texts for years because I knew exactly what kind of beast he was when my father forced me to marry him. Spyware is a shockingly simple thing to work with. Invasive apps masquerade as legitimate ones and then use a phone's or computer's permission settings to spy on its user. It's almost too easy.

So I knew about Marsden's affairs and his gambling debts. I saw Rebecca's message the night Marsden was heading to the barn with Grayson, the contract she'd drawn up asking him to give up all rights to her children. It was horrific to read, but I can't say I was surprised. I'd had my own suspicions about Dr. Carmichael and listened to way too many of his lectures about the genetic dominance of the male sperm within our religious community.

Then Rebecca went a step too far. She forwarded Marsden all of Grayson's disgusting emails to me. I had no idea why Rebecca had to involve me in her little scheme to get Marsden to give up the rights to her kids, and I didn't like it one bit.

I barely had any time to react. I had just gotten home from being at the conference so I could get a decent night's sleep in my own bed when Marsden came barreling into our bedroom and confronted me about the emails, drunk as a skunk. I was able to talk him down and convince him that I never once responded to one of those filthy emails. He believed me.

"Please don't go see him tonight," I begged. But I knew he would do the exact opposite. I knew he would go in there guns blazing and that I needed to control the situation as best I could.

It was always like that between him and Gray, the intense love that quickly gave way to rage and jealousy.

It's true what I told the detective when he interviewed me. Marsden and Gray were always competing for things when we were growing up, including who could kiss a particular girl first, who could take whatever they wanted from her first. It was unfortunately me they both wanted, even though I was a child. They grabbed me on the church playground one day when I was twelve and they were nearly eighteen. They yanked me inside the shed where we kept the balls and playground equipment. It had been Gray who clapped his left hand against my mouth and shoved the other down my pants, putting his fingers so deep inside me I began to bleed. Then Mars lunged toward me. His lips were the first to ever touch mine. Grayson was so pissed he punched Marsden in the gut. They battled it out while I crawled out of the shed on bloodied knees. I confided in my mother that night, hoping she'd help me get some retribution. I told her about the kiss but was too ashamed to mention how Grayson violated me. She immediately told my father, and he insisted that since Marsden was the first to defile me that he would be the man I married. Daddy practically arranged it right then. I hated that man until the moment he took his last breath beneath the pillow I pushed over his face.

So I drove Marsden's blacked-out ass to Grayson Sommers's barn and let him loose. I didn't think he'd actually kill Grayson, but I wouldn't stop him from giving him the beating he deserved.

I waited outside and listened to them brawl, enjoying Gray's cries for help. Then a crack of bone hitting bone and a loud rupture of metal on metal. When I walked in Marsden was sobbing over Gray's broken body, cradling him in his arms.

"We have to call an ambulance," he said, nearly waking up from his catatonic furor.

"Absolutely not, Mars. Get yourself together," I snapped. He blubbered like a bitch boy. "You need to finish what you started."

"I can't," he wailed.

"Then I will."

"There's a camera up there. I think I broke it."

"Then go get it down," I ordered him as I examined Grayson's limp body. He was breathing, but barely. He needed to be put out of his misery and I had to pivot, just like Olivia always told me to do. Grayson was lighter than I expected (he was two inches shorter than Rebecca, like most of the Internet had suspected), but I was also in excellent shape from years of CrossFit and weight lifting. I could easily bench 180. I picked him up and before Marsden could scurry down from the hayloft with the camera I'd impaled Grayson on the blades of the harvester.

I'm not going to lie to you. Watching the life drain out of him sent a jolt of electricity through my body and then calmed me in a way that nothing else ever had. The head of an ax gleamed in the corner; it called to me. As Marsden stared at me in disbelief, I grabbed it and sliced clean through Grayson's right wrist, severing the hand that defiled me all those years ago. I left it inside the freezer next to the sourdough.

"Everyone will blame Rebecca," I assured my husband as I got him into his truck. "No one will ever know we were here."

Marsden was a disaster. He barely remembered anything when we got home.

"Did I do it?" he'd asked pathetically.

"You did," I told him. "But I've taken care of it."

For years Olivia had been counseling me about how to pivot, how to make the best of every new situation to maximize my audience and income. When I had a skin cancer scare a couple of years back, we got sponsorship from three different sunscreens and gained a million followers for my #CancerJourney. Never mind that the tumor was benign. We kept it going for a year until the engagement dwindled. When I couldn't get pregnant recently, I told Olivia I could just make myself seem pregnant with AI and then generate an AI baby. She thought I was joking. I wasn't.

I planned to use my leverage with Marsden over what happened in that barn with Grayson to get him to give me everything willingly, to sign the hotel over to me. To grant me an easy divorce. To just walk away. Olivia agreed, but she told me to be patient, to tread carefully, to let her work behind the scenes. I knew she was trying to decrease the damage and maximize the upside for both of us, for both Rebecca and me. But I also knew her instincts were good, and I trusted her, at least as much as I trusted anyone.

But Marsden became obsessed with the idea of getting rid of Rebecca too. Couldn't stop talking about it. I didn't protest too much.

What did I care? Rebecca Sommers never did a damn thing to help me, just smiled and looked away when I showed up at her house as a child bride. She could have befriended me, taken me under her wing, helped me, but she was too busy building her brand. I'd deal with Marsden afterward. I planted the box of strange pictures of me in the Sommerses' house, just to make sure the police knew what a weirdo stalker Gray really was. I wanted them to think Rebecca did what she did because she was jealous and outraged. I'll admit I had fun taking them. While I was there, I did everything I could to access Rebecca's Cloud storage, where I assumed she had kept the video of Marsden and Grayson fighting in the garage, but someone (I'd later learn it was Lizzie) was in the house and I didn't have enough time. I'd have to deal with it once Rebecca was dead.

I arranged the dinner in the desert, so I'd have a reason to take everyone's phones. I figured either Lizzie or Katie knew where to find Rebecca and had been in contact with her. I used the same little spyware I had been using to watch my husband. In fact, I loaded it onto everyone's phones, all the influencers who came to the dinner. It would serve me well in the future to know what deals everyone was brokering. No one suspected that I'd even touched their devices. They just handed them over like children following a teacher's orders. I had the location of Rebecca's new phone within minutes. Katie had been texting her nonstop about Alice's ear.

I also threw the dinner so everyone would know exactly where I was when my husband kidnapped Rebecca Sommers in case something went wrong. I had thought of everything.

I knew Marsden would fuck up the plan to get rid of Rebecca. He always did. God gave him every physical advantage but forgot to give him any intelligence. He was denser than a big old oak tree.

But it was all to Rebecca's credit that she fought back so hard. And Lizzie's and Olivia's that they went out to save her. Olivia called me afterward. She always did. "You'll have to say the gun was Marsden's. It's unlicensed. They'll never trace it," she said.

"Of course," I agreed. We moved forward from there.

Sometimes I feel like she lives in my brain. I trusted her to do what she thought was best.

"You're getting exactly what you wanted and what you needed," Olivia had said. "It's your time to shine."

Of course I agreed. She gave me the gift I'd been desperate

for. She got rid of my husband. And then I gave her access to all the data I scraped from every major influencer in America. We are the perfect team.

Life is good. Finally. My sisters and I now have control of the hotel. But if I ever want to run it myself . . . Well, I have a plan for that too. I stare longingly at Alice. It would have been nice to make the girls mine. They're delicious. But I'm thinking about adopting. Olivia tells me there's a huge hole right now in the adoption influencing market, just waiting to be filled.

I still want to take down Dr. Carmichael for all the grotesque things he's inflicted on the women here. I discussed it with Olivia and she agreed. Told me to plant the seed with Lizzie. She promised to help it grow.

I have everything I ever wanted. A big life. A big career. Peace and freedom. My fantasies have become my reality.

I saunter over to Lizzie and Rebecca as they chatter away to each other on the dance floor of the wedding.

Stacy walks up to the three of us with her wide lens DSLR camera.

"Exquisite shots. Get closer together." Stacy tilts Lizzie's head to get the perfect angle between Rebecca and me. She brushes a dead leaf off my shoulder.

"Now look at one another and laugh like you're all in on some hilarious joke," she directs us. "Yeah, that's perfect, that's the perfect shot."

#Blessed.

ACKNOWLEDGMENTS

When my second baby was born in 2019, I went weeks with very little sleep. She was fussy and refused to sleep unless I was holding her in a rocking chair clutching her left foot. This left me with a single appendage, my thumb, free to do little else but scroll Instagram. In those bleary hours in the middle of the night, I was served up what felt like a lifetime's worth of gauzy, gorgeous images of "aspirational" motherhood that looked nothing like what I was doing. These women and their homes and children were pristine and perfect-seeming. I very quickly realized that all of them were trying to sell me something. That began my five-year-long journey into reporting on the multibillion-dollar world of influencers on the *Under the Influence* podcast.

It's been a wild ride to say the least, and along the way, I got the idea for this book, a completely bananas, gonzo roller-coaster ride of a thriller set in the world of conservative influencers. I started this project on my newsletter, the Over the Influence Substack. So, I first and foremost need to thank my audience there for their unwavering support of this project and for all their feedback. You are the very best, and I love getting to be in community with you. I also need to thank all the influencers who have worked with me to pull back the curtain on this industry.

Influencing rarely gets the respect that it deserves because it is a business run largely by women and for women, but it has transformed our media landscape and our economies in ways we are only just starting to understand.

And while we are thanking influencers, THANK YOU THANK YOU THANK YOU to the wonderful world of Bookstagram. You are incredible champions of books and the unsung heroes of this industry.

Thank you to all the usual suspects. My tireless editors, Maya Ziv and Manpreet Grewal, from Dutton and HQ, respectively. Thank you to my agents, Byrd Leavell and Pilar Queen, for letting me text you at all hours of the day and night saying, "I have this crazy idea." Thank you to Lauren Morrow and all the queens and kings on my publicity and marketing teams.

Thank you to all my early readers, including Glynnis Mac-Nicol, Casey Scieszka, Sarah Pierce, Carolyn Murnick, Sara Petersen, Chelsea Powers, Flannery Buchanan, Kate Czyzewski, Katie Fulton, and Nick Aster, the last of whom also happens to be married to me.

Don't miss Jo Piazza's gripping and transporting
historical family mystery,

THE SICILIAN INHERITANCE

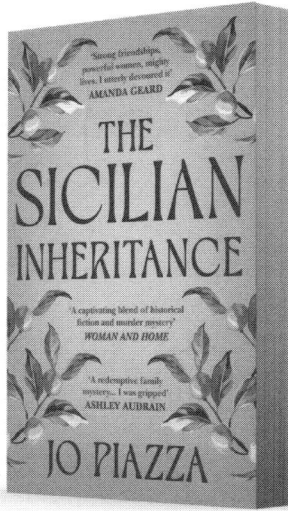

A century-old unsolved murder

A disputed inheritance

A family secret that some will kill to protect . . .

'This rich and complex family mystery is completely addicting!'
Jenny Mollen, *New York Times* bestselling author
of *City of Likes* and *Live Fast Die Hot*

'An addictive family saga with a rich abundance of strong women,
quick wit, immersive history, and page-turning suspense'
Patti Callahan Henry, *New York Times* bestselling author
of *The Secret Book of Flora Lea*

'A gripping story of motherhood, ambition, misogyny,
and female power . . . it is also a great mystery that
kept me guessing until the final pages'
Courtney Sullivan, *New York Times* bestselling author
of *Friends and Strangers*